Wolf Tales

Wolf Tales

KATE DOUGLAS

APHRODISIA

KENSINGTON PUBLISHING CORP.
http://www.kensingtonbooks.com

APHRODISIA books are published by

Kensington Publishing Corp.
850 Third Avenue
New York, NY 10022

All Kensington titles, imprints and distributed lines are available at special quantity discounts for bulk purchases for sales promotion, premiums, fund-raising, educational or institutional use.

Special book excerpts or customized printings can also be created to fit specific needs. For details, write or phone the office of the Kensington Special Sales Manager: Kensington Publishing Corp., 850 Third Avenue, New York, NY 10022. Attn. Special Sales Department. Phone: 1-800-221-2647.

Aphrodisia and the A logo are trademarks of Kensington Publishing Corp. Kensington and the K logo Reg. U.S. Pat. & TM Off.

ISBN 0-7582-1386-7

First Kensington Trade Paperback Printing: January 2006
10   9   8   7   6   5

Printed in the United States of America

My sincere thanks to Margaret and Bill Riley,
owners and founders of Changeling Press,
who provided a fertile birthplace for my Chanku.
And a very special thank you to my agent,
Jessica Faust, who has proved
she is even more persistent than I am.

Part One

Stefan

Chapter 1

Xandi shoved the deflated air bag out of her lap and used her last tissue to wipe the fog off the windshield, well aware it wasn't going to change her predicament. She saw nothing but white. At least it was still daytime. Even so, her hands shook, and her heart raced. She paused a moment, fist full of tissue pressed against the windshield, then forced herself to take slow, even breaths. Hyperventilating wouldn't help one bit.

Look at the bright side. At least it's still daylight. This could have happened at night.

The thought set her heart to pounding even harder.

She'd skidded at least a hundred yards down the hillside and landed in a cushion of thick snow and heavy undergrowth. Her little white sedan tilted to one side, completely surrounded by small trees and shrubs. Thick, fast-falling snow already hid the hood, and most likely the roof as well. She checked her cell phone again. Damn. Still no signal. The narrow gorge she'd fallen into must be blocking her.

Staying in the car was an option, at least until the storm abated, but she'd plowed into the drift hard and deep, and the storm showed no signs of letting up. Already the doors were wedged closed by the weight of the white stuff, and the windows were almost completely covered.

It wasn't like anyone would be looking for her, and even if someone did, who'd be able to find a little white car buried under a ton of white snow? She was going to have to make a decision, and make it soon, before she suffocated.

Xandi grabbed her down coat out of the backseat, made sure her boots were tightly tied, her gloves were on her hands and her hat was pulled down over her ears. Slowly, she rolled the window down, pushing the heavy snow back so it wouldn't fall in her lap.

The irony of the situation wasn't lost on her. She had plenty of vacation time accumulated at work, and she'd taken some of it. She'd told her friends and co-workers she needed to get away, needed to think about making some serious changes in her life. Insisted they didn't need to know her plans, as she would be gone only a couple of weeks and wasn't going far.

Well, she hadn't gone far, not really. She'd made it only about twenty miles out of Portland before the damned diesel had run her car off the road. She wondered if the trucker who'd cut in front of her even had a clue what he'd done.

Wondered if he even gave a shit.

Her hands were shaking as she brushed the wet flakes out of her eyelashes and stared through the open window, up the long slope. Cold. She was just so damned cold. And scared.

"Shut up." She started, surprised by the vehemence in her own voice. This situation didn't fit with the thick flakes of snow and the postcard image of pine boughs bending beneath their weight. It didn't fit with her plans, the reason she'd decided to leave in spite of the storm. It just didn't fit.

Nothing did.

The highway couldn't be too far above her, though it was hard to tell up from down in the current whiteout conditions. Whatever tracks her car might have left were long gone. She hadn't lost consciousness, but she'd sat in the front seat with the deflated air bag in her lap, counting her blessings, for way too long. All the while, the snow kept falling.

Of course, the fact she was still alive after hurtling down the steep slope at over seventy miles per hour deserved a word of thanks. Lately, not much in her life did. She took a deep breath, consciously putting all the crap that was Alexandria Olanet's life behind her, at least for now. With any luck, she'd get up the hill before dark fell and thumb a ride back to town. So much for her great adventure.

So much for taking charge of her life.

Pushing the rest of the snow away from the open window, Xandi clutched her little leather backpack purse in her hand, squeezed her butt through the open window and tumbled out into the swirling snow.

She couldn't feel her hands or her feet, and she'd lost her right mitten along with her cell phone hours ago. Snow swirled in ever-darkening blasts as nightfall approached. Obviously she'd missed the road, but where the hell was she?

Brushing her hand across her frozen nose, Xandi bit back a sob. Tears wouldn't help. It was too late for them, and as cold as it was, they'd just freeze on her face. It was too dark to go any farther, and she was just too damned cold and tired.

Feeling slow and stupid, she looked about her, wondering how she'd go about building a shelter when all she could see was blowing snow and dark shadows.

Damn. It was all Jared's fault. Well, Jared and his blonde nymphet. Would she ever get past the humiliation, the sick-to-the-pit-of-her-stomach feeling? It hadn't gone away, not once over the past week . . . not since she'd walked into her bedroom, the one she'd shared with her fiancé for the past year, and caught him bare assed and buck naked with his face buried between the bitch's legs.

The worst part was the woman's reaction. She hadn't even been upset. No, she'd just grinned at Xandi with a look of feral satisfaction, spread her legs wider and faked an orgasm. It had to have been fake—the timing was too good—but Jared hadn't seemed to mind.

While Xandi stood there in shock, Jared had raised his head, his face streaked with the other woman's fluids, and stared stupidly at her, blinking like the idiot he was.

In a way, she thought, it was a good thing. Okay, so her self-esteem was officially in the toilet, but at least she'd learned the truth about him before they got married. If only she'd listened to her friends. They'd been trying to warn her, had told her over and over to get out before it was too late.

Now, it just might be. Night had fallen. The snow swirled in ever-stronger gusts. She'd stopped shivering, couldn't feel her feet, couldn't move her hands. An almost cozy warmth stole over her. Sighing, feeling more regret than fear, Xandi slowly collapsed into the soft, welcoming snow.

Warmth. The most wonderful sense of warmth, of contentment. Sighing, Xandi snuggled deeper into the blankets, aware of a slight tingling in her toes and fingers, a sense of heat radiating all around her, of weight and comfort and safety.

And something very large, very long, very solid, wedged tightly between her bare buttocks, following the crease of her labia and resting hot and hard against her clit. She blinked, opened her eyes wide, saw only darkness.

Awake now, she felt soft breath tickling the back of her neck, warm arms encircling her, a hard, muscular body enfolding hers. She held herself very still, forcing her fuzzy mind into a clarity it really wasn't ready for. Okay . . . she remembered being lost in a snowstorm, remembered thinking about building a shelter, remembered . . . nothing. Nothing beyond the sense that it was too late, she was too cold . . . then nothing.

The body behind her shifted. The huge cock—at least that much she recognized—slipped against her clit as the person holding her thrust his hips just a bit closer to hers.

Xandi cleared her throat. Whoever held her had obviously saved her life. Everyone knew more heat was given off by naked bodies, but she'd never really thought of the concept of awakening in the dark, wrapped securely together with a totally unknown naked body. No, that really hadn't entered her mind . . . at least until now.

She fought the need to giggle. Nerves. Had to be nerves. But she felt her labia softening, engorging, knew her clit was beginning to peek out from its little hood of flesh, searching for closer contact with that hot cock. The arms holding her tightened just a bit. One of the hands moved to cover her breast.

Neither one of them spoke. He knew what she looked like. She had no idea who held her. What age he was, what race, what anything.

He saved your life.

There was that. She arched her back, forcing her breast into the huge hand that palmed it. In response, thick fingers compressed the nipple. She bit back a moan. Jared hated it when she made noises during sex.

This isn't Jared, you idiot.

The fingers pinched harder, rolled the turgid flesh between them. *Screw it.* She moaned, at the same time parting her legs just a bit so that she could settle herself on the huge cock that seemed to be growing even larger. Then she tightened her thighs around it, sliding her butt back against his rock-hard belly.

She felt the thick curl of pubic hair tickling her butt, rested against the hard root of his penis where it sprung solidly from his groin and clenched her thighs once again, holding onto him. She felt the air go out of his lungs, then the lightest touch of warm lips against her ear, the soft, exploring tip of his tongue as he circled just the outside, the soft puff of his breath.

Shivers raced along her spine. She wrapped her fingers around his wrists, anchoring herself while at the same time holding both of his hands tightly against her breasts. The hair on his arms was soft, almost silky. She tried to picture her hidden lover, but before an image came to mind, he hmmm'd against her ear, then ran his tongue along the side of her throat.

She felt the sizzle all the way to her pussy, felt his lips exploring her throat, his mobile tongue teasing the wispy little hairs at the back of her neck. His hands massaged her breasts, squeezed her nipples, then rubbed away the pain. His hips pressed against her, forcing his cock to slide very slowly back and forth between her swollen labia.

She moaned again, the sound working its way up and out of her throat before she even recognized it as her own voice. The heat surrounding her intensified. Whoever he was, whoever held her . . . she sighed. He literally radiated fire and warmth and pure carnal lust. One of his big hands slipped down to her belly, cupped her mons and pressed her against him. Still gripping his forearm tightly in her left hand, she felt his finger slide down between her legs.

His fingertip paused at her swollen clit, applying the merest bit of pressure. She held perfectly still, afraid he'd stop if she moved, afraid of her own reaction to this most intimate touch by an absolute stranger. She kept a death grip on the wrist near her breast. The fingers of her right hand dug into the corded tendons on the underside of his forearm, and everything in her cried out to thrust her hips forward, to beg him to stroke her, to bury more than just his finger in the moist heat between her legs.

Instead, as her body trembled with the fierce need to move, she held her hips immobile. After a moment that might have lasted forever, he gently rubbed his fingertip around her clit, dipping inside her wet pussy for some of her moisture, then bringing it back to stroke her once more.

She bit back a scream as his roughened fingertip touched her again, the circular motion so light as to hardly register. Her trembling increased, her desire, her barely controllable need to tilt and force her hips against him, to make him enter her.

She didn't care if he used his cock, his tongue, his finger . . . hell, at this point, he could use his whole fucking hand and it wouldn't be enough. She choked back a whimper as he changed the direction of his massage, moving his fingertip slowly up and down over the small hooded organ. Each stroke took him closer to her pussy. Closer, but not nearly close enough.

Her breath caught in her throat when he dipped inside her, swirled his thick finger around the streaming walls of her pussy, then returned to caress her clit once more. A small part of Xandi's mind reminded her she was being beautifully fucked by a total stranger, that her fingers were clutching thick, muscular arms, that she was clasping her thighs around the biggest cock she'd ever felt in her life—and that they still hadn't exchanged a single word.

It came to her then, in an almost blinding flash of insight, a personal epiphany of pure, carnal need and unmitigated lust, that she'd never, even in her most imaginative fantasy, been this turned on in her entire life. Never felt so tightly linked—mentally, physically, sexually—to anyone. She moaned aloud as his finger once more slipped back between her legs. His thumb stroked her clit now, and that one, thick finger plunged carefully in and out of her weeping flesh.

Suddenly, the hot tip of his tongue traced the whorl of her ear, then dipped inside. Shocked, she thrust her hips forward, forcing his fingers deep. His breath tickled the top of her ear, his tongue swirled the interior, leaving it all hot and damp, filled with lush promise.

She thrust harder against his fingers, still holding one of his hands against her breast, forcing the other deep between her legs. She felt the thick rush of fluid, the hot coil of her climax building, building with each slick thrust of his cock between her thighs, each dip of his fingers, each . . .

Without warning, he rolled her to her stomach, breaking her grip on his forearms as if it were nothing. He grabbed her hips and lifted her. Xandi moaned, spreading her legs wide, welcoming him, begging with her body. Eyes wide open, she saw nothing but darkness, felt no sense of space, lost all concept of time. She quivered, hanging at the precipice of a frightening, endless fall.

His big hands clasped her hips, held her tightly. He massaged her buttocks for a moment with both his thumbs, spreading her cheeks wide. She felt her slick moisture on his fingertip, almost preternaturally aware of each tiny spot on her body where she made contact with his.

She wondered how much he could see, if his night vision were better than hers. It was as dark as the inside of a cave, wherever they were. No matter how hard she tried, she couldn't see the soft bed beneath her, couldn't see her own hands.

Couldn't see his.

Yet the link persisted, the sense of connection, of need, of desire so gut deep it was suddenly part of her existence, of her entire world. A link she knew would be forged forever when he finally entered her, filled her with heat and pulsing need.

He lifted her higher, his hands slipping down to grab her thighs, raising her up so that her knees no longer touched the mattress, so that her weight was on her forearms, her face pressed tightly to the pillow.

She expected his thick cock to fill her pussy. Wanted his cock, now. *Please, now!* Her breath caught in short, wild gasps for air, her legs quivered, and she hung there in his grasp, waiting . . . waiting. Hovering there, held aloft, the cool air drifting across her hot, needy flesh. Waiting for him to fill her.

Instead, she felt him pull away, felt the mattress dip as he shifted his weight . . . felt the fiery wet slide of his tongue between her legs.

"Ahhh . . ." Her cry ended on a whimper. He looped his arms through her thighs and lifted her even higher, his tongue finding entry into her gushing pussy, his lips grabbing at her engorged labia, suckling each fleshy lip into his hot mouth. He nibbled and sucked, spearing her with his tongue, nipping at her with sharp teeth, then laving her with soft, warm strokes. Suddenly his lips encircled her clit, and he suckled, hard, pressing down on the sensitive little organ with his tongue.

The scream exploded out of her. She clamped her legs against the sides of his head, peripherally aware of scratchy whiskers, strong jaw. His tongue lapped and twisted, filling her streaming pussy, as she bucked against him. He was strong, stronger than any man she'd ever known, holding her aloft, eating her out like a hungry beast, his mouth all lips and tongue and hard-edged teeth.

He dragged his tongue across her clit once more, suckled her labia between his lips and brought her to another clenching, screaming climax. Once more, licking her now, long, slow sweeps from clit to anus, each stroke taking her higher, farther. His tongue snaked across her flesh, dipping inside to lap at her moist center, tickling her sensitive clit, ringing the tight sphincter in her ass. Gasping, shivering, her legs trembling, Xandi struggled for breath, reached for yet another climax.

He left her there, once more on the edge. Cool air brushed across her damp flesh, raising goose bumps across her thighs and belly.

He lowered her until her knees once more rested on the bed. She felt his hot thighs pressing against her own, his big hands clasping her hips, the broad, velvety soft tip of his cock resting at the mouth of her vagina.

Slowly, with great care and control, he pushed into her. Damn, he was huge. She shifted her legs, relaxed her spasming muscles as best she could. Still, her flesh stretched, the lubrication from her orgasms easing the way as he slowly, inexorably, seated himself within her.

She felt him press up against the mouth of her womb at the same time his balls nestled against her clit and pubic mound. He waited a moment, giving her time to adjust to his huge girth and length, then he started to move.

Slowly at first, easing his way in, then out, stretching her, filling her. Xandi fisted the pillow in her hands as she caught his rhythm. In, out, in again, his balls tickling her clit with each careful thrust. She pressed back against him, forcing him deeper, inviting him.

He groaned, then slammed into her harder. She took him, reveled in the power and strength of her mystery lover, felt another climax beginning to build, knew she would not go alone this time.

She reached back between her legs, grasping his lightly furred sac between her fingers just as he thrust hard against her cervix. His strangled cry encouraged her. Grinning, feeling empowered—feminine and so very strong—she squeezed him gently in the palm of her hand, felt his balls contract, tighten, draw up close to his body.

She slipped one finger behind his sac, pressed the sensitive area, then ran her sharp fingernail lightly back to his testicles. He slammed into her, his body rigid with a fierce power. Shouting a warrior's cry of victory, he pounded into her harder, stronger. She kept a tight but careful hold on his balls, until the hot gush of his seed filled her.

Overwhelmed, overstimulated, she screamed and thrust her hips hard against his groin. Her vaginal muscles clamped down, wrapping around his cock, trapping and holding him close. Suddenly, he filled her even more, his cock swelling to fit tightly against the clenching muscles of her pussy, locking his body close against hers.

Linking the two of them together. A binding deeper than the act itself, more powerful than anything she'd ever known.

He slumped across her back, then rolled to his side, taking Xandi with him. She felt the hot burst of his gasping breath, the rhythmic pulsing of his cock, the pounding of her own heart. Suddenly, inexplicably exhausted, her pussy rippling against the heat of his still amazingly engorged penis, Xandi snuggled close to his rock-hard body and allowed her eyes to drift slowly shut.

Tomorrow. She'd learn who he was tomorrow.

Chapter 2

Xandi rolled over, blinking against the pale morning light, and encountered the hard, cold side of a snow bank. Startled fully alert, she sat up, suddenly aware she was in a tree-shaded rest area at the side of the highway. She recognized it immediately. Her car had gone off the road just a few hundred yards beyond.

Shaking her head, bemused, she looked down at her clothing. One mitten was missing, along with her purse, but otherwise all was as she'd been wearing yesterday when she'd had her wreck.

Yesterday? But . . . She struggled slowly to her feet, and stood, body trembling, trying to remember. She was immediately aware of a tenderness between her legs, that glorious morning-after-a-good-fuck feeling she hadn't known for much too long.

She let out a shaky sigh. Who the hell had she had sex with? Good Lord, she never did anything like that. *Ever!* Even weirder, why was she back here, at the side of the road?

Maybe you were just a lousy lay . . .

No. She knew better than that. Whomever she'd fucked had obviously enjoyed himself every bit as much as she had. She vaguely recalled awakening during the night, feeling searching lips on her breasts, thick fingers buried deep in her pussy.

Thinking about it made her nipples tingle. She knew they were standing up like pencil erasers because they rubbed against her clothing, and she felt the sensation spiral clear down between her legs.

Xandi took a deep breath of bitter cold air, watched the thick cloud of steam as she exhaled, then turned and looked both ways, up and down the long highway. It was still early in the morning, barely past dawn. The sky glowed deep pink in the east, and a coating of ice covered the snow, so that everything sparkled as if covered with pink and gold glitter.

There was no traffic. One pair of headlights far down the road was the only vehicle in sight. She watched the lights grow slowly closer as a thin, wintry sun rose over the mountains and cast a silver-and-gold glow across the snow-covered treetops. Shadows loomed deep and dark in the woods.

The car lights grew brighter, closer, until a large black Mercedes with tinted windows pulled into the turnout. The car sat there for a moment, the engine running and sending thick columns of steam from the exhaust pipe. Uncertain whether to be frightened or glad, Xandi waited, watching. Suddenly the engine shut down. Silence once more engulfed her.

After a moment, the driver climbed out and bowed slightly. He was small and dark skinned, wearing a neat gray uniform with a cap. Xandi bit back an almost hysterical giggle. What a surrealistic trip this has been! A car wreck, lost in a winter storm, amazing sex with a mysterious stranger. And now she was getting rescued by some scrawny little dude in a limousine?

"Miss, would care for a ride?" The driver's voice was very soft, the accent clipped, precise and very British.

Still shaking her head at the incongruity of the situation, Xandi brushed the snow off her pants legs and walked closer to the car. Well, she'd wanted something different, hadn't she? The driver opened a back door. Xandi smiled and thanked him, then slipped into the dark interior of the Mercedes.

He was almost certain she'd scream the moment she realized she wasn't alone. He held very still, hardly breathing, waiting for her eyes to adjust to the dim light here in the backseat. His heart pounded an erratic drumbeat. He was sure she heard it. He rubbed his thumbs over his fingers, wishing there were some way to make his palms stop sweating, some way to calm the racing beat of his heart.

He shouldn't have done this. Should never have risked so much. But leaving her on the side of the road had been the most difficult thing he'd ever done in his life. Hell, they'd barely gotten a mile away before he realized he couldn't—wouldn't—let her go.

She took a great deal of time fastening her seat belt, straightening her coat, brushing her thick hair back from her eyes. Slowly she turned and looked at him. Her beautiful gray eyes widened.

He waited for the look of disgust. The fear. The realization she'd been rescued by a monster.

Her lips parted. She frowned, then smiled. Her hand came up, as if to touch his face.

He grabbed her wrist. Not that. He wasn't ready for that.

"It was you, wasn't it? You're the one who rescued me."

Her voice was soft, the inflection showing just a trace of the Northeast. He suddenly remembered that neither one of them had spoken a word the night before.

No words.

Moans. Whimpers. He'd made her scream, made her sob. Made her cry. Made himself cry, for that matter. But no words.

He cleared his throat, opened his mouth to speak. To tell her she was wrong. That she must be thinking of someone else. Someone whole. Unmarked.

Human.

She pressed her finger against his mouth, as if to explore. He jerked away from her touch.

She blinked in surprise, but she touched him once more, her hand cupping the side of his face. "I know it was you. Don't deny it. Pheromones? Your scent . . . I'm not sure how I know, but I do." She laughed. It was a surprisingly harsh sound. "My pussy knows, that's for sure. I'm getting wet. My muscles are already finding a rhythm—your rhythm—tightening, relaxing. . . ."

The image filled his mind, all that moist flesh, ripening, preparing for him. His sac tightened, his testicles crawled up close to his body. He felt heat and the pulsing throb of the big artery feeding blood the length of his cock. Felt himself stretch, grow. Lengthen.

Her words shocked him. Surprised him.

Turned him on. Dear God, it was all he could do to restrain himself. Didn't she understand what she was doing? What she'd already done? He wanted to rip her clothes off, take her here, in the backseat of the car, with Oliver just on the other side of the tinted glass. Fuck her until she couldn't see straight.

Couldn't see him. "You don't know what you're saying." He had to swallow and clear his throat. "You don't know who I am. What I am."

She smiled, an easy, natural smile that lit up her entire face. "Ah, but I do. You're the man who saved my life. The man who made love to me all night long." She blinked. He was surprised to see her eyes fill with tears. "You're the man who made me feel more feminine, more desirable, than I've ever felt in my life."

He reached up and turned on the overhead light, then grabbed her by the shoulders. His laughter sounded harsh. Painful. "Look at me. Really look at me. Does this turn you on? This face? Yes, we had sex—in the dark. Your back was to me, your eyes turned away. Could you look at me, see me as I am, when I shove my cock up that wet pussy of yours? Would you still want me when I'm tied with you, when my cock swells and traps you against my body, holds you to me like a bitch in heat? Holds you so you have to stare into this face, see this body? Could you do that, little girl? Could you fuck me without the fantasy?"

He growled, released his grip on her shoulders and turned away. "That was inexcusable. I am sorry. I will have Oliver take you home. Please give him your address."

Stunned, Xandi could only stare in silence as he first snarled at her, then turned away in disgust. With her? *No,* she thought. Most likely with himself, though why he should think his amazing countenance would put her off . . . No, it didn't put her off, not at all. The effect was exactly the opposite.

The words he'd said in anger rocked her body. A sensual litany, a promise of unimaginable pleasure: *when my cock swells and traps you against my body . . . when I shove my cock up that wet pussy of yours . . . could you fuck me . . . fuck me . . . fuck me . . .*

Oh, God, yes!

She'd sensed it last night, this link, this need she felt for him. Of course, then she'd merely thought him a man. A normal, albeit very sexy, man. Suddenly the passion, the unimaginable lust, made sense. There was something beyond human, beyond normal desire, with this person. Something her body craved, her mind needed. Something about him that made her whole.

She studied his profile in the dim light of the overhead lamp. He was obviously not completely human, though what he was couldn't possibly be. She glanced at his hands. A man's hands—large, the knuckles big and bony, the nails neatly trimmed, the hair thick across the backs of his fingers.

She remembered the feel of that silky hair. She'd clasped his arms against her just last night. Held him tightly while he palmed her breasts, caressed her between her legs.

Loved her. Passionately.

Now that she could see him, even though he was dressed in a pair of dark pants and a black turtleneck sweater, she realized most of his body must be covered with the silky fur. It wasn't black, as she'd first thought. No, it was more a deep gray tipped with silver. The hair on his head grew long, falling to his shoulders, and it was the same dark gray, also tipped with silver.

What she'd thought was his beard was so much more. The same silver-tipped fur covered his face, his jaw . . . and what could only be described as his muzzle. His nose was dark, his lips almost black. When he curled his upper lip, she saw sharp, white canines.

Even his ears were animalistic, triangular, held close to his head, lying back against his skull as if he were angry . . . or frightened?

Still human, yet very much the beast. An elemental creature, so out of place in the backseat of a Mercedes limousine.

She was a fool to want him. He wasn't human. He wasn't natural.

He was so much more. So very much.

He turned slowly around until he sat facing her. His hands rested on his muscular thighs. His shoulders rose and fell as he took deep breaths, straining the seams of his sweater. She felt his soft sigh as much as she heard the whisper of sound.

"Your address? Please, I would like to take you home."

"No." She shook her head, wrapped her fingers around his right wrist. He started to tug his hand away, but she held on. "I want to go home with you." She looked up at him, forcing him to see her as a woman. A woman who was more intrigued than disgusted with the beast that was so obviously a huge part of him. "I want to make love with you again. I want . . ." She choked up. Couldn't force the words out. "I don't want to lose what you have given me. Please? Take me with you. Whoever—whatever—you are. I need to know . . . more. Do you understand?"

He frowned. His silver-tipped brows drew together over that long, lupine nose. His eyes glowed amber, practically golden in the dim interior light of the car, the pupils narrowed to black, diamond-shaped shards. "No," he said, glancing down at her fingers wrapped tightly around his arm. "No, I really don't understand. Look at me. See what I am. Not who . . . What."

She sucked in a deep, shuddering breath. Let it out. Sensed, somehow, her entire future rested on her answer. "I see what you are, though I have no explanation. I want very much to know who you are." She tightened her grip around his wrist and slowly turned his hand so that it rested palm-side up on his thigh.

"You can't deny that you felt it, felt what happened between us last night." How does one explain a link, a connection, so powerful, so . . . pure? She placed her left hand in his, studied the difference in their colors, the huge discrepancy in size.

She'd known last night that the man holding her was big. She'd had no real sense of his actual size. His hand dwarfed hers, his shoulders were broad, his chest muscles rippled through the black turtleneck. She couldn't even guess at his height, but figured he was well over six and a half feet tall.

She raised her chin and studied his face. Even sitting, she had to look up to meet his eyes. At five feet ten inches, Xandi dwarfed many of the men in her brokerage firm. It was unusual for her to sit close to a man and feel small and petite.

He said nothing, merely watched her with questions in his eyes as she studied him. Suddenly the memory of him taking her, of him seating his huge cock between her legs, of being stretched as he thrust deeply inside, filled her mind. Her pussy clenched in reaction. She felt the warm spiral of desire strike at her very center, knew she must be soaking through her panties just from the thought of making love with this man.

She wondered if he smelled her arousal. If his instincts and abilities were that defined . . . if he was as much the wolf as he appeared.

He stared at her for a moment longer, his nostrils flared, his eyes narrowed, then he leaned forward and tapped on the darkened glass. The window rolled down barely enough to allow conversation. "Oliver. The woman has chosen to accompany me. Take us to the cabin, please."

The driver nodded, the window silently closed, and the big car rumbled to life. Xandi leaned back against the soft leather seat, folded her hands in her lap and shut her eyes in a moment of thanks. Suddenly, she felt his fingers tentatively brush over hers, his callused fingertips slip across the back of her right hand. She held her breath. Slowly, he turned her hand palm up, then closed his fingers firmly, clasping her hand in his. She exhaled, a long, slow breath. Held tightly to his hand. A sense of peace washed over her body, a sense of—finally, after years of waiting—finding her way home.

* * *

Xandi was aware of changes in the road—rough pavement giving way to smooth and then becoming rough again—and of two different times when the car slowed and must have passed through gates, but the tinted windows hid almost as much of the outside from her view as they did the inside from anyone trying to peer in.

Mostly, she was aware of the warm hand in hers, the fingers wrapped firmly about hers. She sensed the inner tension in the man/beast sitting next to her. Neither of them spoke, yet she'd never been so aware of another person in her entire life.

He radiated energy—controlled energy—as if his body might explode at any moment. She wondered what thoughts must be racing through his brain, wondered if he felt regret, anticipation . . . desire?

She should have been terrified. Should have felt some sense of fear, well aware she was essentially acting as an agent in her own abduction. Instead she was pure anticipation and untempered lust. Her body ached with need for him. She felt as if she'd shed some unneeded husk, another body or soul that had ruled her heart and mind for much too long. Shed it like a lizard's skin, leaving her fresh and clean, waiting . . . wanting.

In all her thirty years, she'd never known this sense of rightness before. This pure knowledge that, following this man, learning from this man, was the thing she'd been created to do.

Xandi blinked. The car had stopped. The door next to her companion opened, and Oliver stood to one side. "Sir?"

Her rescuer slipped his hand free of hers and got out of the car, his movements unbelievably graceful for one so large. He held his hand out to Xandi. She tightened her fingers around his and let him pull her gently to the door, then to her feet. She felt awkward and unsure, standing in the bright sunlight in front of a huge redwood home.

She wasn't ready to look at him. Stared instead at the

lovely structure practically growing up out of the snow-covered ground.

It was certainly no mere cabin. Decks wrapped around the home and stretched into the trees, and massive windows reflected the bright morning sun. Snow-capped mountains peeking out above the dark green forest framed the entire scene like an ad for an expensive ski vacation.

Snow covered the ground, so it was impossible to tell what the landscaping might be like in warmer weather, but Xandi imagined azaleas and rhododendrons, spilling masses of color, along with deep beds of ferns.

She was aware of the silence, more so once Oliver climbed back into the limo and drove along a curved driveway to beyond the far corner of the house. Finally, after she had exhausted her view of the home and surroundings, she turned and carefully appraised her host.

In the cold light of day, he was beyond beautiful. She should have felt fear. Most likely, if she had chanced upon him on a darkened street, she would have run screaming in panic. Now her perception of him was colored by knowledge. The tenderness of his kiss, the gentle strokes of his fingers . . . the controlled thrust of his massive cock.

"I haven't properly thanked you," she said, looking directly into his amber eyes. The thought crossed her mind that she could never grow tired of looking at him, of being near him. "I would have died out there. How did you find me?"

He dipped his chin, acknowledging her thanks with a tilt of his head. "I was in the forest. I sensed you nearby, sensed your spirit fading. It was little enough to carry you back here."

"I was miles away from here."

He took her arm and led her up the broad steps without speaking. When he reached the front door, he paused and looked down at her, at her fingers clasped tightly around his forearm. "I often travel far at night. It is my way."

"You saved my life."

He opened the door and waited for her to precede him, closed the door, then turned and leaned solidly against it as if it were an anchor. His hands still grasping the handle, he studied her for a moment. She couldn't read the emotion in his amber eyes, but there was a sense of quiet desperation about him.

"No," he said, his chest rising and falling with a very deep breath. "You may very well have saved mine."

Chapter 3

The room to which he took her was elegant yet very simple, done all in soft shades of gold and green. The bed was large, the bathroom luxurious, with a tub big enough to swim in. He left her there with instructions to meet him for breakfast in another hour.

She took her time bathing, not at all surprised to find a big fluffy robe hanging behind the door when she finally climbed out of the steaming water. A hair dryer lay on the counter, along with a comb and a brush and even a new toothbrush. She dried her hair and brushed it out, then left it hanging loose about her shoulders. She checked a couple of drawers, looking for makeup, then finally gave up and went back into the bedroom, fully intending to put her old clothes back on.

A forest-green gown of softly knitted cashmere lay across the bed. There wasn't any underwear, but she didn't mind. The fabric clung to her body, caressed her flesh. Warmed her. She stood in front of a full-length gilded mirror and studied her reflection.

The style was amazingly simple: a scooped neckline, long sleeves and a natural drape to the gown that followed the flow of her body, emphasizing her rounded breasts and slender waist, her full hips and unusual height. With her gray eyes and dark russet hair, she knew she couldn't have chosen a more complimentary shade or design.

She turned away from the mirror and noticed her purse, the small leather backpack she'd lost the day before. It sat on a table next to the bed. She picked it up, saw her wallet was still inside, that everything appeared to be where it belonged. Sighing, she found her zippered cosmetics bag, put on a bit of lipstick, then set the bag back on the table.

Xandi stared at the bag for a moment, gathering her thoughts. Everything over the past few hours had about it a dreamlike quality, almost surrealistic in nature. She suffered a brief moment of fear, the sense that maybe she should call someone, tell one of her co-workers where she was . . . who she was with. She glanced about the room, suddenly noting the lack of telephone, radio and bedside clock.

Then she smiled. Folding her hands in front of her waist, she took a deep breath. She had no idea where she was. There was no reason to call, no reason for fear. She'd asked for change.

She'd found it.

Now was the time to do something with it.

He sat at a round glass-topped table set in a windowed nook in the large kitchen. She'd expected to find him in a more Gothic setting, at the head of a long table in a darkened, very formal parlor, but the kitchen was exceedingly modern, filled with delicious scents of morning foods. The lighting was bright and cheerful, and the cup of coffee he poured for her smelled wonderful.

Once again, she felt as if she'd been caught in a surrealistic dream, a feeling that wasn't lessened a bit when he handed her the financial section of the local newspaper after she sat down across the small table from him.

Sipping at coffee, reading the paper . . . it could have been any morning in any kitchen anywhere in America.

Except, when she glanced up, the amber eyes of a wolfman watched her.

"You haven't told me your name," she said, sipping her coffee. "I'm Alexandria Olanet. Xandi, for short." She smiled, waiting.

He stared at her a moment longer, took a sip of his own coffee. "I know," he said. "I must apologize. As you've probably noticed, I kept your purse. I read your driver's license, found you on the Internet. You are a very successful young woman. A partner already in your company. You've worked very hard for someone so young. Which reminds me. Do you need to let anyone know where you are? Will people be looking for you?"

"No," she answered without thinking. "I left yesterday for a two-week va—Oh!" She looked up at him, aware she shouldn't give him such knowledge . . . suddenly afraid.

He shook his head. "You need not fear me. I won't hold you against your will, Ms. Olanet. Oliver will take you home whenever you like. You only need to ask." He looked away, as if thinking of something pleasant, then turned back to her. "Spend your two weeks with me. Here, at my home."

"Oh, I can't possibly. . . ."

"Because of what I am." His voice was flat, no longer the rich baritone she'd found so full of life.

"No," she said. "That's not the reason at all. I was going to say I couldn't possibly intrude, even though I want to stay. More than you can imagine I want to stay. Please, tell me your name. I can't keep thinking of you as my rescuer, can I?"

She smiled and, without thinking, reached across the small table and placed her hand over his forearm. He didn't pull away this time, though she felt his muscles tense. He merely stared at her fingers, was still staring when Oliver came into the kitchen with a bag of sweet rolls from a bakery in Portland whose name Xandi recognized.

"Morning, Miss. Sir." He set the bag in front of them, turned and opened the oven door and drew out a warmed quiche and a platter of sausages and bacon. After quickly setting out silverware and placing the food in front of the two of them, the small man turned to leave. "If you don't mind, sir, I'll be leaving now. I'll return in the morning."

"Enjoy your visit with your family, Oliver. And thank you. We'll be fine."

Xandi watched as Oliver left the room, then turned back and faced her host. "Okay. You've sidestepped my only question long enough . . . my only question for now, that is. Your name is . . . You can fill in the blank any time you'd like."

"My name is not so mysterious." He turned his hand and actually grasped her fingers in his. "My name is Stefan. Stefan Aragat."

"Aragat? That name's familiar. Wasn't there a—?"

"A magician. Yes, a very famous, very powerful magician. An extremely egotistical, misanthropic fool of a magician."

Xandi looked from their linked hands to his face. He was actually smiling, his lip curled back, his sharp canines unable to disguise the self-deprecating humor. "Unfortunately, he pissed off an even more powerful purveyor of the black arts. A wizard, actually. A very old, very potent wizard. Aragat didn't have the patience to learn control of the powers he hoped to gain. Without control, one often makes mistakes. Very. Serious. Mistakes."

He released her hand, picked up the plate with the quiche and offered it to Xandi. "Please. Help yourself. Don't let the meal grow cold."

"You did this to yourself?" She took the quiche without even looking, loaded her plate with bacon and sausage, even grabbed one of the warm sweet rolls.

"Unfortunately, I have only myself to blame." He filled

his plate as well, then took another swallow of coffee. "It was not a pleasant experience, especially at first, when I was limited to life on four legs and an appetite for uncooked, very fresh meat. Really pissed off some of the local farmers and just about got me shot on more than one occasion. I've tried reversing the spell, but obviously my success has been limited. At least I regained a mostly human body. Thank goodness I got my hands back. It was damnably hard to zip trousers with paws. Not to mention brush my teeth."

Xandi almost spewed her coffee. She grabbed the linen napkin and jammed it over her mouth. "I'm sorry, it's just . . . I'm sorry. I shouldn't laugh."

He chuckled, sighed, then took a bite of sausage. "Actually, it feels good. To laugh. I haven't had much to laugh about for the past five years."

"Five years? It's been that long? Ya know, I think I remember an announcement that you'd decided to retire. I thought you were moving to Europe—Liechtenstein or some other little country where rich people like to go."

"That's the announcement I had Oliver put out. Then I came home to lick my wounds, literally. Oliver has been with me since I was very young, just starting out in the business, in fact. Thank goodness he stays, as I'm not quite fit for public viewing. For a long time I actually worried that if I were captured, I'd end up in a zoo. I had trouble speaking at first. It wasn't easy until I was able to shift some of the more wolfen parts through a number of spells.

"You're the first person who's been in my home since my . . . mishap. You are the only person besides Oliver who has seen me." He stared at her, long and hard. Xandi felt her nipples tighten, knew they raised the soft fabric of her gown.

She lowered her head, unwilling to let him see the unbridled lust that must be quite visible on her face. Once again, she wondered if he sensed her arousal, if his animal instincts were finely honed enough to scent the liquid even now pooling between her legs.

Quietly, she finished her meal. Stefan did the same. She wondered what he was thinking, if he felt the same rush of desire as she did, experienced the deep, gut-churning need that thrummed through her veins.

She hoped so. She wanted him. Wanted him in the light of day, face to face, filling her. Loving her. She wanted domination by the beast as much as by the man. Again . . . and again. And again.

He snarled, a wolfen sound, a low growl that started deep in his throat and leaked slowly, menacingly, to his lips. Xandi immediately jerked upright, looked into his amber eyes.

Saw the need she felt reflected in their depths. She carefully wiped her mouth, folded her napkin and placed it beside her knife. Then she stood up and held her hand out to him.

Without a word, Stefan rose as well. He took her hand and led her down the long, sun-bright hallway.

Her fingers were slim yet very strong, clasping his hand tightly even as he led her. He heard the blood rushing in his veins, smelled the rich, lush scent of her desire, knew her vagina was beginning to pulse, the lips at its gate to swell. His cock stretched, grew in girth and length, until he was aware of its restricted position down the left leg of his pants. The fabric brushed against his erection with every step he took. His heightened senses felt each thread, each tiny imperfection in the material, almost as pain.

His room was only at the end of the hallway, a mere fifty feet from the kitchen. He almost didn't make it, so strong was his need. When he finally opened the door and led her into his bedroom—his den—his sanctuary, she was trembling, reassuring him with her physical reaction that her need was every bit as strong as his.

He started to tilt the blinds, to darken the room, but she stopped him. "No. I want to see you. I want to know who takes me so high, who loves me so well."

He almost cried. He'd wondered if any woman would ever want him, would ever desire him. He'd been celibate since the change, unwilling to risk discovery—or rejection. To think that he'd found a woman who embraced him, who found this beast attractive. It was more than he could have ever dreamed.

She turned in his arms and placed her hands on his waist, slipping her long fingers beneath his sweater. He shivered when she raised the hem along his chest, revealing the soft gray fur that covered him. He'd thought it ugly, animalistic, but there was no denying the fascinated light in her eyes when she saw him.

He raised his arms and bent at the waist, allowed her to tug the sweater over his head before he straightened once more. He felt naked, standing there with his furred body in plain view, but she leaned close and nuzzled her cheek against his chest, then found his nipple with her tongue.

"Ahhh." The cry escaped without warning. He choked it off as she licked his taut nipple, circled it with her tongue. He felt the sensation in his nuts, felt the shock of her touch like a coiling flash of lightning. She nipped at him, and he almost cried out again, but he found some semblance of control, just in time.

She touched him all over, running her hands over his torso, across his back. She seemed to be fascinated by him, turned on by his bestial appearance . . . by him.

Suddenly her fingers were fumbling with the snap at his waist, trembling, tugging at the zipper. He grabbed her shoulders, needing something solid to hang onto, something to keep him from falling to his knees.

Last night had been a fantasy, a wonderful interlude with an unknown woman.

Today was a miracle.

After a moment's struggle, she found the zipper, tugged it slowly down, released the pressure holding his damned cock in place. It practically jumped out of the opening, all glistening animal cock that it was. He might have changed his hands, but the penis still looked like something a dog would sport . . . a very large dog. He wondered if he'd ever get used to the sheathlike foreskin, the strange shape, the extra-sensitive surface of this organ.

He glanced at Xandi. She was staring at him as if mesmerized. Her tongue slipped out between her lips, licked both top and bottom, and retreated back into her mouth. He was trying to come up with some way to get that tongue to touch his cock when she suddenly dropped to her knees and pulled his slacks down over his hips.

Completely free now, his cock bobbed just in front of her face, the foreskin pulled back close to his body. She leaned over without any hesitation at all and licked the length of him. His knees almost buckled. He tightened his grip on her shoulders, and she looked up at him and smiled.

He was still trying to figure out the meaning of that grin when she leaned closer and took him in her mouth.

Mother of God! Only her sturdy grasp on his hips held him upright.

Her fingers dug into his butt cheeks, her mouth encompassed his cock, and her damned tongue danced the length of him, licking and tickling until he wanted to cry.

He moaned instead. More of a whimper, actually. Not very manly, but all he was capable of at the moment.

Her fingers squeezed and stroked his butt, her mouth did amazing things to his cock, and he thought his balls might explode from the myriad sensations.

She took him deeper, her mouth squeezing and milking him, her fingers digging into the crease of his ass. He was afraid he might lose it, afraid if he did, that damned knot in his dick would choke her. Silently cursing his regret, he slowly withdrew his cock from between her lips. She leaned over and licked the length of him. He jerked in response. She did it again, and her fingers found the tight ring at his ass and began to probe and press.

It was all he could do to step back out of her reach. "My cock isn't human," he said, knowing the regret in his voice would be more than obvious. "If I come in your mouth, if I lose control, the knot, the part that tied us together last night . . . I'm afraid it could choke you. I can't risk that. Please?"

She licked her lips, as if tasting the few drops of precum he knew she must have found, then nodded. He helped her to her feet, slipped his pants completely off and stood before her, naked. Human. Wolf. A combination of two species, unique among man and beast.

He expected anything but the look she gave him, the blatant lust radiating from her beautiful eyes, the thrust of her breasts peaking against the soft gown he'd left for her.

Without thinking beyond now, Stefan leaned closer and grabbed her gown in his fists, bunching it at her waist and pulling it over her head. She stood there in front of him, her breasts high, the nipples turgid, pointing out of the dark areoles as if begging for his mouth.

He reached for her, lifted the warm weight of her breasts in his palms and immediately lost himself in the feel of silky flesh against his callused fingers. Leaning over, he suckled first one nipple, then the other. She moaned. Her body swayed closer to his as he circled her nipple once more with his tongue, then released her with a quiet little *pop.*

She blinked, her wide gray eyes soft and unfocused. He took a moment longer to look. Her belly was slightly rounded, her hips shapely and full. The dark tuft of curls at her center had been neatly trimmed, enough so that her protruding clit showed through the damp thatch of hair. There was moisture on her inner thighs as well, proof of the arousal he'd scented even as they had breakfast.

She wanted him. Even knowing, seeing, who and what he was, she wanted him. Her body couldn't lie.

"Oh, my," he said, not even trying to hide his eagerness, his hunger. It was there, in his voice, in the catch in his breath, all the longing, the need, the lust. He started to say something, but the words wouldn't come. He swallowed, and finally choked out, "You're beautiful. Perfect. Mine."

He held out his hand to her, tugged her closer. She came willingly, breasts swaying, lips full and pouting. Her hair flowed over her shoulders in thick, shining russet waves, a dark, radiant cape. Her gray eyes sparkled now with laughter as much as with lust. Stefan felt his blood rise, knew his heart raced and the animal in him was barely under control.

When she drifted into his arms, raised her lips to his and kissed him full on his mouth, he let the beast loose.

Chapter 4

It was the most natural thing in the world to raise up on her toes, wrap her arms around his neck and kiss him. His mouth might have been more lupine than human, but Xandi already felt as if she knew the man within. She tested the seam of his lips with her tongue.

He parted them for her, teased her tongue with his, drew her into his mouth. It was different . . . the same . . . amazingly sensual, this kiss that was more than a kiss, with a man who was more than human.

She pressed her hips against him. She was just enough shorter than he was that his hard cock, still damp from her mouth, rode against her belly. The soft fur covering his chest abraded her nipples, and she wanted to dive into him, be a part of him.

He wrapped his arms around her and fell back onto the bed, then rolled both of them so that he was over her. She lay there beneath him, smiling up at the beast hovering over her. She sensed his indecision, his disbelief, that she could truly want him in this form.

Some small part of her mind wondered the same thing. What was she that she could so desire a beast? What strange lust made her loins ache, her pussy weep, her heart race?

He dipped his wolfish head and licked her jaw, his long tongue trailing across her cheek, finding her ear. She shivered, then laughed. "I imagine you can do wondrous things with that tongue," she said.

He growled and nipped at her ear, then moved lower along her body. He stopped at her breast, suckled first one nipple, then the other. She felt the sharp curve of his tongue feathering the very tip, then the stabbing clip of his teeth before he laved her, licked her entire chest with that slick, hot tongue.

Whimpering, gasping tiny, frantic little breaths, she lifted her hips, searching for his cock, but it jutted straight forward, out of her reach. Stefan nuzzled her belly, lapped at the nest of curls between her legs, licked the crease between thigh and groin.

Slick moisture flooded her pussy. Her vagina pulsed, deep, rhythmic contractions, but there was nothing to contract against. She moaned, a deep, guttural plea, then reached for his shoulders and pushed him down, down closer to her needy, hot pussy.

He laughed, then dipped his head and licked her from asshole to clit. One long hot sweep with his tongue. Then he sat up, kneeling between her widespread thighs, and grinned at her, exposing his huge canines, the tip of his tongue.

The blend of man and beast was no more evident than in this posture. The beautifully molded body, the strong chest and powerful arms, the rampant cock all swollen and damp, the alert, forward-pointing ears, the amber eyes with their feral gleam, the teeth and muzzle of the wolf.

Waiting. Watching. Laughing silently at her. She bucked her hips, unable to reach him, then pounded her fists against the tumbled blankets.

"Shit. Oh, shit. You're not going to do that and stop. I won't let you!" She tried to look furious. Burst out laughing instead. "Down, boy. Down!" she ordered, shaking her finger. "Behave, or you're going outside."

He blinked, as if her command caught him by surprise. Then he grinned, dipped his head and licked her once more. Thoroughly. From one end of her crotch to the other, with a quick pause to dip his tongue deep within her streaming pussy.

She didn't move. Couldn't. Could merely hold herself immobile and experience something she'd never, not in her wildest fantasies, imagined. His long tongue moved inside her, curled and licked the walls of her pussy, then flicked her swollen clit before lapping once more across her mons.

When he raised his head, her juices covered his muzzle. Xandi's heart was pounding so hard, she was afraid it might explode. Her vagina contracted over and over, but her climax hovered just on the other side of sensation.

Stefan cleared his throat and grinned at her. She'd already grown used to his canine version of a smile. "Tell me, mistress. Are you interested in obedience training?" he asked. He stretched his tongue around his muzzle and licked his mouth clean, as if emphasizing his animal side. "I should warn you, I don't do well on a leash."

She could barely catch her breath to answer. Humor was almost out of the question at this point. She gave it a try. "Maybe just a collar? When I tell you 'down,' though, I expect you to obey."

"Ah, down? Like this?" Once more he dipped his head. This time he slipped his hands beneath her buttocks and lifted her closer to his mouth. Her legs hung limply over his arms. She whimpered as he lapped carefully, licking her slowly, thoroughly, not missing a single spot between her legs—except her clit.

"Oh, God . . . yes . . . like that. More. Please," she whimpered. "More." She clutched at the bedding, arched her hips, hoped like hell he'd find her button, but he laved everything else instead. Her pussy throbbed, her juices flowed, until she was barely aware of his fingers moving across her buttocks, finding the crease between her cheeks, rubbing the tight ring of muscle at her ass.

Suddenly his tongue found her clit as his thick finger breached her anus. Too much! Too fucking much! Screaming, she arched her back and clamped her cheeks tightly against his hand. He held her immobile, his tongue stroking her clit, then diving into her pussy, his finger pumping in and out of her backside, finding a slow and sensual rhythm in counterpoint to her frantic attempts to thrash and twist.

He brought her down slowly, whimpering and gasping, her legs quivering, her pussy streaming, as her orgasm settled into a slow, rhythmic pulsation.

She gazed at him through half-lidded eyes, waiting, hoping. He couldn't possibly think they were through, could he? She watched as he sat back on his heels, his huge cock glistening deep red in the filtered light streaming through the blinds. The smooth fur covering his body glistened as well, the silver tips of his amazing pelt catching the sunlight like diamonds.

Xandi reached out and touched him, her fingers barely connecting with his cock. It jumped at the brief contact. Stefan growled, deep in his throat. She looked up at his face, startled by the sound, but his head was thrown back, his eyes tightly shut, his mouth twisted into a snarl. She knew immediately it was a sound of desire, not anger, of an almost desperate need for her to touch him.

Slowly she encircled his penis with her fingers, holding his thick cock carefully in her hand. His hips thrust forward, an involuntary move, she thought, but it was more than obvious he wanted her. Badly.

She arched her hips and scooted closer, placing the very tip of his penis against her swollen, wet labia. Still grasping him, she swept his cock back and forth between her legs, coating him in her fluids. He groaned, then leaned closer, easing just the tip into her welcoming pussy.

He moved slowly, carefully, but she urged him on with slow undulations of her hips. She took him this time without any trouble, fitting him deep inside, until the broad head of his penis rested solidly against her womb, the weight of his testicles pressed snugly against her ass.

His face was lifted up, his eyes closed. He panted, as if struggling for control. She looked at him, at the wolven countenance of a man so far removed from the beast, yet so much a part of the creature, and felt the first true stirrings of real emotion, of passion beyond lust, of need and caring and warmth.

She knew he hurt, knew he hated the animal countenance he'd cursed himself with. She found it exotic, intriguing, sensual. She spread her legs wider, lifted her hips to force him more solidly against her cervix, then grasped his lean hips in her hands. "Open your eyes, Stefan. Look at me the way you want me to see you. Please? Open your eyes."

Slowly his breathing eased, and he settled himself between her legs, then he looked at her. There was a wild gleam in his amber eyes, a look that told her he was close, so close, to the edge of whatever kept him human, whatever remnant of his soul controlled the beast.

Xandi reached up and swept her fingers across his muzzle, feeling the sharp prick of stiff whiskers beside his nose, the sleek line of his jaw where the strong muscle blended into his throat. "I want you, Stefan. You. The way you are. The way you feel in me. The way you touch me." She paused and turned his head so that he looked at her directly, his bright canines gleaming in the morning light, the pink curve of his tongue visible between his teeth.

"The way you look, Stefan. I love the way you look."

An expression of what could only be pain filled his eyes, but he began to move, his hips slowly thrusting deep inside, his strong hands grasping her waist. She caught his rhythm, joining with him, man and woman, mating in a dance older than time, hips thrusting, hearts pounding, as he increased the tempo, picked up speed, filled her.

In this position, she felt him even more than she had last night. His cock was hot, burning her with each slick penetration, rubbing her sensitive flesh, bringing her closer and closer once more to her peak.

His breath exploded in short, sharp gasps. Close, so close, to her own orgasm, Xandi struggled to stay with him, watched his chest swell, his jaw clench. Suddenly he threw back his head and shouted, words unintelligible, a victory cry, as she felt him grow, felt the swelling in his cock slip past her thickened labia, filling her, locking the two of them in a climactic knot.

She fought a moment's panic that he was too big, that she'd tear, that he'd hurt her, but the link was there, once again, the connection that was more than mere sex. The moment she felt it, her body reacted—her muscles stretched and adjusted, holding him deep inside, squeezing each spurt of semen out of him. Connected, mind and body, in total sync, her own climax slammed into her, the coil of heat practically exploding across her body, wringing a long, strangled cry out of her.

Panting, gasping for air, Stefan collapsed forward across her chest. Xandi wrapped her arms around his neck, holding him close, stroking his neck and shoulders, kissing the side of his face. She tasted salt on her tongue, knew she cried, but wondered if the tears were all hers, or possibly Stefan's as well. He shuddered in her embrace, took a deep, quavering breath, and that question was answered.

His cock still pulsed, deep, rhythmic undulations against her womb. Her own muscles spasmed around him, matching his cadence, holding him tight.

After a while, he raised his head, blinking owlishly as he stared down at her. "Are you okay?"

"No, I'm way beyond okay." She ran the backs of her

fingers along his jowl, reveling in the silky touch of his fur. "How about you?"

She could almost feel the relief. She could also still feel the hard knot of his swollen cock filling her.

"Amazing. Absolutely amazing. I haven't done—" he shook his head, looked away, shut his eyes tightly for a moment, then turned back to her—"this. Not in the past five years. Not since I . . . changed."

She held his face in her palms, his beautiful wolven face, all sharp teeth and gleaming eyes, and looked directly at him. "We'll do it again. And again. I have never felt like this. Never. Never this connection, this mind-and-body experience that's so totally soul-deep. Not with anyone. I will not let you go."

"I felt it, too," he whispered, turning his head to lick her palm. "I was so afraid I was alone, but I felt it, felt you." His hips rocked against the cradle of her thighs, probing her, touching the mouth of her womb with his hard cock. No longer swollen, but still erect, he loved her once more. She wrapped her legs around his hips and held him close.

They sat quietly in front of the fire, sipping an excellent Cabernet Franc, watching the flames dance. Xandi's two weeks were almost spent. Her car, slightly dented but still functional, sat in the driveway where Oliver had left it after towing it out of the deep canyon where she'd gone off the road. It was as if they waited now, for something, unsure what that something might be.

Xandi couldn't stand it any longer—the suspense, the need to know. They'd made no mention of tomorrow, never discussed a future. "What next?" she asked, resting one palm over his beating heart. "What are we going to do?"

His arm tightened around her shoulders, and she felt him sigh. "I don't want to lose you, yet I can't, in good faith, tie you to a beast."

She laughed. "Ah, but I love being tied to a beast. You've shown me an entirely new type of pleasure, one, I fear, I've become addicted to." She paused a moment, gathering her thoughts. "You can't force me to leave, you know. I can be tenacious." Xandi snuggled closer to his warm, familiar body. A body she'd learned to crave over the past days and nights of sensual exploration. "I have . . . feelings for you, Stefan. Very strong feelings. Stronger than I ever imagined."

He tightened his arms around her. "I'll not hedge mine, Alexandria. I love you. You have given me a reason to live, to search for an answer to my dilemma." He smiled at her, brushing the tangled hair back from her eyes. "You are the woman I never thought I'd find, the one who has reminded me that humanity is more than just appearance. It is the soul, the spirit, the very essence that makes one a man."

He looked away again, but when he turned back to her, his eyes were filled with resolve. "I told you it was my own hubris that turned me into a beast. What I didn't tell you is that it was a very powerful wizard who actually did the deed. All he asked was my apology, my admission that I was a fool, and he would give me back my humanity."

He sighed, then smiled at her. "It has taken me five long years to realize I was wrong and he was right. I owe him that apology, whether he returns me to my former self or not. I've decided to try to find him, to beg him to forgive me for my insolence. He merely offered to teach me, but I thought I was more than he. It wasn't his fault I was a fool. It will, however, be my fault if I don't let him know I've finally learned my lesson."

"Take me with you." Xandi turned in his arms, grabbed his shoulders and forced him to look her in the eye. "Take me on your quest, Stefan. I can't imagine being parted from you. Not now, not ever. You've become a drug my soul needs to survive. A part of the very cells that keep my heart pumping, my brain functioning. Please. Take me."

"And what if, when the journey is over, I am nothing more than Stefan the Magician, a normal man with insubstantial powers? The face of a human, the strength of an average man. Will you love me when I am no longer the wolf? Will you still want me?"

She ran her finger along his bare chest, circled his navel and traced the length of his growing penis. "Ah, Stefan, yes. I'll still love you. But when you ask him to return your humanity, do you think you could keep just this one small remnant of your life as a beast?"

Laughing, he grabbed her, rolled her onto her back, used his hand to spread her legs wide. "We'll make that a priority, my love. Hopefully he'll consider it a little souvenir of my life as a wolf."

PART TWO

Alexandria

Chapter 5

The black Mercedes took the steep mountain road without effort. Alexandria Olanet struggled to keep her eyes open, but the journey had been long and difficult, emotions between her and the enigmatic man sitting beside her practically off the chart.

He'd been silent the better part of the trip, an uncommunicative partner on a quest that would likely change both their lives at the most elemental of levels. She studied him, sitting there next to her on the wide backseat, through half-shuttered eyes, almost afraid to let herself consider what lay ahead.

It was difficult enough to explain what had already transpired. When she'd called her office and informed her partners she was taking an extended sabbatical, they'd asked her very few questions. Of course, they thought she was still smarting over her failed engagement. Little did they know how thankful she was to have gotten out of a disaster-in-the-making.

Now she wondered if she was about to enter another. Stefan Aragat was more than a mystery—more than a man, for that matter. He stared out the window, one elegant hand resting beneath his chin, the long fingers with neatly trimmed nails supporting a face that was, for want of any other description, pure wolf. Grizzled muzzle, sharp canines, fur-tipped ears pointed forward, searing amber eyes—even though his body was tall and strong and almost completely human, beneath the tailored slacks and dark gray silk shirt was a coat of gray fur tipped with silver and the strong, violent heart of the wolf.

And, of course, a most amazing cock.

Xandi almost laughed out loud. She would never grow tired of that amazing tool of his, all part and parcel of a package caught halfway between wolf and man. She'd fallen in love with a creature beyond anything her imagination might have created, a creature hell-bent on changing himself back to human.

Would it be the same, making love to Stefan as a man? Merely thinking of the wolf taking her, of that amazing cock penetrating her, swelling inside her pussy and trapping them together in unbelievable orgasms, made her hot. Made her pussy weep and her muscles clench in frustrated need.

What was wrong with her, she wondered, that she would desire the wolf as much as, if not more than, the man?

Stefan stared blindly out the window, thinking of the man they were rushing to meet, and of the woman beside him. Xandi had been unusually quiet as they wound their long way up the mountain in the chauffeur-driven limo. Of course, so had he, though there was so much he wanted to say to her.

She'd turned his life upside down over the past two weeks, ever since she'd literally stumbled into his world. Alexandria Olanet—Xandi—of the sweet lips and even sweeter body, a woman as fascinated by his bestial qualities as she was by the man inside. How was she going to feel when he returned to his human form? Would she love him as much? Would her fascination and insatiable sexual appetite remain just as powerful after he found his humanity, or was it the wolf in him that excited her?

Even more worrisome, what was she going to think of his darker side? The desire and passion even he didn't understand? The needs he felt, even now, with a lovely woman close beside him.

Desire linked to Anton.

Stefan's shoulders dipped, and he closed his eyes. He would know the answers to all his questions once this long journey ended. He'd contacted the wizard—his mentor, Anton Cheval—and told him he was returning, but nothing more. He'd reached the wizard through a spell of his own making, using the amazing mental link he had with Anton, the same link he shared with Xandi.

He still hadn't admitted to the woman he loved that their ability to read one another's minds wasn't unique. Nor had he told her of the dark desire he felt for Anton. Of the dreams that awakened him night after night with his cock erect and his body wanting another man. Would she still love him, or would she think he was—Hell, even he didn't know what he was. Man? Beast? Bi? Gay? Straight?

Damn. He was such a fucking coward! For five years now, he'd lived as part man, part beast, tortured by erotic dreams of another man—and so afraid of those dreams, he'd chosen half a life, rather than face the desire he felt for Anton.

Anton. Shit. What was wrong with him? He'd never lusted after a man, never thought of another man sexually. This need, though—this sexual desire—was somehow intrinsic to his very existence, to his nature. How could he explain it to Xandi when he didn't understand it himself? The dark desire, the sensual need and the overwhelming hate that seemed to coexist with every thought of the man who had been his mentor?

His master?

The man who had cursed him.

He'd told Xandi there would be penalties to pay, punishment to endure, but he hadn't told her everything. Fear of his own desires, pure and simple, had kept him away from Anton. Those same desires now moved him forward. Stefan felt a growing sense of expectation, a dark, purely sexual need for subjugation, a desire to submit totally to Anton.

He pictured the wizard—darkly handsome, his lean face and amber eyes mesmerizing, intensely intelligent. Thoughts of Anton had haunted his nights for five years now, filling Stefan's dreams with a combination of carnal longing and murderous intent. Five long years of celibacy, of waking in the dark of night sweating, panting, painfully erect and thinking of Anton, of his elegant hands on Stefan's body, of his mouth, his cock. Dreams that shamed him, excited him, confused him.

Was that unnatural desire part of the curse that left him half man and half beast, or was it a truth about his nature he'd not known before Anton?

When Xandi entered his life and made love to the beast, she stilled the dreams. Stilled them, but didn't end them. He shuddered, feeling Xandi close beside him, sensing the wizard up ahead. Would she hate him when she learned the truth? When she discovered a side of him to which he himself still couldn't admit?

As the car drew closer to Anton's home, Stefan's sense of dread grew and expanded. This wasn't going to be easy, not with Xandi beside him. Since the first time he saw her, he'd loved her, had reveled in their sexual and mental compatibility. She made him more powerful, more male. More in control.

Was he about to lose all of that to Anton? Would he lose Xandi as well? He swallowed and felt the muscles in his throat constrict, as if someone were choking him, cutting off his air.

I can do this. I will beg his favor and submit. I have to.

I want to.

Oh, God, how I want this.

It went against his nature, against everything that defined him.

A dark thrill coursed through his body. His cock swelled against the restricting fabric of his slacks. *No. What defines me has changed. I have changed. Xandi loves me as I am. Her love empowers me. Yet Anton's love draws me. Must I lose one to gain the other?*

Must I lose who I am now to regain my humanity?

He took a deep, steadying breath. Held it. Let it out and felt his shoulders relax.

Sighing, he took Xandi's cold fingers in his and held her hand tightly against his thigh. Afraid, anxious, expectant. Confused. But not alone. No longer alone.

Xandi remained quiet as the car followed the twisted road to the wizard Anton's home. High in the mountains of Montana, the location was a mere X on the map Stefan had found on his breakfast table this morning.

Neither of them had any idea how Anton had gotten the map and instructions into Stefan's home. The simple sheet of handwritten directions and the map, placed discreetly next to the salt and pepper shakers, had merely hinted at the wizard's power.

Stefan was his usual silent self, but Xandi sensed conflicting emotions roiling beneath his outwardly composed exterior. Relaxed he might appear, but she knew he was as tense as a well-strung bow. She sensed his raw power tempered by an underlying hint of fear. He reached over and took her hand, squeezed her fingers, then held them against his thigh.

She sighed and moved closer to him. He might not say anything, but she knew he needed her, for companionship, if for nothing else. Why did he seem so conflicted? Something else bothered him, something she couldn't quite sense. She squeezed his hand and settled close against his side.

Xandi was still contemplating his moods when they pulled into the drive of the wizard's home. Palatial in design, the house managed to look as if it had been hewn from the very trees and mountains that protected it, as if the rock had grown out of the earth, not been laid by the hand of man.

She felt Stefan's resolve strengthen as the car rolled silently to a stop. He straightened his shoulders and lifted his chin, then nodded with an almost regal bearing when the driver opened the door for them. An old servant in a faded blue robe met them at the top of the broad staircase leading to a large, intricately carved wooden door. He bowed and stepped aside, leaning heavily on a carved staff. With a terse nod, he invited them in.

Stefan strode through the door like a man on a mission. Xandi followed quietly, curious at Stefan's unexpected show of bravado. He'd been almost humble when he'd cast the spell to contact Anton the night before. Humble and penitent, as if well aware of the pain his arrogance had brought him.

Xandi realized she preferred that side of him. This attitude, as if he were looking for a battle, put her off, unsettled her.

The old man abruptly appeared just ahead of them, blocking their path. His voice trembled as if with palsy, his hand on the head of the staff shook. "Stefan Aragat. You seek the wizard. Why?"

Stefan drew himself up, standing straight and proud, glaring down his long, lupine nose at the old man. "You can look at me and ask that? I want him to return me to my human form."

"Ah. I see." The old man moved closer to Stefan. He tilted his head and looked up, frowning. "Do you truly regret your hubris? Do you accept your blame for his actions? Do you understand humility? That is the lesson he wished to teach."

"Of course I do, but I wish to discuss this matter with Anton, old man. Not with his servant."

Xandi drew away from Stefan. She shivered from a sudden chill, and her gaze shifted nervously from the proud tilt of Stefan's head to the answering gleam in the old man's eyes. She backed against the wall, sensed a building power within the room, an aura of shifting light and darkness. Didn't Stefan feel it? How could he be oblivious to the anger, the darkness, the seething cloud settling all around them?

Then she saw it, the slight curl to Stefan's lip, half smile, half snarl, the same expression on the old man's face as he nodded in understanding.

Suddenly it all came clear to Xandi. Stefan challenged the old man! He *wanted* a fight. What the hell was he doing?

Stefan recognized his mistake the second the words left his mouth. He'd stormed in here all full of bullshit and bluster, his heart pounding in his chest, his passions running high and hot. Wrong. So damned wrong he wasn't even close to right. He needed to get the hell out of here, now, not force the issue while Xandi stood beside him. What the hell was he thinking? He turned and reached for her, but a voice filled the room, reverberated within the walls, bounced off the high ceiling and left his sensitive wolf's ears ringing.

Stefan spun around. The old man held his staff high. Power flashed in a sparkling aura around his body. There was no weakness in him now.

Of course! Stefan had wondered if the old man was Anton. He had his proof now. Wasn't this exactly what he'd wanted? At least what one side of him wanted. Stefan blinked, recognizing his desires for what they were, finally understanding how powerful his needs had become.

"Have you learned so little, Stefan Aragat? Have the last five years taught you nothing? I had hoped better of you. You truly are an arrogant bastard."

The extent of his error struck home with the precision of a radio-controlled missile. *Oh, shit.* He never should have pushed Anton with Xandi here. He barely had time to raise his hands in apology—the shift was instantaneous. One moment he faced an angry old man in a faded blue robe, the next he cowered beneath the snapping fangs of a ferocious black wolf. Before he had time to react, the wolf caught Stefan's shoulder between powerful jaws, twisted his body and bore him to the ground. Stefan landed face down, hard, the air rushing from his lungs in a powerful gust, leaving him dazed and disoriented.

Snarling and snapping, the wolf caught his shirt and ripped it away from his back, clawing at Stefan's flesh, rending it with his sharp claws. Stefan's pants went next, stripped from his writhing body as he fought desperately to stop the vicious, snarling attack.

Abruptly, he stilled beneath the wolf as understanding slammed into him. This was exactly what he'd wanted all along. Not merely to submit, but to be *forced* to submit, forced to take the punishment due him. Being forced absolved him, allowed him to exorcise the wizard from his mind, the dark desires from his dreams, without admitting his acceptance.

Xandi screamed. The sound cut off sharply in mid-howl. Frantic, Stefan twisted his body and saw her, unexplainably naked, caught against the far wall as if by invisible shackles, her arms raised, her legs spread wide, her mouth open in shock and fear.

Xandi! He must protect her. Now was not the time to deal with conflicted passions and dark dreams. Stefan twisted beneath the wolf, turned and snapped his own jaws, reached for a handhold on the thick fur. Each grasp was torn loose, each twist left him more at the mercy of the beast. Suddenly Stefan felt a sharp probing between his legs. Something hot and wet jabbed his balls, the soft flesh near his anus.

He'd expected this, feared it, wanted it, but not now, not like this, not with Xandi watching.

Not with a wolf!

Desperate, he twisted harder, writhed and jerked in a frantic attempt to shake his attacker loose. But a heavy paw forced his head to the ground, another, claws extended, raked his back and thighs, and he felt the screaming agony of penetration, felt the creature's thick cock forcing entrance.

"No! You bastard! No!" Snarling, snapping impotently, he fought the more powerful wolf, his hips twisting and turning to shove the beast off, but the creature thrust harder, his thick cock stretching and tearing his flesh to find entrance. Burning, stabbing pain took his breath, forced the air from his lungs. Gasping, twisting impotently, his actions only drove the creature's huge cock deeper into his virgin ass. He threw his head back in an agonizing cry . . .

. . . and looked directly into Xandi's gray eyes. Caught there, her gorgeous body held against the wall by invisible bonds, her eyes wide, her lips parted.

The creature slammed against his buttocks, and Stefan felt the agonizing length of the wolf's cock piercing deep and hard, the pulsing inside his own body as tissues and muscles adjusted, accepted.

He bowed his head, his shame complete. Xandi would watch his subjugation, stand witness to his weakness. Stefan ceased his struggle in a tacit admission of defeat. He should never have fought this, should have knelt and accepted what was his due . . . what he'd desired all along. He dipped his head farther, closed his eyes, as sharp claws caught his naked hips, as the creature behind him pressed home with short, jabbing thrusts, until his huge cock found its home, deep within Stefan's body.

Suddenly, the beast went still. Stefan felt almost preternaturally aware of the solid cock pulsing hot and hard inside his ass, of his bare knees resting on the thick carpet, his trembling arms supporting his own weight as well as that of the wolf. He held his breath, afraid to move, afraid to bring back the agonizing pain, just now beginning to subside.

He took long, slow breaths through flared nostrils, controlling the expansion of his lungs. As his body shifted and adjusted to the intruder, a familiar warmth suffused his skin, heated his loins. He felt the first stirrings of desire, fought the impulse to spread his legs wider, to welcome the cock deeper, to press his hips closer.

Shamed, humiliated beyond belief, Stefan fought the all-too-familiar hot arousal pulsing through his blood, the ache in his balls as his cock rose, stretched, engorged, in response to the unfamiliar fullness of a thick cock penetrating his ass. The creature withdrew slowly, pulling back so the head of his penis teased the tight ring of muscle, then carefully slipped back inside, pressing hard and deep. The wolf found a slow and steady rhythm, sliding in and out, deeper with each careful thrust, intended now to arouse, not to punish.

Shamed, betrayed by his own body, Stefan recoiled as the creature's testicles brushed against his own, a stark reminder of his position beneath the more powerful male. His mind roiled with memories, thoughts of pride and arrogance, of fear and desire, all brought down to this, to the steady thrust and grind of a hard cock filling his ass, of hot breath against his back, all while Xandi watched. He wanted to weep for the shame, but at the same time, his body reacted, adjusted, accepted . . . submitted.

Memories of dreams filled his head, dreams so much a part of his nights these past five years, he'd learned to welcome them. Dreams of Anton and the passion he'd felt for the man, the admiration for his mentor, the hatred. So many conflicting emotions, swirling now, filling his head, his heart.

Sharp claws scraped Stefan's sides. The cock drove deeper, each powerful thrust threatening to topple him forward, a further reminder of the other's strength. A reminder of his own responsibility, of his own failings. Would Xandi still see him as a man? Would she want him after this?

Will it even matter?

Mastered by the stronger wolf, Stefan bowed his head in complete submission. He adjusted his stance, holding steady against the powerful assault.

Then it was a man taking him, a man's muscular thighs pressed against his, a man's belly rubbing against his buttocks. He wanted to feel revulsion, to experience disgust, but his own cock grew harder, stronger, his own body reacted as it found a rhythm to match Anton's. Moaning, more aroused than he could ever remember, Stefan shuddered beneath the steady thrusts, no longer able to deny his nature or the passion clouding his mind.

He raised his head. Xandi watched him, her eyes wide, lips parted, hands trapped against the walls, her naked breasts rising and falling with each labored breath, her nipples pointing at him, proudly erect. A suspicious glistening shimmered now between her legs, dampness clumped the reddish pubic hair covering her mons. No! It couldn't be . . . she wouldn't . . . but she was aroused, deeply aroused, as aroused as he was, a participant, not merely a witness to his shame.

Stefan shuddered. He should feel betrayed, shouldn't he? Betrayed by the woman who found his humiliation exciting.

He should, but he wasn't. His gaze locked with Xandi's, his mind a confused and twisted mass of sensation, of lust and passion, of humiliation and pain. And he realized she was there, her own thoughts twisting with his, struggling to understand the myriad sensations, the emotions and passions that engulfed him.

She experienced this act with him! He was aroused, and she knew it, felt it, reveled in it. He shook his head, looked back at her, felt her grow stronger in his mind, the link they'd discovered during lovemaking building now, filling his thoughts, feeding his passion. The cock plunging deep within his bowels no longer burned with each stabbing thrust. Now it caught him in a dark, carnal rhythm, a rhythm that seemed to take on the beat of his heart, the rush of blood through his veins, a rhythm he shared with Xandi. A rhythm he knew deep in his heart, knew in his body as well as his mind.

He knew! Somehow his body knew this act, understood the deep bonding between males of his kind, comprehended the role Xandi played in who he was, what he was yet to become. Making him accept, welcome, know this was the Master's way. It was the only way that Stefan might learn and understand.

Anton was there, his thoughts mingling with Stefan's, sharing his knowledge, his understanding, answering more questions than Stefan knew to ask. So many lessons. So much to understand. So many unknowns, all tied to the Master imposing his will on Stefan, imposing his will in the way of their kind. A great glow seemed to surround them, a glow that grew out of the tableau of watching, sharing woman, subjugated male and alpha wolf. Finally Stefan knew and understood. He spread his knees wider, braced his hips to meet Anton's deep, penetrating thrusts. Eyes still focused on Xandi, shoulders straining to hold himself steady, he welcomed the man's cock into his now-willing body, welcomed the subjugation, welcomed both Xandi and Anton in his mind.

A hand grasped his swollen cock. Strong, masculine fingers encircled his sensitive flesh, stroked him in fierce counterpoint to each stabbing penetration. The other hand stroked his flank, then grasped his testicles, so that he was totally governed by his Master, completely under Anton's control.

Flexing his shoulders, Stefan strengthened the mental link with Anton, felt the deep love and admiration of the other man, the passion as well as the need and confusion in the woman. He felt the first contraction in his balls, the tightening of his muscles, the huge knot growing in his wolf's penis as his orgasm slammed into him.

Anton's hand closed tightly around his cock just behind the knot. His other clamped down on Stefan's balls, squeezing him to the point of exquisite pain. Arching his back, he felt the hard pulse of the wizard's climax, the hot seed filling him, the fast, hard thrusts as Anton mastered him. Shuddering through his own climax, shaking with his release, arms trembling with passion spent, Stefan collapsed.

Anton released his grip on Stefan's genitals and backed away just as he fell. The wizard's flaccid penis slipped easily from Stefan's body. Without a word, Anton turned and left the room.

There was no pain beyond the rhythmic clenching of his muscles in the aftermath of orgasm. No humiliation. No feeling of any kind, other than the knowledge that what had happened had to happen. What Anton had done to him was not meant to humiliate or destroy. No, it had been a lesson. A very graphic lesson, an act of love as much as an act of dominance, a sharing of knowledge that had more than rocked his world.

Stefan raised his head, almost afraid to look at Xandi.

Free now of whatever spell had trapped her, she knelt before him, her knees spread wide, her nether lips pouting and moist. She reached her hand out and touched his shoulder. Stefan felt the link strengthen between them and knew immediately that the knowledge Anton had given him had not been shared. Xandi didn't know. Still, he sensed compassion, love, need—overwhelming need.

There was no pity. He couldn't have borne pity. He needed her passion. It was his, not Anton's. She could have chosen the alpha wolf. She chose Stefan. She needed him. He felt desire rolling off of her in waves of heat, in the racing beat of her heart pounding in his ears, in the ripe, musky scent surrounding her body.

He covered her hand with his, pulled her fingers from his shoulder and kissed them. Then he carefully stretched her out on the thick carpet and knelt between her legs.

She moaned when he covered her labia with his mouth. Arched her back and cried out when his lips suckled her clitoris, then raised her hips to meet his mouth as his tongue swept the weeping walls of her vagina. He licked and suckled, scraping tender flesh with his teeth, lifting her hips with his fingers spread wide across her buttocks.

He found the cleft between her cheeks and probed gently with clasping fingers, lifting and licking, letting his thoughts of love and passion mingle with hers, drawing her closer to him, mentally and physically, until his wolven tongue stretched deeply inside, licked the walls and tissues, covered the sensitive bud, bathed the fleshy lips.

Suddenly her body stiffened. She cried out, a long, low keening wail that reminded him of a wolf's howl, a desperate, needy cry that turned to choppy, whimpering sighs and pants. He brought her down slowly, steadily, his tongue a silken caress on sensitized flesh. Her thighs quivered, her hands grabbed for his head, his shoulders, stroked his back, fluttered over his scalp, across the tips of his wolven ears.

Finally he knelt over her and drove his cock slowly into her waiting folds. She welcomed him with raised knees and thighs spread wide. He thrust into her once, twice, then buried himself as she climaxed once more.

The clenching, grabbing undulations of her pussy caught

his swollen cock, sucked it deep and hard, until his own orgasm burst out of him, the huge knot at the base of his penis slipping through her tight opening, linking them, holding them together.

He felt her thoughts in his mind again, her mental sighs of release, her love, her myriad questions. He lowered himself to one side, their bodies still tied, his cock pulsing in rhythm with her muscular contractions. Her slim arms wrapped around his neck, her face burrowed into the hollow between his neck and shoulder. He heard as much as felt the soft exhalation of moist breath against his muzzle.

He brushed her hair back from her face. Nuzzled her forehead, her lips, the closed lids protecting her eyes. Why didn't she look at him? The link was gone now. The sense they'd been two bodies with one mind, then a single body, a single mind. Now she closed her eyes and sighed against his throat, and he wondered if she felt shame for him. Felt pity. Regret.

"I love you," she said. Her lips moved against his throat, and he wanted to weep. "I'm not sure what happened here tonight. I'm not sure I even believe what I saw. But I do love you."

He couldn't ask for more. Not now. Later, maybe. Later he would tell her what it meant to be part of the pack. What it meant to be female when the alpha male demanded his rights.

What would happen when Anton decided it was his time to claim Alexandria.

Chapter 6

His clothes were shredded, hers just gone. Xandi sat up and covered her breasts with crossed arms as the door at the far end of the room opened.

"Oliver? What the hell?" Stefan leapt to his feet as the familiar figure of his servant crossed the room carrying two terry-cloth robes. "You're supposed to be visiting your family. What are you doing here?" He took the robes Oliver offered and handed one to Xandi. She was thankful Stefan stood in front of her, providing some protection from Oliver's view.

"This is my family, sir." Oliver refused to meet Stefan's eyes. Instead he nodded his head and turned away, giving them both privacy to cover themselves. "The Master will explain. First, though, I will show you to your room. Follow me." On that cryptic note, Oliver directed them to a staircase leading to the upper floors.

At the base of the stairs, Xandi placed her hand on Stefan's forearm. "Are you okay?"

He laughed. "Other than a really sore ass, you mean?"

"I . . ." She closed her mouth. Awkward didn't begin to describe how she felt.

He covered her hand with his own. "It's okay. There is so much I need to tell you." His eyes were very bright, his expression almost carefree. "I'm fine. Now." He leaned over and kissed her. "I know you don't understand, but what Anton did was inevitable. It makes sense now. Eventually, it will to you, too."

She hoped so. For now, nothing made sense. She knew she must be in shock. She'd seen an old man turn into a wolf. That was impossible, wasn't it? But the man she loved was also a wolf. Impossible. There was no such thing as half man, half wolf . . . yet Stefan walked beside her. Had made love to her.

She should have felt outraged over what was essentially the assault of her lover, yet in the midst of the act, she'd sensed Stefan's desire, had actually felt his passion, even as he submitted.

She'd been every bit as aroused as Stefan.

Shaking her head, confused and filled with questions, she followed Stefan and Oliver up the stairs.

An hour later, freshly bathed and dressed in a soft, deep red velour pantsuit she'd found waiting for her in the bathroom, Xandi held tightly to Stefan's arm as they once more followed Oliver. He led them down the stairs and along a wide hallway, to what appeared to be a library on the lower floor.

A man sat in an overstuffed chair by a large window, his face partially hidden in shadow. He was impeccably dressed, his black hair swept back from his forehead and tied in a neat queue at the back of his neck. His elbows rested on the arms of his chair, and his long fingers were steepled in front of his lips. He nodded to Stefan, acknowledging his presence, then smiled at Xandi.

His beauty when he smiled almost took her breath away. It was an ageless beauty she would never have expected from a man capable of doing what he had done to Stefan. Then she'd seen only the predator, the wild eyes and snarling visage of one man showing his supremacy over another. She'd not seen this man, but still, she knew, it was the same person, the wizard Stefan seemed to both love and fear.

Anton greeted them with a reserved nod of his head, the sweep of his hand directing them to a low couch near his chair.

Following Stefan's lead, Xandi sat close to him on the comfortable couch. "Master." Stefan inclined his head in greeting, but offered no subservience in his manner. Xandi did, however, sense the respect Stefan held for the other man.

A respect she'd certainly not noticed in him earlier.

"Please introduce me to the lady." Anton's eyes, eyes the same unusual shade of amber as Stefan's, focused directly on Xandi. His voice was deep, melodious. Powerful. Surprisingly, she sensed a subtle link, the same link she'd learned to associate with Stefan. Xandi knew her surprise showed on her face, though she tried to keep her expression under control.

"Master, I would like to introduce Alexandria Olanet. Alexandria, this is Anton Cheval, the wizard I've told you of." As if the scene in the great room had never occurred, Xandi found herself shaking hands with the wizard. His grip was firm, the flesh warm. He held on, covering her hand with both of his, when she tried to pull away.

"My dear, it is a great pleasure to meet you. I sense your questions, and I understand them. They will all be answered." He glanced at Oliver, waiting quietly in the doorway. "Wine for my guests, please, Oliver?"

Still holding onto Xandi's hand, Anton turned his gaze on Stefan. She was surprised by the honest concern in his voice when he said, "I must ask you. Are you all right?"

Stefan dipped his head, this motion a subtle acknowledgment of the other's superiority. "Yes, Master."

Anton gave a quick nod, and Xandi realized that, with this brief exchange, the two men had put the morning behind them. Forever. She wondered if she would ever do the same. The image of Anton fucking Stefan, first as a wolf, then as a man—the look of pure animal lust on the faces of both men—no, this would stay with her.

Her pussy clenched, and she closed her eyes, willing her restless body to be still. Anton's fingers stroked her hand. He tilted his head and looked deeply into her eyes.

He knows. He knows what's in my mind. She shuddered, aware of a deep pulsing in her vagina, the brushing of the taut points of her erect nipples against the soft velour shirt. Anton looked away, but there was a slight smile on his full lips. A look of satisfaction.

Once more he addressed Stefan. "Does the word *Chanku* mean anything to you?"

Stefan shook his head. "No. Should it?" He glanced down, as if studying Xandi's hand, still cupped in Anton's, then reached over and carefully pried her fingers free of Anton's grasp. "No disrespect intended, Master."

"None taken. She is quite beautiful. She is also very special. More special than you realize."

Oliver entered the room with a chilled bottle of white wine and three long-stemmed glasses.

"Thank you, Oliver. I will pour." Anton nodded, and the smaller man left the room. "Oliver has been in my employ for almost ten years."

He paused, as if giving Stefan time to consider the implications. Xandi watched the play of emotions on Stefan's face, read his understanding and acceptance.

"So, you have watched me all this time?" The corner of his lips curved up in a wolven smile. "At least it explains the map. I wondered how you placed it on my table. I wondered if your powers had grown beyond all understanding." Stefan took the glass of wine Anton offered him and handed it to Xandi, then took a second for himself. "So, Oliver never was my servant. He was your spy. Why?"

"Because you are Chanku. You are the most powerful one I have been able to find, and I could not risk losing you." Anton's eyes blazed, and he took a swallow of his wine, as if to calm himself. "I will explain, something I should have done five years ago, when I confirmed what you were. My only excuse is that I was still learning then. Still trying to understand all the implications."

Anton paused, set his glass down and clasped his hands in front of him. "There was an ancient race, a wolven race, that coexisted with early humans in the Himalayas, long before the advent of villages and towns, before man began to settle in communities. Legend calls them Chanku, but they no longer exist as the people they once were."

"What do you mean by *wolven*? Animals that coexisted with people, the way dogs do now? Or are you talking about werewolves? They don't exist." Xandi clutched her wine glass. She already knew Anton's answer. Sensed exactly where this conversation was going. But why? How should she know? Why should she know the word, the name *Chanku*?

Know that the Chanku were much more than wolves, much more even than humans?

Anton nodded, and she was certain he read her thoughts. "No, my dear. Not werewolves. Those are mere creatures of myth and legend. Still, I knew you would understand." He turned to Stefan. "You do as well. However, you are more stubborn than the woman." He smiled once more at Xandi, and sighed. "He'll believe me eventually. It's okay." When he looked back at Stefan, he was smiling as if he'd just shared a private joke with Xandi.

"The Chanku, like the fabled werewolves, have the power to shift their bodies from human to wolf and back again. In our case, though, it's nothing paranormal, not supernatural. We don't need a full moon or any type of spell, nor must we remain under cover of darkness. It's physical, actually, all based on a small part of the brain near the hypothalamus, an extension of that organ that exists only in the Chanku, an insignificant bit of flesh that without certain nutrients, loses its ability to function."

He stood up, as if the information spilling out of him controlled his movements. "I discovered the history of the Chanku during my studies of arcane sciences, learned of the grasses once common to the area that is now Tibet, grasses that have the ability to draw certain nutrients from the soil in precise percentages, nutrients perfectly formulated to stimulate this small organ. It, in turn, exerts influence on the functions in the body needed to shift."

Anton wheeled around and pointed his finger at Stefan. "You thought I turned you into a wolf as punishment for your arrogance. You were only partially correct. I gave you the nutrient in sufficient quantities to allow you to make the shift. You didn't understand how or why it happened, nor did you understand the changes in your very nature. It frightened you—I frightened you—so you blamed me and left before I could explain. Without the nutrient, you were unable to shift back to human form. It wasn't your magic that helped your partial shift. It was the residual effect of the nutrient still in your system. Not enough to complete the shift, it left you caught between man and wolf."

Anton paused in his tirade, took a deep breath and faced Stefan, once more in control. "I frightened you then. I was wrong, but I let my own arrogance get in the way of the truth. I exposed you to your nature without explaining the background that might have allowed you to accept what you were. I won't make that mistake again. You will stay here. You and Alexandria. You will learn the way of our people. You will both be given proper amounts of the nutrients, and you will find your true selves."

Stunned, Xandi turned to Stefan. "*Selves?*" She licked

her lips, stared up at Anton, hovering over them. "*Selves?* I . . . I don't understand."

"Yes, you do. You understand much more than you're willing to admit." Anton knelt in front of Xandi and took her chilled hands in both of his. "How do you think Stefan found you? Lost, dying in a blizzard? He sensed you. Sensed a kindred spirit. You carry the genes of the ancient ones. The link when you make love with him?"

Xandi blushed and turned her head. How could he possibly know?

"Don't hide from me, Alexandria. I felt you. I know you were there, a part of both of us, of both Stefan and myself. When I covered Stefan, when I penetrated his body, what did you feel?"

Xandi blinked. Her eyes stung with unshed tears. How could he know?

"Xandi?" Stefan turned her so that she had to face him. "It's nothing to be ashamed of. If anyone should feel shame, it should be me, for dragging you into this without proper warning. I suspected what might happen with Anton. I wanted it. I should have told you. I am so sorry." Stefan brushed her hair back from her eyes. "You were there. In my mind, so much a part of the experience that I felt your desire. Your passion."

"I was there." Tears were coursing down her cheeks, and she felt the sense of brotherhood, as well as the desire. Desire from both men? It was too much, too powerful. She looked from Stefan to Anton, then back at Stefan, at his beloved wolven features. Looked at him and felt the sense of kindred, of belonging, she'd not known before.

Suddenly the words came tumbling out of her. "I should have been horrified, but I wasn't. I watched the old servant turn into a wolf, saw the wolf force you to the floor, tear your clothing from your body, and I couldn't move. It was the wizard's power holding me against the wall, but instead of fear, instead of the horror I expected . . . oh, Stefan! I was getting so turned on, I could hardly stand it! When he entered you, I felt you inside me—felt your cock filling me. When he shifted to human form, my senses seemed to shift, and I felt Anton's cock deep inside me, and I didn't care! Stefan, I didn't care that another man was fucking me!"

She burst into tears, and Stefan pulled her into his lap. Anton sat back on his heels and brushed her long hair back from her face, his free hand resting on Stefan's shoulder.

"It's okay, sweetheart." Stefan rubbed his muzzle against her hair. "It's okay. I think you were supposed to feel this way. Anton? Maybe you need to be more specific. There are things I think I understand, but I'm not sure if I can explain them to Xandi."

Anton sat close beside them, one hand still on Stefan's shoulder, the other hand brushing the hair back from Xandi's face. She found it oddly soothing, comforting, to be curled tightly into Stefan's lap, yet sharing connections with both men.

"The Chanku are a polyamorous race. I found old writings that corroborate what my instincts tell me are true. We mate for life, but we share our mates within the pack. The alpha male rules by physical domination when necessary, but it's usually the female who leads the pack, whether in human or wolven form. It's her decision whom she will take for sexual pleasure, whether it be only one or all the males. Often the women have sexual encounters with other females in their group, though they love one male above all the others. Chanku females can only be impregnated while in wolf form, and then they can choose when to reproduce. I have no idea how that works."

"How do you know these things?" Xandi took the handkerchief Stefan pressed into her palm and wiped her eyes. "How do I know you're not just making this up?"

"I can show you the scrolls. You might even be able to decipher the language. Is it necessary? Alexandria, look at Stefan. Isn't he proof enough? You saw me shift from man to wolf and back to man. Look into your heart and deny the truth of what I'm telling you." Anton stood up and paced restlessly about the room.

"I know my assault of Stefan, my domination of him, frightened you. I apologize to both of you, but it was necessary. Fear, anger, passion—all those emotions were necessary. I had to find a way to overload both of you at the same time, create such a backlash of emotions that you wouldn't fight the link. It was the only way I could make you understand. The only way to make you feel your true self."

He stopped in front of Stefan. "You wanted what happened today. Wanted me to fuck you, to take the responsibility out of your hands and turn your fantasies into reality. You've wanted me all these years, just as I've wanted you. I've felt your need at night, sensed the passion in your soul on those sleepless nights when you raced through the forest. I wanted to explain, but you had to come to me. Do you understand?"

Stefan's shoulders drooped. He sighed audibly and nodded. Anton continued his pacing. Xandi felt Stefan's acceptance, as well as her own. This was just one more side of the man she loved. Anton turned abruptly, knelt before Stefan and Xandi. Grabbed their hands in his and held them tightly. "You are both Chanku. As am I. We are among the few of a dying race. We must find the others. We must give them their legacy before it's too late. Please. Rest. Stay with me as my guests, as my brethren. My only family. Learn your heritage and help me save our people."

He bent slowly, placed a kiss on each of their hands. His amber eyes glittered with unshed tears, and his voice cracked, overcome with emotion. "Save me as well," he said, raising his head. "Please. I need you both."

Chapter 7

Xandi heard Stefan's footsteps just outside the door. He'd been down there with Anton for over two hours now, while she'd spent the time in their room, overwhelmed by the events of the day. She still wasn't certain how to deal with her conflicted emotions, her attraction to both Stefan and Anton, but she'd sensed Stefan's need to spend time with the wizard, to find answers for many of the questions she knew he had. How to complete the shift from wolf to human, for one thing. How to master the ability to shift, something Anton obviously did with great ease.

How to explain the obvious sexual desire coursing between two seemingly heterosexual men.

Questions she'd never once dreamed of asking, not in her life before Stefan. Questions—and answers—that now deeply affected her. The door opened quietly. "It's okay," she said. "I'm awake." She stepped out of the shadows near the window. Stefan crossed the room quickly and drew her into his arms.

"I didn't want to wake you. Damn, Xandi. I am so sorry to have dragged you into all this."

"I asked to come, remember? If what Anton says is true, I had to come." She kissed his throat, the side of his muzzle. She had seen him as a man, not as a beast, from the beginning. If what Anton said were true, it explained so many things—her ready acceptance of a beast as her lover, for one thing. They truly were kindred spirits. "Did Anton answer your questions?" She didn't add, Did he answer mine? She didn't need to.

"The combination of minerals our bodies need to shift has to be a regular part of our diets. We should both be capable of shifting within a few days. I ahead of you, most likely, as I've had the stuff before. Anton is an amazing man."

"You're very forgiving." Xandi slipped away from Stefan's embrace. "You've obviously forgiven Anton for his assault on you. I'm not so certain I can forget what happened this morning."

"Are you able to accept what happened?" Stefan ran his hand across the smooth fall of her hair and pushed it behind her shoulder. "Will you accept me?"

Xandi thought about it, about the throbbing intensity of her reaction to what she would always think of as Anton's rape of Stefan. She looked at Stefan and blinked back the thick flow of tears, then her words tumbled out, one after the other. "My problem is accepting me."

She grabbed his shoulders, holding onto him as if he were a lifeline. Her one remaining grasp on reality changing with each beat of her heart. "Don't you understand, Stefan? I wanted to be part of it. Oh, God, I thought he was attacking you, and I still wanted both of you inside me. I wanted to feel what you were feeling, to feel Anton fucking me hard and fast, the way he fucked you. I'm aroused now just thinking of it. I can't get the image out of my mind. It's like a disgusting porn flick, only I see it through eyes of love, of lust and desire, like I've never felt in my life! What's happened to me, Stefan? Why would I react like this?" She burst into tears, sobbing raggedly. Stefan's arms held her tight, his breath warm on her cheek, and she wondered if she would ever understand what had happened.

"Anton explained it, my love. You heard him. It's our nature. The nature of the Chanku. We are extremely sensual beasts. It explains so much! We are what we will be. You could no more keep from becoming aroused by what you saw than I could control my arousal when Anton penetrated me. I was afraid to tell you, but I've wanted him since I first met him, felt drawn to him, but I didn't understand it. Hell, I'm not gay. Men don't turn me on. But Anton did, and it scared the shit out of me. I came here knowing full well I was going to get fucked. Anton was right. I wanted him to force me, because I was too afraid of admitting what I wanted."

He sighed, and his breath was warm and moist against her neck. "I love you, but there's another thing you need to know as well. Anton wants you, too. Not as his life mate, but to solidify the bond within the pack. I should be jealous as hell, but I'm not." He laughed and rubbed his muzzle against the side of her face. "He didn't expect you. Oliver never suspected you were Chanku. Anton was trying to figure out how to separate us until he met you and recognized your nature. I think you were a shock for him. The choice, of course, will be yours, but you have two men who want to make love to you."

He tilted her chin up so that she was forced to look at him. Her body trembled, but there was no fear in her. Not now. Not with Stefan holding her in his arms, telling her with his calm, understanding voice that she would finally, after years of wondering, discover her true nature. She thought of his words, of the deep conviction he shared with her, and realized she accepted the truth.

Just as she would soon accept Anton.

Stefan watched as Xandi dug into her rare steak with obvious relish. He'd watched her carefully over the last week, well aware of the subtle alterations taking place within his own body as the added nutrients in his diet wrought the desired changes. Obviously, the minerals worked just as well for Xandi.

She'd eaten very little meat when they first met. Now she preferred her beef blood rare, just as Anton and Stefan did. She'd taken to long days in the woods, disappearing for hours on end. When she returned to the house, she said little, but it was obvious from the flush to her skin and the sweat soaking her jogging suit that she had run long and hard.

Both of them had noticed increased perception, better hearing, a more sensitive sense of smell. At night, they'd come together almost frantically, their sexual encounters lasting for hours and leaving the two of them spent and exhausted. There'd been no further mention of Anton joining them, but Stefan knew it was just a matter of time.

The wizard master had become the proverbial elephant in the parlor, though in this case, Stefan thought of him as the wolf at the bedroom door.

Waiting. Ever patient.

Stefan had run out of patience. He was eager to attempt the shift, felt the strength coursing through his veins, and wondered when Anton would say he was ready. Wolf first. Then human. Finally he would once again be human.

He wondered what Xandi would think when she finally saw the real Stefan Aragat, when she would feel the need to shift as well. Wondered what it would do to the two of them. As a wolf, she would become the leader of this small group. She fought it now, fought the rightful position Anton had explained she would soon hold. A position where even Anton would defer to her needs, her wants.

Would she still want Stefan? He shifted his gaze away from Xandi and caught Anton watching him. The wizard blinked, then smiled and nodded.

Stefan felt the stirring in his mind, the tentative thoughts as Anton linked with him.

You grow stronger every day. I don't believe Alexandria

is ready, but I feel the strength of Chanku running through your body. Tonight. After she sleeps. We would not want to frighten her should you have any problems with the shift.

Stefan nodded. *I agree. I'll come to you once she's asleep.*

Xandi seemed distracted tonight. Stefan watched her from his side of the bed as she carefully slipped into her silk gown, turned out the lights and crawled in next to him. She reached for him in the darkness. He wondered if her night vision had grown as acute as his had over the past few days.

"Yes," she said, snuggling close against him. "I don't need the lights at all." *Nor do I need words. I can hear your thoughts, my love. In my mind.*

I wondered. Then that means you've kept yours blocked from me. Why?

Because I'm afraid. I know what you and Anton intend to do tonight. I heard him asking you to meet him after I fall asleep. How am I going to sleep knowing the danger you risk?

If you're there, I'm afraid you'll distract me.

He ran his tongue slowly along the line of her jaw, showing her exactly the kind of distraction he feared.

You're right. I know that. It's something you have to do alone. Please, Stefan. Distract me more.

He sat up next to her and slowly removed the gown she'd just slipped on. Her body shimmered golden beneath his enhanced vision, the perfect circles of her nipples and the triangle of dark hair between her legs drawing him like a magnet.

He leaned over and licked a trail from one taut nipple to the next. Xandi sighed and arched her back. He trailed his fingers along her slightly rounded belly, parted the curls guarding her vagina and dipped one finger inside her moist center. The muscles immediately grabbed him, held his finger inside. He added another finger, slipping very slowly in and out, licking and sucking at first one nipple, then the other.

She reached for him, but he caught her hand. "No," he whispered. "This is for you. Only for you. Anton said I would be better prepared if I remained celibate tonight. He didn't say that applied to you."

He opened his thoughts, letting Xandi feel what he felt when he touched her, taste what he tasted as his tongue made a licking, lapping journey across her breasts, along her torso, across first one thigh, then the other, before he settled himself on his knees between her upraised legs.

Her knees were bent, and he pushed her heels almost back to her buttocks, opening her wet heat to his searching tongue. He knelt there a moment, knowing the night breeze would cool her hot, moist skin, sharing the sensation of need and desire coursing through both their bodies.

When he knew she could wait no more, he dipped his head and ran his long, canine tongue the full length of her pussy, ending with a tight swirl around her engorged clitoris. She bucked her hips and whimpered when he sat back on his heels. Her hands fisted the cool sheets. She raised her hips, silently begging for more.

This time he lifted her buttocks in his hands, palming her fleshy cheeks, forcing her legs wider apart until she was completely open to him, her labia red and swollen, her sex weeping with need. His own cock had become a thing apart—hard as stone, thick and erect. He felt it brush against his belly.

Damn. He wanted nothing more than to plunge into her, to bury himself in all that heat and moist womanly flesh, but on this he would obey the wizard. Instead, he dipped his head between her legs and licked her long and hard, his tongue plunging into her slick vaginal passage, his teeth resting sharply against her clit. He inhaled her scent, the deep musky smell of woman and desire. His cock wept, and his hips thrust shamelessly, but he ignored his own need and feasted on the woman.

Suddenly her knees pressed against the sides of his head, and she arched against him. He grabbed her buttocks in a bruising grip, kneading the flesh with strong fingers, holding her close against his mouth.

His tongue plundered her spasming muscles, swept the inner walls of her pussy, lapping and licking through her first orgasm, bringing her almost immediately to a second, higher peak. She cried out, a long, low keening wail. Her entire body went rigid.

He glanced up to watch her face. Her lips were parted, her eyes tightly shut, her hair plastered in strings about her face and neck. He'd never seen anything more beautiful, more arousing, than Xandi in the throes of her climax. His cock and balls ached, and it was all he could do to control his own longing to mate, to fight the almost overwhelming desire to plunge deep into those hot, wet, ripe tissues.

He sighed, willing his raging erection to behave itself. He gentled his licking, suckling assault on her pussy, careful to caress her oversensitized clit with the lightest, softest pressure possible. She held her knees tightly against him, then slowly allowed her body to relax. Her legs fell limply away from his head. Her breath came in long, satiated sighs, the aftermath of passion and pleasure.

Stefan felt her questing thoughts once again, experienced a sense of laughter. When he raised his head, his muzzle soaked with her fluids, she was smiling at him. "I am so thankful Anton only needed you to remain celibate tonight. Thank you, my love."

She reached out and touched his brow, swept his hair back over his ears. "Be careful. For me."

He covered her body with his and kissed her lightly on the throat, nuzzled her ear, then planted a kiss on her lips. Her tongue came out and licked the side of his mouth, and he sensed her tasting herself. Stefan kissed her once more, then rolled away from her inviting body. It was the hardest thing he'd done in a long time.

Suddenly all that Anton promised couldn't compare to the sweet gift of Xandi's love. "I promise," he said, dressing quickly. "I'll be back as soon as I can. Wait for me." He leaned over and kissed her once more, then left their room. When he closed the door behind himself, Stefan felt Xandi's love surrounding him, protecting him. Smiling, he went to meet the wizard.

Xandi turned on the faucets in the large shower and stood beneath the pounding water for a long time after Stefan left. She'd learned it was one way to separate herself from the constant barrage of thoughts within the wizard's home. She doubted either man realized the extent of her mental acuity. After just one day of Anton's special nutrients in her diet, she'd begun hearing the others' thoughts. Even Oliver's mind was an open book.

She'd learned quickly to block out things she didn't want to hear, but it was impossible to completely prevent herself from eavesdropping on private mental conversations between the men. She'd already admitted to Stefan that she'd learned tonight he would shift, that Anton would help him. She knew Anton didn't believe she was ready.

Xandi hadn't tried it yet, but there was no doubt in her mind she was ready. Her skin seemed to crawl at times. Her bones felt almost fluid, liquid, until she brought her errant body under control. Only one thing held her back. Her period was due any time, but Anton had told her to expect very little blood.

Now that her body was becoming more and more Chanku, her reproductive organs would be changing. Instead of shedding the unneeded lining of her uterus, she would be sending out powerful pheromones, making her irresistible to the males. Though reproduction was by choice—the female Chanku must consciously act to release an egg for fertilization while in wolf form—males of the species were attracted by a female in heat much as any canine male is to one of its own breed.

She understood that shifting for the first time would be easier during her menses because her body's hormones and basic chemical makeup would be perfectly aligned for the change. But once she gained her lupine form, the men would come—both of them. They would come for her. Two drop-dead, gorgeous men, unable to fight their need to mate the alpha female.

She would have the final approval of a mate, but her own lust would be running high and hot. Did she want to risk something she knew to be inevitable? Sex with both Anton and Stefan, whether in human or animal form? Two virile, handsome men intent on giving her pleasure?

Laughing aloud, Xandi tilted her face up to the stinging spray and let the water cascade over her throat and breasts. She must be mad. She had to be completely insane to think she'd even hesitate over such an amazing possibility.

Chapter 8

Stefan stood facing Anton, picturing the sight they must make—two powerfully built men of similar height, one covered completely in a coat of silver-tipped fur, the other sporting the standard male hair growth, on chest, belly, groin, legs. He should have felt uncomfortable, naked, alone with the man who had introduced him to his first homosexual experience, the two of them together in the midst of a small clearing surrounded by towering pines. He should have, but he didn't. Instead, he was filled with anticipation. Excitement thrummed through his veins, pounded in his chest.

He'd been erect, his cock as hard as stone since leaving Xandi's side. When Anton directed him to disrobe, the wizard had glanced at Stefan's cock and nodded approval. There'd been nothing sexual in his perusal, merely the acknowledgment that Stefan was ready to attempt the shift. Anton's cock had been only partially tumescent, yet Stefan's erection was proof his blood was running hot and high, that his entire system was primed and ready to explode.

Moonlight cut between the trees, bathing the area in a silver glow bisected by stark shadows. Stefan put his clothes aside and followed Anton's directions, to empty his mind of all thought, to sense the forest around him, to open his mind to Anton's.

I want you to join me, to be a part of my thoughts when I make the shift. Feel what I feel, sense what I do. Then do exactly the same. Don't fight the sensation. You will feel vertigo, a massive distortion of perception as your body adjusts. It's normal. Remember, do exactly as I do.

Anton's words sounded loud and clear in his mind. Stefan nodded his agreement. His breath caught in his throat. There was something totally elemental about this moment, this sharing with the man he'd grown to love.

He felt Anton's hands resting lightly on his shoulders. Stefan reached out and placed his own palms against Anton's warm flesh.

Close your eyes. Concentrate on what I feel. What my body does.

Stefan's fingers trembled against Anton's shoulders. He sighed, took another deep breath. Opened his mind, forced his body to relax.

Felt Anton begin to shift.

Naked, Xandi watched the two men from her hiding place in the thick ferns that grew beside the small meadow. Her enhanced night vision made the moonlit meadow as bright as day. Her perceptive mind picked up Anton's thoughts as if he spoke aloud.

She closed her eyes and felt the changes within Anton's body as well as Stefan's, then mimicked them in her own. Her limbs turned loose and fluid, her muscles lost their tone, her bones no longer shaped her frame. It felt like it took hours, but lasted mere seconds, the subtle changes blossoming, racing through veins and arteries, crossing synapses, altering flesh and bone in a million different ways, repatterning her body, her blood, her very brain.

Disoriented, she shook her head, suddenly aware she viewed the ground beneath her long muzzle. Sitting back on her haunches, Xandi held one large paw up to her face, inspecting the thick toenails, the dark pads. Her coloring was not the same as Stefan's. The fur covering her body was a deep russet, the same shade as her own hair. She stared at her foot for a long time, mesmerized by the difference from its human counterpart, then realized the night around her had come alive with sound and movement. She blinked, turned her head, aware her long ears shifted to catch the sounds from the meadow.

Moving with quiet stealth, she rose slowly to her feet and peered through the shrubbery. Two dark wolves stood nose to tail in the midst of the meadow, sniffing one another like a couple of large dogs. She would have laughed if she hadn't felt the urge to join them. Stefan's identity was obvious, the silver tips of his fur already familiar to her, the wolven head essentially unchanged.

Anton was black all over. Only his eyes gleamed amber in the moonlight. He raised his nose and sniffed the air, turning to stare directly at Xandi. She held perfectly still, well aware her scent could give her away. She'd taken the gamble, hoped that her period would wait until tomorrow. She hadn't considered the fact her scent might already be loaded with the pheromones Anton had warned her about.

She drew back into the shrubbery, hoping to remain hidden. Stefan still seemed unaware of her presence, but Anton knew. His voice came into her mind, his thoughts directed solely at Xandi.

Are you sure this is what you want? You have put yourself at great risk, Alexandria. I sense your heat is only hours away. It will be hard enough for us to control our lusts in human form. Impossible as wolves.

Xandi took a deep breath and stepped out of the thick overgrowth. *Let me run with you tonight. I promise to shift back before it's too late. Please.*

Xandi? Stefan's hackles rose. He stepped between her and Anton.

It's okay, my love. I couldn't wait. She opened her mouth, her long tongue lolling out in her closest approximation of a flirtatious grin. *I want to run with the wolves tonight.* She turned and dashed into the forest, her tail waving high as a flag. Anton and Stefan raced close behind. Leading the two males, running through the thick woods with her senses alive and her instincts more powerful than she'd imagined, Xandi finally knew the true meaning of freedom.

There was nothing sexual in their run through the dense forest, but it was by far the most sensual thing Xandi had ever experienced. Racing with forelegs out-stretched, ears flattened against her skull, nostrils flaring to catch the myriad scents surrounding her, she felt as if this amazing body were one huge nerve ending, sensitive to anything and everything she passed.

The steady sounds of Stefan on her right and Anton on her left, the two huge males keeping pace with her smaller, fleeter body, gave her a sense of power she'd not felt be-fore. Her perception of all around her was different, no longer quite so human, though she realized her humanity still ruled her thoughts. Her lungs drew in huge drafts of air, her eyes saw through the moonlit night as if it were high noon, and her long legs were powerful enough to leap small streams, bound over fallen logs, even outdistance the two larger wolves pacing her.

They ran for hours, covered miles. At one point they chased a rabbit into the ground, finally giving up on the terrified creature when it cowered beneath a huge fallen tree, out of their reach. Laughing, tongues lolling, the three spun away as if losing the race had been their plan all along. But Xandi knew she would have killed the tiny creature without a second thought. She'd salivated during the hunt, snapping ferociously at Stefan when he'd gotten between her and her prey.

For a brief moment she wondered how her human self

would be affected by the changes wrought in her tonight, but the worry fled on the night wind, fled with the sheer exuberance, the complete exhilaration she felt in this amazing body.

Snapping joyfully at Anton, she sped off ahead of the two males through the thick woods. They followed close behind, one on either side. It wasn't until the sky began to lighten on the eastern horizon that Anton turned their mad run through the forest back in the direction of his home. Exhausted now, feet no longer so swift, breathing not as smooth and effortless, Xandi padded along behind the two males. Only Anton's tail was still held high. Stefan's drooped behind him, as did Xandi's. Even with the long runs she'd taken over the past days, she had to admit her conditioning needed improvement.

They reached the broad lawn behind Anton's home just as the sun crested the mountains to the east. Exhausted, legs quivering and tongue lolling, Xandi collapsed in the cool grass, with Stefan close beside her. They lay close together, panting, eyes half closed, as the morning unfolded. Xandi wondered if Stefan relived the hours past. Finally she sent a questioning thought his way.

He answered her almost immediately. *My God! Did you ever imagine?*

Never, not in my wildest dreams. Anton? She looked around, searching for the wizard, but he was nowhere to be seen. *I wonder where he's gone?*

He'll be back, you know. He wants you.

I know. How do you really feel about that? Xandi leaned closer and nuzzled Stefan's muzzle. *You know I want both of you, don't you? Is that so wrong?*

Before Stefan could answer, Anton the man, walked down the front stairs. He'd obviously showered and shaved. Dressed in a pair of black jeans and a snug tee shirt, his feet bare, his long hair hanging loosely behind him, he looked relaxed and at home.

Xandi suddenly felt sweaty and dirty, almost embarrassed by her wolven form. Stefan sat up on his haunches, obviously wondering what Anton intended.

"It's time for you both to shift back to your human forms. I think you're capable of doing it without my help." He nodded first at Stefan, then at Xandi. "Can you reverse the process?"

Xandi went into her mind, realized she could sense her humanity as an image that drew her out of her wolven body. This time she was hardly aware of the vertigo, merely a change in perception as her vision shifted from that of the wolf to that of the woman.

Stefan watched her, and she sensed his mind following her patterns. Suddenly his bestial body seemed to waver, to shift. The silver-tipped fur disappeared, the face altered and adjusted, and for the first time Xandi saw Stefan, the man, standing before her.

Naked, without the fur covering his body, he was more beautiful than anything she could imagine. Strong and muscular, his lean chest powerfully sculpted with a mat of silver-tipped hair stretching between his flat, copper-colored nipples, muscles rippling across his abdomen, he had the body of an athlete in his prime.

His face, though. She reached up and touched the side of his face, running her fingers along his jawline, tracing his full, sensual lips, threading through the long hair hanging to his shoulders. Black, shot through with silver, thick and straight, it framed his face perfectly. She'd never seen his face, only vaguely recalled what he looked like from his publicity shots while he was still performing as Aragat the Magician.

There was something familiar, though, something that made her turn and stare at Anton. The resemblance was extraordinary. "You could be brothers," she said. "You look so much alike."

Anton shook his head. "No. Possibly distant cousins,

but I've checked our lineage. The resemblance is purely co-incidental." He nodded at both of them, smiling. "Bathe, dress, join me for breakfast. We have much to discuss." He bent close and lifted Xandi's chin in his lean fingers, stared into her eyes for a long moment, then leaned closer and kissed her.

Though she'd expected something like this, she was startled by her body's reaction, the immediate shock of desire that settled in the pit of her stomach, swirled about until it settled in her pussy, deep in the heart of her sex.

He backed away, stared at her for a long moment, then turned and went back into the house. Almost afraid to look at Stefan, Xandi finally turned toward him.

He was smiling. His look was tender, his head tilted to one side, his amber eyes glowing in the morning light.

Feeling lighter than she could remember, Xandi kissed Stefan on the lips, then led him up the stairs to their room.

Chapter 9

Stefan followed her into the oversized shower. Exhausted, exhilarated, confused, Xandi stepped aside to let him enter. His body was hard, the muscles pumped up from their nighttime run, his cock erect, bobbing close against his body. The feral look in his eyes was very much that of the wolf, obviously possessive, broadcasting his need to dominate, to hold.

His hunger slammed into her like a fist to the solar plexus—desire so hot and elemental, it practically sizzled across her nerve endings. She raised her arms beneath the sharp spray from the shower, wrapped them around his neck and opened her mouth to his.

For the first time, she kissed human lips, felt the solid thrust of his tongue inside her mouth, tasted the flavors of the man, not the beast. His long fingers clutched at her hips, and she clung to him, raising her legs up to clasp them tightly around his waist, her body ready for the hard cock surging into her.

There was no need for foreplay, no reason to prepare her body for his assault. Their entire night had been foreplay, the end result here, now, in the shower, with the steam rising and the hot water bathing their fevered bodies. Her flesh practically sizzled from the current racing between them, the shared need, the passion running so hot and hard, she felt like a marionette on strings, as if her arms and legs moved courtesy of the hand of someone greater than both of them.

His cock stretched the slick walls of her vagina, reached deep inside, then slowly withdrew before filling her again. She pressed her breasts against the thick mat of hair covering his chest. The texture was much coarser than the wolf's pelt she'd grown familiar with, and her nipples peaked, tightened, with each new contact. She experimented with the sensation, rubbing her breasts slowly across his chest as the steaming water cascaded over their writhing bodies. She felt the sizzle race from nipple to clitoris, as if a direct line of power and sensation existed between the three points of pleasure, a connection beyond the physical, beyond sex.

His hands squeezed her buttocks, and he raised her higher on his cock. Muscles in his arms and chest expanded with the effort, and she felt herself responding even more to his arousal. He was human, but the instinct to mate, to mark her as his, was something primal, something more of the beast than the man, something dark and carnal and so damned intriguing.

She responded as the beast, clawing at his tense shoulders, nipping his jaw, clinging to his straining body, as he thrust deep and hard, driving her higher, further than he'd ever taken her as beast.

Sobbing, crying, Xandi felt his sharp teeth against her neck, his fingers holding her with bruising strength, his hard cock driving deep and fast, taking her over the edge, filling her with his hot seed, pumping into her over and over again, until both of them shuddered beneath the stinging spray.

Stefan slid slowly down the shower wall until he sat on the floor with Xandi sprawled across his lap. She raised her head to kiss him once more. His body trembled in counterpoint to hers. His pulse beat visibly in the huge vein at his neck. His nostrils still flared with each deep breath, but his eyes were troubled. "Are you okay?" He slicked her wet hair back with one hand, then glanced down at the water swirling down the drain. His eyes widened.

Xandi followed his gaze and understood the heat that had taken her, the overwhelming carnal desire still pulsing through her veins. A watery pink stain flowed from beneath them, swirling in a perfect spiral before disappearing down the drain.

She'd started her period, a simple thing to a woman.

A powerful event for the alpha female of the pack.

It was time. She'd known this was coming, known she must make her decision. Anton said the female took all the males in her pack sexually, that the drive to mate would be strongest during her heat. She knew instinctively he was right, knew that as alpha female it was her choice to breed, to produce an egg for fertilization.

She'd felt the first stirrings during their nighttime run, had recognized the deeply rooted drive that led her to race the two males through the night, her tail held high, her actions teasing, playful. She'd reveled in her own sexuality, celebrated her power as female, as future leader.

Playtime was over. Was she ready? What about Stefan? "How do you feel about it?" she asked. There was no need to explain. Stefan's arms tightened around her, and he rested his head atop hers. His cock still filled her pussy, and she felt him complete the link, his thoughts moving easily within her mind.

I do not want to share you. Never. Yet I know Anton is right. The bond of the pack will be strengthened with your mating. We are sensual, sexual creatures. Creatures of the flesh. I understand it now even more, after the run tonight, the bond we share with Anton. We love with great passion. We hate just as passionately. Share your body with him if you must, but please, save your soul for me.

Xandi rose up and kissed him. She heard his unspoken request, though they'd never mentioned children. *You have my soul. You have my heart. I control whether or not a mating results in young. Already my body responds to my wishes, and I do not wish children now. This new self is so fresh, I'm still a child myself. When the time is right, my offspring will be yours. This promise I give you, Stefan Aragat. I love you.*

She felt the tension leave his body with her pledge, but Xandi remained taut and anxious. She sensed Anton in her mind, knew he waited for the two of them. It wasn't merely Alexandria the wizard wanted. No, he wanted more. He intended to once more exert his dominance over Stefan. Though Anton's intentions were for the good of the pack, Xandi understood his personal desire for power as well.

She kissed Stefan's lips, wrapped her arms around his body, sensed the knowledge in his heart. Felt his strength, his resolve.

Then she shared Anton's intentions with the man she loved.

He already knew. Xandi understood the quiet nod of his head, accepted his intentions. Stefan knew what Anton wanted, what the wizard expected. She understood the confident look on his face—he had no fear of Anton now. Knowledge gave him power.

Xandi dressed carefully for their evening meal with Anton. She'd never dressed for seduction before. Not really. Of course, if what Anton said were true about the alpha female during menses, she wouldn't need seduction. She would merely need to attend.

She chose a simple, sleeveless, dark green dress with a scoop neck and fitted bodice that emphasized her breasts. The slim, form-fitting skirt hugged the curved lines of her hips and ended just above her knees. She decided against wearing a bra, but she did pull on a skimpy pair of bikini panties, not far removed from a thong.

She had no need of a pad or anything to protect her clothing. The metamorphosis over the past week had been complete. Her period this time was totally unlike anything she'd experienced before, when fully human. Other than the first tiny show of blood when she and Stefan made love, there'd been no other spotting of any kind, just as Anton had predicted. There was, however, a subtle, musky scent on her body, one she'd never noticed before. She knew Stefan was well aware of it. When he was close, it was obviously all he could do to control his hands. His nostrils flared each time she walked by. She felt his desire burning hot and ready beneath his skin, knew he was drawn to her as much by her scent as by the emotional feelings he already had for her.

Her body thrummed with sensual urges. Her skin felt ultrasensitive. She was aware of the simple movement of air across her bare arms, of the heat from the lamp near the bed. Her hearing was superacute, so Stefan's heartbeat echoed in her ears, and she was almost certain she heard the whoosh of blood through his veins. The air around her seemed to crackle with energy, but she was unaware whether it originated from Stefan or her.

He wore simple black slacks and a white long-sleeved shirt, with the sleeves rolled back past his forearms. His black-and-silver hair was long, like Anton's, and he'd pulled it behind his head and tied it with a band just above his collar. She wanted to tug the restraining band loose, let his hair flow free around his face. She wanted to feel it brushing across her breasts, tickling the sensitive flesh over her ribs, tangling with the thatch of russet hair at the apex of her thighs.

Xandi glanced at the clock, though her senses had become so acute she knew they were running early. Oliver hadn't even started the grill. She would have smelled the gas flame, though the kitchen and patio were on the far side of the house from their room. Tilting her head, she winked at Stefan.

He cocked one eyebrow, then opened both eyes wide as she slipped to her knees in front of him and brushed her knuckles across the fly of his slacks.

The fabric immediately bulged outward.

"Um, Xandi, don't. We need to get down to the dining room. Aren't you hungry yet?"

"Oh yeah," she whispered. "I'm real hungry." She leaned closer and blew a draft of hot breath against the fabric, then reached up and undid just the zipper on his slacks. No underwear. Grinning, she slipped her fingers in through the opening and wrapped them around the solid length of his cock.

His very human cock. She hadn't been able to take him in her mouth until now, not with the risk of his huge cock choking her when the canine knot formed. Now, though . . . now he was totally human, his penis, though large, not so large she needed to worry about the size.

She licked the tip. He jerked his hips and laughed, but it was a strangled, half-sobbing sound. She tasted him again, wrapping her tongue around the silky tip, then following the thick vein all the way to his testicles. She felt his tesicles draw up close to his body, all the incentive she needed to take him fully into her mouth, to suckle him deep and hard, using her tongue and lips, strong cheek muscles, even her teeth.

He groaned again, and this time his hands fisted in her thick hair, as if he anchored himself against her. She found a rhythm, sliding his hot length in and out of her sucking mouth, tonguing him, nipping at the tip, then holding him hard inside, exerting all the pressure she could. He tried . . . she knew he tried to maintain, to keep from coming in her mouth, but she took that control, took it away with her mouth, her hands, stroking his balls, the sensitive flesh between his testicles and anus, all through the zippered opening in his slacks.

Stefan choked off a strangled moan. His body stiffened, his hips thrust forward. His cock was hard and hot inside her mouth, and she clamped down on him with teeth and lips, sucking hard, harder, swallowing the thick jets of semen as he gave himself up to her.

Long after he'd finished, long after the last drops of come had spilled from the tip of his penis, long after that huge erection had softened, only then did she stop her licking and kissing, her gentle suckling, as she brought him down. Using her tongue to remove every trace of his seed, she gently tucked him back inside his slacks and carefully pulled the zipper up.

Stefan stared down at her, his expression shell-shocked. She smiled up at him and took his answering smile as the gift she'd expected. Then she rose to her feet and looped her hand casually over his forearm. Together they walked to the large dining room, their secret safe between them.

Anton rose immediately when they entered the room. He set down the glass of red wine he was holding and walked forward to greet them, his hands outstretched.

She heard the low growl beside her and smiled to herself. She and Stefan had already had this conversation. He would start no fights this evening. She would not switch, and neither would he. As long as she remained human, the allure of her scent would not be overwhelming to the men. If they became wolves, nothing would stop them.

The quiet growl made her feel protected, desired.

Anton acknowledged it as well. He dropped his hands and leaned forward to give Xandi a quick kiss on the cheek. He paused there a moment, and she heard him inhale a long, slow breath. When he stepped back, his eyes glinted with amber fire beneath the subtle overhead light. He glanced quickly at Stefan, then back to Xandi, with a fixed smile on his face. His nostrils flared.

"Dinner's ready," he said, breaking into the charged silence. "You're right on time." Anton turned and walked back toward the table, but Xandi thought his usually fluid movements looked almost stiff, as if he forced himself to walk away from her. He pulled a chair out and nodded at Xandi, then turned toward the kitchen. "Oliver, our guests have arrived. You may serve."

Xandi found herself seated next to Anton and across from Stefan. The comfortable camaraderie from the night before was gone. An ominous silence hung over the large dining room. Oliver quietly served their steaks and a quiche. The meat was, as usual, blood rare. Xandi knew the quiche contained the grasses and other nutrients their bodies needed.

She cut into the meat just as Oliver turned on the CD player. The soft strains of a Johann Strauss waltz took some of the edge off the tension building among the three of them. Anton ate almost mechanically, a far different host than the urbane wizard to whom she'd grown accustomed. Xandi glanced at Stefan, but the question was in her eyes, not in her mind. She didn't know how to converse mentally with one man without the other hearing.

Stefan's eyes held a warning. He ate steadily as well, but his demeanor, while watchful, was much more relaxed. Xandi sipped her wine, studying Anton over the rim of the crystal goblet. He focused all his attention on his food, but she noticed his breathing appeared somewhat labored. There was a noticeable tremor in his large hands.

Without warning, Anton shoved his chair back from the table. He ripped at his shirt, tearing it down the front of his chest, sending buttons in all directions. Xandi slapped her hand over her mouth to stifle a scream as Anton tore away the rest of his clothing and shifted, his body writhing through the change from man to wolf in less than a heartbeat.

Xandi shoved her chair back from the table as Anton

leapt in her direction, snarling and snapping his jaws. Before she could throw up her hands in protection, Stefan was there, shifting before her eyes, blocking the attacking wolf, shoving him back with hands that were paws, with sharp teeth and strong jaws clamped just beneath the larger wolf's throat.

Afraid to shift, Xandi backed out of the way. She should have stayed in their room, not allowed the two males to scent her while they were together, not during her time, when instinctive lust could override their civilized minds.

Anton struggled to gain the upper hand, but Stefan was quicker, his emotions under control. Like viewing a nightmare in replay, Xandi watched as Stefan, his shredded clothes falling away from his body in tatters, forced Anton beneath him. He held Anton down with slavering jaws gripping his neck and both forelegs wrapped around his upper body.

Both wolves were aroused by the battle, their huge cocks glistening red and swollen, but it was Stefan this time who had the strength, Stefan who drove into Anton, forcing entrance despite the other wolf's struggles. At the moment of penetration, Anton yelped and snarled, but he quickly dipped his head in acceptance and acknowledgment of Stefan's superior strength.

Stefan's hips thrust forward, at first making sharp, jabbing strokes, then easing back and slowing his pace once he seemed to realize Anton had truly yielded. The shift of the two men was almost simultaneous. As Xandi watched, one wolf dominating another became two men, almost identical in appearance, their bodies lean and beautiful, their long hair swinging with the rhythm of their joining. Stefan knelt behind the wizard, his eyes closed, a look of pure pleasure on his face, as he stroked in and out of the other man. Anton held himself up, knees spread wide, arms outstretched, his body sliding forward with each powerful thrust of Stefan's hips.

Stefan reached around Anton's waist and grabbed the wizard's swollen cock, massaging it in time with his slow, steady strokes. Xandi slowly peeled her dress down over her hips and stripped off the tiny bikini panties. She rubbed her palm across her rigid nipples with one hand, pressed hard between her legs with the middle finger of her other hand. It wasn't enough. Not nearly enough.

She knelt beside Anton, her fingers still buried inside her streaming pussy. Anton's eyes were closed, his lips parted in what might have been pain, but was more likely pleasure. She leaned over and kissed the corner of his mouth. Anton's eyes flew open. Xandi took the opportunity of surprise to kiss him again, this time slipping her tongue deep inside his mouth.

Anton reached up with his left arm and wrapped it around her neck, holding her closer for their shared kiss. "I'm sorry," he whispered. "I'm so sorry . . . I . . ."

"I know." She trailed kisses along his shoulder, kissed the line of taut muscles along the side of his ribs, then sat back on her heels to watch. She was barely conscious of her fingers slowly circling her clitoris, dipping into her wet pussy, then stroking her clit once again. She caught the rhythm the men shared, stroking herself in time with Stefan's deep penetration of Anton.

They were beautiful to watch, the two men, their lean bodies glistening with sweat, their muscles straining with each thrust and draw. Anton's eyes were closed, his mouth twisted in a tight grimace of pain and pleasure as Stefan's thighs slapped against his buttocks. Stefan's eyes were mere slits, his mouth slightly open, his fingers now grasping Anton's hips, his long hair swinging across his shoulders with each powerful thrust.

Xandi felt her desire growing, knew her climax was mere seconds away. Stefan picked up the pace, slamming his cock into Anton, his hands holding Anton in place as he filled him. Anton threw his head back and cried out, his shout turning to a long, low howl of pleasure, the sound of the wolf. His erect cock seemed to swell, to beckon Xandi. She reached out and grabbed him, held on tightly, squeezing the hard flesh, pumping Anton's cock in time to Stefan's deep, penetrating thrusts, while her left hand stayed buried in her own hot pussy.

Anton stiffened, just as Stefan cried out and drove forward, almost knocking Anton over. Xandi watched the thick spurts of semen spatter the carpet in front of Anton as he climaxed, knew Stefan filled the other man with his own ejaculate. She sobbed with her own orgasm, felt the muscles clenching her fingers and wished it had been Anton's cock, Stefan's, that of either of the men she loved.

Panting, arms trembling, Anton carefully lowered himself to the floor, rolling away from Xandi. And in a heartbeat, it all made perfect sense. Why hadn't she figured this out before? She shook her head and smiled, first at Stefan, then at Anton. She let her gaze linger on the wizard. "Okay," she said, with enough force that both men looked up. "It's bullshit. That's enough. I have finally figured it out, you know? This is the last time. No more."

Anton squinted and stared at her. Stefan still looked a bit dazed. "You don't get it, do you?" she said, rocking back on her heels. "All this domination crap. You, Anton, jumping on Stefan when he already wanted you. Now Stefan saving me from Anton's wild impulse. It's all bullshit." She wiped her damp fingers on the thick carpet. "You're both so damned afraid to admit what you really want. Don't you get it?" She glared at Stefan and then at Anton. "You love each other. You desire each other. That doesn't make you less manly or any less than what you are. It makes you more. Quit hiding behind all this macho shit and make love to each other the way you want to."

Xandi stood up and planted both hands on her hips. "You both need to bathe. Together might be a good way to start. Then you need to spend some time together, getting past your hang-ups. Learn to touch one another with love, not under the guise of doing battle. In the meantime, I'm going to run. Alone. I'll be back in a couple of hours."

She shifted before they had time to react, taking her lupine form with all its musky scent and powerful pheromones, well aware neither man had the energy to pursue her now. With a sharp yip, she raced down the long hallway and through an open door, out into the freedom of the dark forest beyond.

She returned around midnight, when the quarter moon hung high in the sky and light spilled from the huge bay windows in the den. Anton and Stefan must be awake. Shifting into her human form, Xandi went directly to the room she shared with Stefan. The huge bed was empty. She had expected as much.

She was smiling, humming to herself, when she stepped into the shower. There was still one more thing she needed to do before this night could end. One more thing before the beginning of a new day.

Chapter 10

Xandi dried her hair and wrapped herself in a light silk robe. She let out a short sigh of regret for the lovely dress she'd worn earlier, the care she'd taken preparing for her role of seductress. Anton's unexpected response to her scent while she was still in human form had shocked but not completely surprised her.

He'd admitted earlier in the week he had been years without a woman. Not until he'd taken Stefan, in what was more a show of dominance than lust, had Anton broken his celibacy. She wondered if Stefan realized she'd orchestrated their lovemaking this evening as much to ease his sexual tensions before dinner with Anton as to share their love?

Things could so easily have gotten out of hand at dinner. As it was, everything had been perfect, though not entirely planned. Smiling, Xandi tightened the belt to her robe and padded barefoot down the long hallway. Her life had certainly taken some odd turns in the past few weeks.

The image of Stefan's powerful body pressed up against Anton's equally strong male form filled her mind. Her nipples peaked, and she was aware of the charge of heat and moisture in her pussy. A perfect example. She'd never thought watching two men having sex would arouse her.

Tonight she'd practically come without even touching herself at the moment Stefan had penetrated Anton.

Xandi stopped just a few feet from the closed dining room door and opened her thoughts. She sensed both men just beyond, sensed the subtle shift in power. Stefan maintained his newly won dominance over Anton. Their night of sexual discovery obviously had not ended when she left the room, but it had left Stefan in control. Smiling, Xandi pushed the door open. Did Anton realize his night of exploration was far from ending?

Well, she was doing it for the health of the pack, wasn't she? Grinning even wider, Xandi stepped into the dining room.

Anton and Stefan sat near the fire, each with a glass of cognac. Both men were casually dressed, their shirts unbuttoned and hanging out at the waist. Stefan had chosen a leather wingback chair. Anton sat alone on one end of the long black leather couch. Xandi noticed bites on Stefan's throat, red marks such as he had often left on her neck during lovemaking. The comfort level between the two men was high, the pervasive sexuality between them both sensual and seductive.

Thank goodness she'd had the few hours' long run to sort things out. It was so much easier to make decisions as a wolf. Her civilized upbringing and middle-class mores faded into the pure, elemental world of a creature of the night.

Stefan noticed her first, stopping in mid-sip, his crystal goblet of cognac tilted against his full bottom lip. He smiled. "You're back. Anton and I were just wondering if we should go search for you." There was no condemnation in his voice.

"Actually, we were going to flip a coin. The winner would be the one who searched." There was such a look of longing in Anton's eyes that Xandi's stomach did a quick flip.

Later. There was time for that later.

Stefan poured a glass of the amber liquor and handed it to her. Xandi sat next to Anton, facing Stefan. "I needed to think," she said, taking a sip. The cognac went down her throat like golden fire. Suddenly, her thoughts were even clearer than they'd been earlier.

"This has been a most amazing week." She stared into the liquid depths of her drink. "I came here with Stefan, looking for answers for him. Instead, I've found answers to questions that have plagued me all my life. Questions about my desires, my wants . . . my basic nature. I've also realized many things I held as truths went against my innermost feelings."

She looked up then, smiling at both Anton and Stefan. "I've learned, most graphically, that love, the abiding emotional and sexual love we all need and want, isn't always just between a man and a woman. It can be just as strong between two men." She paused, hoping she was putting her thoughts into the right words. "Or, a woman and two men."

Stefan nodded, urging her on. She turned toward Anton and saw the hope in his eyes. "I've known you only a week, Anton, but the bond between us is strong. Instinctive, almost. I imagine it's the wolf in me that understands this. The human woman certainly couldn't figure it out, though I felt a bond with Stefan the very first night we met, even before I'd seen his face." She smiled and tilted her head toward her lover. "By the way, have I told you what a handsome face it is?"

His soft chuckle warmed the atmosphere even more. "If anyone had told me I would be aroused by the sight of two men making love, and that's exactly what you two have done, for all the dominance and power plays, I would have denied it. If anyone had even suggested I would want to be part of that love, I would have thought they were crazy. I was so wrong."

She sighed and shook her head, her heart almost bursting with the overwhelming emotions, hers and theirs. "I love both of you. I realize I need both of you. The time may come, as our pack increases, that I will want another mate as well. As might you. Whether it's the wolf in me or just who I am, I realize this is my new reality. I hope you can accept it . . . accept me."

Stefan set his empty glass down, stood up and leaned over Xandi. "I love you," he said, kissing her very gently on the lips. He turned then to Anton and ran his palm in a caressing stroke from the wizard's brow, along the smooth fall of his hair, to his shoulder. "I love you as well. Both of you, in equal measure. But it's been a long day for me, and I imagine the two of you have much to—" he paused and winked at Xandi—discuss. Good night. I'll see you in the morning, if not before." Without any sign of self-consciousness, Stefan leaned over and kissed Anton on the mouth, gave him a last squeeze on his shoulder and left the room.

Anton's expression was one of pure disbelief when he looked up and stared at Xandi. She almost laughed out loud, but instead, she took one last sip of her cognac and reached for Anton. "For the good of the pack?" she asked, taking his hand. "That was the reason you gave me for polyandrous relationships within a wolven pack. It's more than that, Anton. I do love you. You have made it possible for me—and Stefan—to finally know our true natures. You have given us our lives. That is a gift without price."

Anton stood up, his lithe body moving with the grace of a dancer. He stared intently at Xandi, his amber eyes glowing with desire, the corner of his mouth tilted up in a slight smile. "I feel as if I've been caught at my own game." He shook his head as he placed both hands on Xandi's shoulders. "It's not a game, though, Alexandria. Do you mean what you say? Your scent is driving me wild. Thank God Stefan stopped me tonight, or I would have raped you without any thought to your humanity, to your own needs and desires. Right now, if Stefan and I hadn't exhausted ourselves fuc—making love—I'd be ripping this robe from your shoulders and driving into you whether you wanted me or not."

"Ah, but I do want you." Xandi wrapped her arms around Anton's neck and stood on her toes to kiss him. "Only I want you on my terms, in my way . . . at least this first time. I take my role as the alpha female quite seriously." She tested the seam of his full lips with the tip of her tongue, plunging inside when he parted for her. His arms tightened around her back, and she felt the huge bulge of his cock pressing against her belly.

This was not Stefan, yet the need she felt, the desire for Anton, was almost identical. She dipped her shoulder so that he could tug her robe off of her, and when she was completely nude, she posed before him, her body offering the kind of lush invitation she knew he needed.

Anton felt as if he'd entered some sort of dream state. For five long years he had thought only of Stefan, of the torment the young magician suffered because of his unwillingness to learn, of his own almost visceral sexual reaction every time he was close to the younger man. Their confrontation a mere week ago had left him dissatisfied, angry over his own loss of control. He'd not been able to read Stefan's true feelings, had hoped like hell he hadn't broken the other man's will or, even worse, made an enemy of one of the very few left of their kind.

Now this woman, this perfect, sensual, intelligent woman, not only embraced the beast within him, but within herself as well. His mouth moved over hers. His hands stroked the smooth, satiny flesh of her back. She was perfect. She was everything he'd dreamed of.

She was Chanku. He fought the urge to shift, to take her as a wolf.

He controlled his need, subjugated it to her will. She had offered herself in her human form. He must honor that, no matter how difficult. He ran his hands along her smooth back and sighed against her mouth. It was a truly pleasing form, this human body of hers.

Her hands slipped across the front of his shirt and shoved it back over his shoulders. He quickly shrugged out of it, then shoved his pants off. But he'd forgotten about his shoes. Laughing, feeling ridiculous and silly, he ended up on his butt, looking up at Alexandria.

This view wasn't bad at all. She stood before him, legs spread wide, hands on hips, fighting a smile and pretending to glare down at him while he sat on the floor all tangled in his pants. The fleshy lips of her pussy pouted between the neatly trimmed thatch of auburn curls, and her scent caught his nostrils, her essence arousing in the extreme.

Almost in a trance, he felt the smile leave his lips as he shoved his pants and shoes off his feet in one swift motion, then leaned over to taste her with his mouth. Her fingers tangled in his hair as he ran his tongue lightly across the soft flesh of her belly, but she moaned aloud when he swept over the tiny protruding clit, barely peeking out of the mat of soft hair.

She was hot. So damned hot. And her flavor was sweet and succulent, seasoned with the essence of her time, her heat. He lapped at the thick labia, licking and sucking at her swollen flesh, well aware when her arousal loosed the lubricating fluids, readying her for their joining.

Her legs trembled, and her hands clenched tightly in his hair. Shaking himself free of her grip, Anton stood up and grabbed her in his arms, lifting her off her feet as if she weighed nothing at all. She looped her slim arms around his neck and smiled at him.

He carried her to the long couch in front of the fire and stretched her out on a soft afghan. She was perfect, a woman unlike any he'd ever known. A female of his own species.

Alexandria smiled at him, held her arms up to welcome him. Anton settled himself between her legs, and his cock was so hard and sensitive it felt alien to him, as if some other entity had empowered him with this sense of lust, of deep, carnal desire for a woman of his kind.

For Alexandria. Gone were thoughts of Stefan, of any other partners he might have known over his past fifty years. There was only Alexandria and her pouting lips, her pussy welcoming him, begging him to enter.

When he angled his cock to meet her, when he touched her moist center, he almost wept. This was the feeling he'd wanted, the knowledge he'd begged for. For all his power as wizard, as wolf, as mentor and as Master, this was the one thing that had eluded him—the perfect match of male and female, of alpha wolf and mate.

In the back of his mind, he knew she belonged to Stefan, but she was granting him this time, this moment, without thought of any other male. Anton found entrance and thrust hard and deep, then held himself there, deeply entrenched in her hot, wet passage, his cock squeezed by her strong vaginal muscles, his senses overwhelmed by the scent of her heat, her season, this time she shared with him.

This was what it truly meant to be part of the pack, to be one with the alpha female. He wanted to weep, to bow his head in thanks for such a gift, but he withdrew slowly and filled her once again. She lifted her hips, welcoming him, and he found his rhythm, their rhythm, until the only sounds were the slick slap of belly to pubis, of his breath and hers, of soft moans, slight gasps, the rush of her heart, the pounding in his, and they crested, both of them finding completion together, joined in a single heartbeat, a final thrust, a single sigh and a groan.

Almost in a trance, Anton held himself over Alexandria, his hips pressed tightly between her legs, his cock deeply embedded in her welcoming pussy. Her muscles spasmed around him in a sweet rhythm, and he felt his seed filling her. There would be no young. He accepted that. She was pledged to Stefan. Knowing that, he accepted her gift and honored it. She would be a true leader, one who welcomed all to the pack.

He let his arms go loose and fell to one side. Alexandria cupped his face in her palm, leaned close and kissed him. "Thank you," she whispered. "I love you." She nuzzled his cheek with hers, ran her lips across his throat. They lay together as their heartbeats slowed, as their breathing returned to normal. Finally Alexandria raised herself up on one elbow and kissed him. "I need to get some sleep," she said. "It's been a long day. Come with me, please. The bed is large, and I know Stefan is waiting."

Anton leaned back. He had to see her, had to know she wasn't teasing him.

Her gray eyes stared back intently. He shifted to one side and sat up. Alexandria slipped from beneath him and grabbed his hand. There was no subterfuge, no sense of jealousy, nothing to make him feel anything beyond loved. Wanted.

Anton squeezed Alexandria's fingers and rose to stand beside her. She tugged his hand, led him up the stairs and along the hallway to their bedroom. The room where Stefan waited for both of them.

Better than any dream he might have had, more potent than any fantasy . . . this was real. This was the way he had hoped it would happen—had hoped but had never dreamed. Squeezing his fingers around Alexandria's small hand, Anton followed her to Stefan.

PART THREE

Anton

Chapter 11

Anton came fully awake between one heartbeat and the
next. He lay still in the darkness, surrounded by the
warmth of the two people he loved most in the world.
Stefan curled beside him in wolven form, while
Alexandria, all warm and sensual woman, sprawled across
his lower torso. Her soft lips, slightly parted in sleep,
rested against his belly.

Anton listened to the steady beat of hearts, the comforting rush of blood through veins, and knew something else
had dragged him from slumber, some shift in the air, some
sense of disquiet in his mind.

Almost two weeks of odd, intermittent dreaming. Now
three nights in a row. He couldn't blame three nights of
strange dreams on Oliver's cooking.

He closed his eyes and concentrated, shifted his senses
beyond the human range, to grasp the part of him that always remained the wolf.

Nothing.

A lingering sense of unease, the visceral memory of a
terrible scream? He wasn't sure. The sensation passed, his
eyelids grew heavy. He stroked Alexandria's tousled hair,
rested his other hand on Stefan's furred shoulder and
willed his body back to sleep.

* * *

Keisha Rialto stared at her clasped hands and tried desperately to believe her therapist. The woman's soft voice, trained to soothe and comfort, rolled across her tense shoulders without any of the desired effect.

"The dreams are a manifestation of your anger, your fear . . . and your pain. You've blotted out the worst of the attack. That's how the mind protects us. You didn't kill those men, Keisha, no matter what your subconscious wants you to believe."

Dr. Wilson, the therapist, leaned closer and placed a comforting hand on Keisha's shoulder. "We're dealing with two separate incidents. Your beating and rape had nothing to do with the fact a rival gang chose that particular time to attack the men who harmed you. Though unintentional, that very attack may have saved your life. You were an unfortunate witness to a brutal triple homicide, but no matter how empowering it might be for you to believe it, you're not the one who killed the men who assaulted you. They were killed by vicious dogs, animals trained as weapons."

Dr. Wilson paused, and her choking swallow was audible in the small room, her voice barely a whisper. "Horrible, vicious dogs."

Keisha raised her head and caught the look of horror on the therapist's face. She knew the woman had seen police photos of the apartment, knew exactly how awful the scene had been. Dr. Wilson must be remembering those pictures now. The carnage was imprinted on Keisha's mind with a stark clarity she'd not been able to forget, images of the torn and bloodied bodies of three men, the men who had held her captive and repeatedly raped her, who had subjected her to unimaginable atrocities over a twelve-hour period.

She'd barely regained consciousness when the police broke through the door, yet the images of those eviscerated, mutilated bodies were burned into her mind. The room covered in gore, herself a battered, bloody mess, her once tightly braided hair hanging in blood-soaked tangles around her face. The police were amazed the dogs hadn't touched her. They'd killed her attackers in what had to have been a maelstrom of terror without harming Keisha.

The images were the things of nightmares, but her nightmares were worse. In her dreams, she was the killer. Each night she replayed the same visuals—of herself rising up, turning on her attackers, changing into a huge rampaging wolf, an intelligent agent of death, all claws and teeth and powerful muscle.

She still tasted the hot blood, felt the joy of the kill, the thrilling satisfaction of strong teeth tearing throats, of powerful jaws ripping apart the bodies of the ones who had hurt her. Each night she repeated the heinous acts, acts made no more acceptable by the fact the men had practically killed her with their assault.

She gestured frantically at the therapist. "I know what you're saying must be true, but the dreams aren't going away. If anything, they've become clearer, more graphic . . . more like a memory than a dream." Keisha grabbed the doctor's hand and held on as if to a lifeline, her coffee-brown fingers a stark contrast to the other woman's pale flesh. "Last night I awakened in the garden. I was naked, and there were scratches on my arms and legs. Scratches, as if I'd been running through thick brush. I have vivid memories of streaking through Golden Gate Park—only I wasn't human. I was a wolf."

Dr. Wilson blinked in surprise and stared down at their clasped hands. "Goodness! You haven't mentioned somnambulism, though sleepwalking isn't uncommon during periods of extreme stress. Has this happened before?"

Keisha slowly released her grip on the therapist's hand. "I don't know for sure. At least two other nights. I don't know anything anymore. Look at my hair!"

Her expression one of pure confusion, the woman stared at Keisha. "What about your hair?"

"I have it braided by a professional. It's supposed to last for at least a couple of weeks. The mornings after I dream, the braids are undone. It's always been very curly, but it's getting straighter. It's longer. What's happening to me? What am I going to do?"

Blinking owlishly, obviously at a loss for words, the doctor glanced down at her notes. "Have you gone back to work?"

Keisha felt the subtle withdrawal, the woman's struggle to remain professional.

"I see you're a licensed landscape architect. You have your masters degree in . . ." She paused a moment, reading through her notes. "Ah, here it is—landscape architecture and design, with a strong background in botany." Dr. Wilson smiled gently at Keisha and took a firm hold of both her hands. "You've spent seven years training for your profession, so you must obviously love what you do. I would think the beauty of working with growing plants and flowers would be every bit as healing as talking to me. It's going to take time, dear. I can't ask you to forget an event that's obviously too powerful to be forgotten, but I can ask you to accept the fact your life was spared, that you're mentally strong and in good physical health. Your body is recovering. Your mind will heal as well, and at some point the dreams will go away." She patted Keisha's hand. "I want you to work on those exercises I gave you. Keep a record of any other nocturnal events that might occur. Just jot down whatever you recall when you awaken." Dr. Wilson sat back and folded her hands in her lap, a sign their session had ended. "We'll talk again next week."

Keisha stood silently on the corner of Polk and Van Ness in the heart of San Francisco and waited for the bus.

People of all ages passed by on either side, some smiling in her direction, others brushing past as if she didn't exist. They didn't know. None of them knew what horror she'd seen, what fears still filled her heart.

She knew she looked perfectly normal, knew she projected an air of success, of control. She'd better—she worked damned hard at it. Anyone who noticed her would see an attractive young woman of color, tall and slim, dressed in a neat navy blue pantsuit, her shoes and bag perfectly coordinated and obviously expensive, her hair tightly braided and ending in a neat little bun at the nape of her neck.

Not a hair out of place. Everything under control.

Professional, successful . . . normal.

Little did they know.

Dr. Wilson said she would heal. She'd have to if she wanted more than a pale imitation of life.

The bus pulled to a stop, and Keisha climbed on board. She paid her fare and moved to an empty seat near the middle of the bus. A supermarket tabloid lay on the seat, and she shoved the newspaper to one side.

The graphic photo and even more graphic headline leapt out at her, left her skin clammy and her heart pounding a staccato beat. *Werewolves Kill Rapists, Spare Victim.*

The photo covered the top half of the front page, with the snarling visage of a rabid wolf superimposed over the grainy black-and-white. Keisha recognized it immediately and knew it must be a picture from the police files. The faces and torn throats of the men were obscured, but it was obvious they'd been badly mutilated before they died. There was little to identify the location. She didn't need any more than this.

Keisha would never, not for the rest of her life, forget the filthy apartment where three men had died an unspeakable death.

The same place where Keisha Rialto lost her soul.

* * *

Alexandria Olanet stretched herself awake, eyes narrowing against the bright sunlight streaming through the window blinds. She reached for the man beside her and found thick, coarse fur instead. The huge wolf raised his head, amber eyes twinkling in the morning light. With a wide yawn, he rolled over on his back and stretched. Front legs rippled and took form, becoming hands. Back legs lengthened, shifted, until they were sleek and muscular, with long, narrow feet. Finally, the wolven head slowly morphed into the human visage of the man Xandi loved most of all.

She leaned over and placed a very chaste kiss on Stefan Aragat's lips, a kiss that shifted, just as his body had done so easily, into something deeper, more sensual.

Something hungry and demanding. Stefan's lips were warm and mobile beneath hers, his tongue searching, exploring the space between her lips and teeth, tangling with her tongue and finding a rhythm that mimicked the lovemaking that had kept them busy most of the night.

Busy with Anton.

Xandi pulled slowly away from Stefan. "Where's Anton?"

"I'm here."

Both Stefan and Xandi turned as one. Anton lounged in the open door, his shirt unbuttoned and hanging open, his soft denim jeans hugging his slim hips and muscular thighs. He held a steaming cup of coffee in one hand, a newspaper in the other.

Xandi rose up on one elbow and smiled. "You're up early."

Stefan leaned over and nipped her shoulder. "Why don't you join us?"

"Please, Anton." Xandi held her hand out to the wizard.

He hesitated a moment, then shook his head and smiled

with the expression of a man who has willingly lost his battle. He set his coffee and the newspaper on the bedside table, slowly eased out of his shirt, then unzipped his jeans and slipped them down over his hips.

Xandi licked her lips as his dark thatch of pubic hair came into view, then the solid length of his partially erect cock. Damn . . . so beautiful! His body was all silk and steel, smooth skin over taut muscles, the body of a predator.

She'd tasted him last night. She'd tasted Stefan as well, two men of very similar appearances but totally different flavors. Stefan was fire and hot spice, while Anton reminded her of dark forests and musky woods.

Anton discarded his pants and sat on the edge of the bed. He leaned over Xandi's shoulder and kissed Stefan, but his palm found Xandi's breast, and his stroking fingers brought her nipple to a tight peak. Xandi reached for Anton's growing cock, sighed and lay back against the cool sheets, sandwiched between her men.

Anton's tongue tasted Stefan's smooth lower lip, then found entrance into the hot, wet cave of his mouth. Alexandria's breast filled his palm, her hands were doing wondrous things to his cock and balls, and Stefan's tongue dueled gently with his.

He tried to recall what had brought him into the bedroom in the first place, but Stefan's hand suddenly found his ass, squeezing him hard, drawing his body closer to Alexandria's. She tilted her hips just so, her grasp on his cock tightened, and he shifted just enough to help her guide him into her warm pussy.

Her mouth found his nipple, and she suckled hard, nipping him almost to the point of pain. Stefan broke their kiss just as Anton felt her soft gasp of breath. He knew Stefan had entered her backside, easing his way slowly inside that tight opening.

Anton fought every instinct that told him to thrust hard and fast into the woman. Instead, he held still, sensing her muscles clenching and stretching around him, feeling the shift and twist of her body as she accommodated Stefan's huge cock as well as his own, each finding a home in its own, separate sheath.

Anton felt the smooth glide of Stefan's cock riding against his. A shudder raced through him from the pure, unadulterated pleasure of a woman's hot sheath surrounding his cock and the unbelievable sensation resulting each time Stefan thrust slow and deep into her backside. Alexandria moaned and sucked harder on his nipple. Her hands clutched him around the ribcage as he found his own rhythm, alternating stroke for stroke with Stefan.

Stefan swept his hand along Anton's thigh, across Xandi's back, then turned Xandi just enough so he could suckle her breast. There was a soft *pop* as her lips broke suction with Anton's nipple. She arched her back, giving Stefan better access to her breast.

Anton leaned close and drew her other nipple into his mouth. Neither he nor Stefan had shaved this morning. Their beard-roughened chins scraped Alexandria's pale breasts as each man sucked and nipped. Anton matched Stefan's rhythm, driving deep inside Alexandria as the other man withdrew, then slowly reversing.

He'd long had fantasies like this, fantasies where he loved both a man and a woman at the same time, but nothing he'd imagined came even remotely close to the reality. Anton drew Alexandria's nipple deep into his mouth and wrapped his tongue around the taut flesh, sucking hard. He felt her stiffen, heard the soft, keening cry, as her first orgasm claimed her, felt the thick slide of Stefan's cock against his own as the other man buried himself completely inside his mate, buried himself so hard and deep his balls pressed against Anton's and his muscled arms drew both Anton and Alexandria into a tight, shuddering embrace.

Anton let his mind open, found Stefan, found Alexandria, felt the passion in their hearts, the hot rush of need, the multiple sensations of Stefan's cock buried deep inside Alexandria, the smooth rush as his own cock slipped deeper into her pussy.

Connecting their minds, Anton shared the sensual images surrounding him, the wonder of his cock sliding against Stefan's, the even greater wonder of Stefan and Alexandria's love, a love that made room for a man without a mate of his own.

Anton wanted to last, he tried to hold out, but the trembling woman in his arms, the hot rush of her fluids bathing his cock, Stefan's deep groan as their balls pressed together when he hugged the three of them into a tight, hot, shivering mass of flesh, catapulted Anton into his own release.

He arched his back and drove deep inside Alexandria, her tight pussy an even tighter sheath with Stefan's cock pressing hard against his own.

Too much!

Once more . . . please . . . once more!

Gasping, crying out, Anton felt his testicles contract, felt the hot coil of life-giving seed burning the length of his cock, felt each spasm and contraction deep inside Alexandria's hot sheath. The sensitive head of his cock found the hard opening of her womb as he filled her. She cried out once more, her thighs clamping hard against his, her pussy milking every last drop of seed, taking him deep inside, taking Stefan, holding both of them.

Loving both of them.

Heart and mind. Body, soul . . . still, it wasn't enough.

She was Stefan's mate.

She was the leader of their group.

She would bear a child only for Stefan.

Stefan.

Shuddering, still trembling in the aftermath of orgasm, Anton slowly withdrew.

Aware once more of the reason he'd come back to their room in the first place.

Chapter 12

Anton poured himself another cup of coffee and leaned against the counter. Both Alexandria and Stefan, freshly showered, were mesmerized by the article in the cheap supermarket tabloid. Finally, after a long moment, Alexandria raised her head and swept the thick fall of auburn hair back from her eyes.

"You think she's one of us, don't you?"

Anton nodded his head. "I've awakened a number of nights now with the sense that something is wrong. Not a true nightmare, just a strange sense of unease. I saw this when we picked up groceries yesterday and felt a strong compulsion to buy it."

Stefan grinned. "What? And here I thought this was your regular reading material."

Anton groaned. "Right . . . like I want to read about four-headed babies and alien abductions? I don't think so. This—" he pointed at the lurid headline and photo, and took a deep breath— "this sort of thing gets my attention. What if the woman is the wolf? What if the stress and fear of the attack forced her to shift? Imagine her now, alone and traumatized, possibly even unaware it happened."

"That's awful." Alexandria shook her head. "I can't imagine the horror of this attack, if it's real."

Anton nodded. "I think it's real. I also think it's what has been disturbing my sleep. I believe she is able to shift, and I somehow sense when it happens." He carefully set his coffee cup down. "Enjoy your breakfast. We're flying out to San Francisco in about two hours. You'd better get moving."

Xandi shook her head, grinning, as she, Stefan and Anton left San Francisco Police Department headquarters with the name and address of the rape victim. "Your powers to mesmerize the detective were, to say the least, mesmerizing."

Anton smiled and winked at her as he carefully folded the slip of paper and put it inside his wallet. "Hey, when you're good, you're good. Don't ever doubt it, woman. I am good."

Stefan punched him lightly on the shoulder. "Don't get cocky. He was so busy looking at Xandi, he wasn't even paying attention to you."

"That's how I got him." Anton rubbed his fingers over his chest. "I convinced him Alexandria was the victim's sister and was desperate to get in touch with her."

"She's black, Anton. I'm not." Xandi shook her head, amazed. Sometimes Anton's powers appeared limitless.

Anton stopped, his look serious and somewhat withdrawn. "In a way, my dear, if I'm right, you are sisters. I believe she is Chanku. She is also recovering from a horrible trauma. I hope that not only will she accept us as family, she will also allow us to help her."

Xandi slipped her hand around Anton's arm, linked her other with Stefan and hugged both men close to her. "Take us to her, Anton. We'll figure out how to help her once we find her."

Nibbling on a long blade of yellowed grass she'd plucked from a planter in her studio, Keisha stared blankly at the drawing in front of her. The job of a lifetime—the design for a memorial garden in Golden Gate Park—and all she could see were the terrified eyes of men awaiting their own brutal death.

A small, filthy apartment, awash in blood and gore.

A nightmare vision from the wrong point of view—not through her own eyes, but through the eyes of a berserk predator—a snarling wolf gone mad.

The men deserved to die. She wondered if she would ever move beyond the horrible memories—memories of their violent, horrible acts, which left her bruised, torn and bleeding. They'd planned to kill her. She knew that, felt it with every bit of her soul. But why did she continue to believe she was the one who had turned the tables and murdered them instead?

Impossible.

Late afternoon sun streamed through the French doors of her workroom, casting long shadows across the clutter and comfortable bits and pieces of her work, her life. What had always brought her peace now merely distracted. She rubbed her sweaty palm across her forehead and bit back a sob.

Therapy wasn't helping. The comforting words of friends and co-workers merely reminded her she was still a victim, still in need of being handled with kid gloves.

She was not a victim. She refused to be a victim. She'd worked too hard all her life, paid too many debts, fought too many battles, to get this far.

Her father might have been an excellent gardener, a job he loved until the day he died, but he'd never been respected for all his skill and knowledge. She was a landscape architect, a licensed professional, already gaining notice in a very competitive market. It hadn't been easy, and damn it all, she was not going to lose sight of her goal now.

Success lay so close, the designs spread across her draw-

ing board the key to the prize she'd worked for since the
first time she'd seen a professionally designed garden and
fallen in love with the beauty of nature.

Nature shaped by the hand of man.

And the hands of men have taken it all away.

"Damn." Flinging her pencil to the floor, Keisha stood
up and paced about the room. Suddenly aware she was
pacing in the pattern of wolves in a zoo enclosure, she
came to a trembling halt.

A bell chimed on the ground floor. "Who the hell?" She
brushed her hand across her forehead, threw the mangled
piece of grass on which she'd grown in the habit of chew-
ing into the trash and straightened her work smock before
heading down the stairs. She looked through the small
peephole and saw an attractive young white woman on
the front porch. The woman appeared to be alone. Keisha
slowly eased the door open. The woman smiled and held
out her hand.

"Ms. Rialto? My name is Alexandria Olanet."

Keisha nodded, aware the tiny hairs on the back of her
neck were standing upright. Her heart leapt into over-
drive. The hand she held out to the stranger trembled, then
stilled as the woman's fingers tightened around hers. She
stared at her fingers, firmly clasped in the woman's grasp,
and was aware of a sense of calm, of peace, she hadn't felt
now in weeks.

Wide-eyed, she raised her chin and studied the stranger.

The woman's voice was soft, well modulated. "You
don't know who I am, and you have no reason to trust me,
but I'm here to help you." Without waiting for an invitation, she stepped into the brightly lit foyer. "I probably
should have called, but you would have told me not to
come."

Keisha stepped back, allowing the woman farther into
her home. "Why? What do you want with me?"

"I know what happened in that apartment two weeks

ago. I know how those men died. You need to know the truth."

Keisha's blood ran cold. She backed against the wall, her breath lodged in her throat, and it was all she could do to keep from screaming. "I think you'd better leave before I call the police."

"Please." Alexandria held her hands out as if in supplication. "I mean you no harm. You're kin to me, and I want to help."

"Kin? Shit, woman. You're white. We're no more kin than—"

The woman didn't look crazy. No, she looked as if she meant what she said. Maybe she was one of those religious fanatics who went around trying to save people from the devil.

"We're sisters of the heart, you and I." She stepped closer to Keisha. "I've not suffered as you have, but I know about the wolf."

This woman was definitely nuts. "What wolf? That's all tabloid garbage. It was pit bulls—trained fighting dogs—that killed those men. That's all it was."

The woman nodded. "I know that's what you want to believe. In your heart you know differently."

"No." Keisha's throat seemed to constrict around the word. "The police report said—"

"The police report is wrong. You killed those men. They deserved to die, and you killed them."

"No!" Keisha backed away, edging slowly toward the phone in the hallway.

The woman merely shook her head and sighed. "I should have thought this through . . . figured out a better way to approach you . . ." She smiled, almost self-consciously, at Keisha. Then she started to melt. That's the only way Keisha could explain it. She melted, right there in the marble foyer of Keisha's new townhouse apartment.

Keisha opened her mouth to scream. No sound

emerged. Her legs began to shake, her hands trembled so much she couldn't grab the phone, and if she'd thought of it in time, she would have closed her eyes. Instead, they were open wide and saw it all, saw the beautiful auburn-haired woman sort of ripple and melt and fold in upon herself, until there was a pile of clothing on the floor and a full-sized she-wolf standing in the foyer.

Keisha did what any right-thinking young woman would do under similar circumstances.

She fainted dead away.

"Maybe that was a bit abrupt." Xandi slipped the work smock off the young woman's shoulders and loosened the top buttons on her blouse to make her more comfortable on the soft leather couch. Anton had carried Keisha's limp body into the living room within seconds after she fainted, reacting instantly when Xandi's mental cry of alarm brought him practically crashing through the door.

Stefan sat across the room, his fingers steepled under his chin, his amber eyes thoughtful. "There really isn't another way. Poor thing has had a horrible experience, one shock following another. Tell me one easy way to explain that she's also a shape-shifting wolf who just ruthlessly killed and partially devoured three men. Personally, my love, I think you did just fine."

Xandi brushed a few loose tendrils of Keisha's dark hair back from her eyes. The woman's eyelids fluttered but remained closed. Xandi sighed and shook her head in dismay. "I came into my heritage in a world filled with love. Keisha hasn't had that option. It's been forced upon her— violently. Her body still hasn't recovered from the assault, her mind doesn't accept the attack. We need to proceed more gently with her. I really blew it."

Anton moved closer, gliding silently to a spot beside the couch. He knelt beside the unconscious woman, his entire demeanor one of worry and solicitude. "She's so beautiful,

so frightened. She doesn't understand any of this. She
wants to—she's very intelligent, very open to new ideas—
but all of this scares the hell out of her."

"How do you know?" Xandi cupped Anton's jaw in
her palm. "I tried to read her, but her mind is closed to me.
Do you understand her thoughts?"

"This close, her mind is practically melded with mine."
Anton shifted back on his heels, but his palm still brushed
Keisha's hair. "I think we've had a partial link for the past
couple of weeks, hence the dreams keeping me awake. I
feel her thoughts, her fears. She's terrified of the truth,
afraid that what you told her actually happened. She does-
n't want that. She's not violent by nature, or so she be-
lieves. That's why the idea of the wolf in her is so
frightening."

"Can you calm her?" Xandi studied the woman's face.
She looked almost as if she'd been caught in the midst of a
scream—her jaw was tense, her lips twisted. "I keep thinking she'd be more comfortable with a woman, especially
since her assault, but not if we can't link. Can you help
her, Anton?"

He nodded his head. "Leave me alone with her. Take
Stefan and go see the city. Golden Gate Park is only a
block away. Enjoy the gardens . . . whatever. Don't try to
link with me. I need time completely alone with her."

Xandi nodded. Stefan rose to his feet and held out his
hand. She placed hers within his firm grip and followed
him to the door. "We'll take about an hour, Anton. You've
got my cell-phone number if we wander too far for a mental connection. If you need us sooner, just call."

Just call. Such simple but special words to a man who
had spent most of his life alone. Anton stroked Keisha's
shoulder, but his thoughts followed the couple walking
down the long hallway. Stefan and Alexandria. Mates,
lovers, two people with enough love to share not only

their bodies, but also their hearts and souls with a loner such as Anton.

Who would have guessed? He projected peace and warmth, calm and contentment, to the unconscious woman, but part of his thoughts remained with Stefan and Alexandria. He wasn't actually jealous of what they'd discovered with one another, but damn if he didn't want the same thing for himself.

He sensed their love and laughter, their concern for Keisha, even their concern for him, as they strolled the busy streets of San Francisco. Smiling, basking in the feelings still so new to him, he turned his mind back to the unconscious woman. She was beautiful. Her skin was very dark, an all-over coffee brown, with hair that was black and thick, braided into neat little rows of braids stretching back from a high forehead.

He wished she'd open her eyes. He hadn't seen them yet, wondered if they were the same amber as his and Stefan's, or deep gray like Alexandria's. Whatever color, he knew they would be perfect.

Everything about her cried out to him.

Chanku.

Anton raised his face to the heavens for a brief prayer of thanks. He had found her, and she would survive. How many of their kind were out there, lost and afraid, unaware of the power just beyond their fingertips?

Unaware of the sense of brotherhood, of family?

He tried to focus on specific images in her mind, but found only a jumbled litany of fear, nightmarish snapshots of the faces of her abductors, the bloodied room and the torn bodies, all of it intermingled with the beauty of her work and the lush gardens she designed.

He took her limp hands in his, concentrated on her thoughts and projected a sense of belonging, of brotherhood, of peace and acceptance.

He felt her slight flicker of awareness, the tightening reaction of fear, then heard her sigh quietly. Her tongue slipped between her full lips, and she licked first the upper, then the lower one, moistening them. Anton thought his heart might stop altogether as she slowly, cautiously, opened her eyes.

Anton smiled when he recognized the flash of green in their amber depths. Hers truly were the eyes of a wolf.

It took her a moment to focus, and he used every one of his mental tricks in that brief span of time to reassure her, to make her feel safe and protected. He felt the tension go out of her grasp and knew it was working, at least for now.

"Are you all right?" Anton kept his voice pitched low, professional. He kept a firm but comforting grip on her hand.

Keisha scooted back on the couch and sat up, looking around as if trying to find the wolf, but she left her hand within his grasp. Held it, in fact, as if it were a lifeline.

"Who . . . ?" She glanced down at their hands, then back up at Anton.

"I'm a friend. You can trust me. The others have gone. I asked them to give us some time. I know you have a lot of questions." Anton stroked her hand, projecting soothing thoughts. "Alexandria felt terrible about frightening you, but she knew of no other way to convince you."

"You mean . . . I really did see what I thought I saw? That woman turned into a wolf?" Her voice squeaked on the word.

Anton smiled. "Yes, you saw her turn into a wolf. It was not a parlor trick, not a figment of your imagination. It's something all of us are capable of doing."

"Us who?" Carefully, Keisha extricated her hand from Anton's grasp.

Regretfully he let her go.

"Chanku. We are all of that race, an ancient race—you, me, my friend Stefan and the woman you saw, Alexandria.

Others as well, though I've not located them yet. Long before I read the article in the paper, I had sensed your existence. The tabloid story merely pointed me in the right direction."

Keisha stared at him as if she still thought he might be totally nuts. Anton let his thoughts surface in her mind.

Maybe this will help. Our people can communicate over short distances with the power of our minds, over longer distances under certain circumstances. I know you can hear me. See if you can answer.

"Holy shit." Keisha shook her head. "I hear you in my head."

You can speak to me this way as well. Try it.

How? Her simple question touched his mind, an erotic feather-stroke across his senses. Anton shivered at the brief contact.

Just like that.

Her eyes grew round and wide. *You mean you can hear me as well as I can hear you? How come I've never been able to do this before?*

Most likely you've not had anyone listening. Do you believe me now?

Well, I'm beginning to think either you're totally nuts or I am. She smiled.

Anton realized she was so caught up in the magic of telepathy, she'd forgotten her fear. He silently reassured her, built on her sense of achievement.

He'd never seen anyone more lovely, not even Alexandria in all her wolven glory. He told her so, let Keisha see herself as he saw her—skin like dark silk, sparkling yet wary amber eyes, a lush and sensual mouth that begged to be kissed, full breasts he wanted to nuzzle and taste.

Keisha arched her eyebrows and scooted away from him. The artery in her throat fluttered with her increased heart rate. Anton sensed her fear and immediately clamped down on his sensual thoughts.

I'm sorry. I was out of line.

She stared at him, obviously not certain whether he was worthy of her trust.

He shook his head, held his hand out to her in apology. "I am sorry. I have no right, especially after all you've been through. You're a beautiful woman, and I let my thoughts go a bit astray. The Chanku are a very sensual race."

Keisha nibbled on her upper lip a moment, then seemed to come to a decision. "Tell me more about this ancient race of yours. I'm of African descent—one hundred percent, as far as I know. I can trace my ancestors back to the Ivory Coast in the mid–seventeen hundreds. Both my parents are gone now, but as far as I know, there aren't any white people in my heritage. How can I be part of some other race I've never heard of?"

"I don't know. Somewhere in your past is the blood of Chanku. There's not a lot of information about the race as a whole, but I sense it very strongly in you." Anton stood up and paced about the room, gathering his thoughts. "I learned of my own heritage practically by accident. I was a magician, a very good one. I wanted more. I wanted to be a true wizard, a master of the arcane arts. To achieve this goal, I studied. I went to libraries all over Europe, read scrolls in their ancient languages, immersed myself in the writing of scholars and practitioners of wizardry."

He leaned against the edge of a large table, crossed his ankles and folded his arms across his muscular chest. "A lot of it is pure, unmitigated bunk. Even the old stuff. However, some of what I learned led me to Tibet, where I was allowed access to some very old records of ancient civilizations. There was a single reference that caught my eye. It was the word Chanku. I felt as if that word unlocked some secret part of my mind. It literally stopped me in my tracks."

Chapter 13

Keisha understood the part about being stopped in your tracks. Watching this absolutely drop-dead-gorgeous guy pacing around her living room as if he owned the place was a surrealistic experience. Though she couldn't control her intense fear of men when he was close enough to touch her, she could certainly admire him from across the room.

His dark hair fell well below his collar, and his eyes were the same unusual shade of amber as her own. He had the high cheekbones and shadowed jaw of a top fashion model, and he moved with the grace of a dancer, all long limbs and lean body. His shoulders were broad, stretching the dark knit of the shirt he wore, and sleek muscles rippled along his arms, across his chest. As tall as she was, he was so much taller, so much stronger.

She wondered if she'd ever be able to let a man come close to her again. The image of her abductors slipped unbidden into her thoughts, and she shuddered.

"Are you okay?" Anton knelt in front of her, his look one of concern and caring.

"Yes . . . I was just thinking . . ." Her thoughts drifted, her heart pounded, as Anton drew closer. He smiled and backed away.

It's okay. I respect your need for space. I want you to

know I will never hurt you. None of us will. We under-
stand your fear. With time we will make it go away.
I don't know if I'll ever be the same again!

Anton stood up, still smiling, as if Keisha's cry had never entered his mind. "Once you fully understand Chanku, you'll realize you need never fear again. You will discover new strengths within yourself and within the links you share with others of our kind. We are strongly connected and just as strong individually. Like the fabled werewolves, we have the power to shift our bodies from human to wolf and back again. It's nothing paranormal, not supernatural. We don't need a full moon or any type of spell, nor must we remain under cover of darkness. It's due to a physical anomaly, a small part of the brain near the hypothalamus, actually, an extension of that organ that exists only in the Chanku, an organ that without certain nutrients loses its ability to function."

Keisha stared at him for a long moment, weighing the veracity of his words. "If what you're saying is true, how could I have shifted? How could I have suddenly, without any warning, turned into a wolf?"

"Fear. Adrenaline. The body's need to survive. I don't really know. For the rest of us, it takes a special diet. When I was in Tibet, I learned there were plants once common to the area that have the ability to draw certain nutrients from the soil in precise percentages—nutrients perfectly formulated to stimulate that special part of the brain, which in turn influences the functions in the body needed to shift. I was drawn to the plants, not realizing my body craved what they offered."

Keisha thought of the small shipment of exotic shrubs and grasses that sat, at that moment, in the little green-house in her backyard. Some even grew in the decorative planter in her studio. They were shrubs and grasses common to the lower reaches of the Himalayas. She'd seen them at a demonstration, had felt oddly drawn to them, had created her entire memorial design around these varieties of plants of which she'd never before heard.

Could something in her own genetic makeup have forged the immediate connection she'd felt for the odd selection of plants?

No. Absolutely not . . . but what if? The suspicion lingered in her mind.

She took a deep, steadying breath. "I'm a landscape architect. I work with a lot of imported varieties. Possibly some of those . . ."

"Only if you eat them." Anton shrugged, but there was a twinkle in his eyes. "Been nibbling on your plants much?"

Keisha felt the tension slowly ebbing from her body. Whoever and whatever this man was, he was handsome and sexy and trying so hard to help her relax.

"Actually, yes." She stood up, took a moment to gain her balance and walked slowly toward the backyard, immediately feeling more at ease. "I tend to nibble when I work. Come see if anything looks familiar."

She sensed his attraction to her as she brushed past him. Her muscles tensed when she felt the warmth of his body, the reaction involuntary and irritating. Her insides felt twisted, tied in knots. He was attractive, intriguing. She was drawn to him, wanted to know more about him, but at the same time was repulsed by his very maleness.

Before her attack, she'd always thought of herself as a sensual woman. She liked sex. Always had. She wanted to want someone again, wanted to know that rush of sexual excitement, the tingling awareness of her own sexuality. Frustration stiffened her gait as she led him to the back of the house and into the small garden.

Had her sexuality, her need to touch and be touched, been beaten out of her forever? Sighing, Keisha knelt down and brushed her hand across a soft, yellowed grass growing in tangled clumps around the low steps leading to the greenhouse. "I liked this so much, I planted some of it in my own yard and even have a planter of it in my studio. The rest is for a project I'm working on—a small memorial garden in Golden Gate Park."

Anton rolled a few blades of the grass between his fingers, looked up and smiled, then followed her into the greenhouse.

Immediately, the space seemed too small, the air too heavy—damp and warm and close. Keisha backed away from Anton. He stepped away as well, giving her more space. She sighed and shook her head, well aware he knew why she'd reacted the way she did. "I imagine it will take time. I'm still recovering. I'm sorry. I don't want to feel like a victim, but even more, I don't want to make you feel like a pariah."

"I understand, but more importantly, I know this is only temporary. You will heal."

Anton turned away and stared intently at the rows of flats, each one filled with soft grasses, stunted and twisted shrubs, and small, flowering ground covers. When he raised his head, he was smiling once again.

"Your choice of plants alone would convince me of your heritage. Each one of these, in very small amounts, is an integral part of the Chanku diet. I have most of them growing at my own home. Do you have any idea what made you choose these particular varieties?"

His eyes sparkled, and his smile broadened, changed his entire face. She'd thought him handsome at first, but she hadn't realized the man was downright breathtaking. Literally. Damn. It was such a stupid cliché, but Keisha had to remind herself to breathe.

"I . . . I don't know exactly why I chose them." She did, though. She knew exactly why she'd picked these particular plants. They'd felt right. That was all. When she'd gone to the wholesaler's and looked across the vast array of growing things, this selection of plants had practically called out to her.

Her choice of just the right plants for her various designs had brought her numerous awards. Keisha had always figured it was her extensive knowledge after years of education and training. Was it merely that odd sixth sense she'd always wondered about? Something beyond her normal, human skills? Or was she merely fulfilling the needs of Chanku?

Startled by her weird train of thought, she looked away, knelt down and patted dirt around a small bush. Her heart fluttered, and she felt terribly self-conscious, unbearably aware that her mind was in turmoil, that she was alone in a small, isolated greenhouse with a stranger. She concentrated on the grains of sand clinging to her fingers instead of the powerful man standing, once more, almost close enough to touch. "The garden is a memorial to a group of Sherpas who died leading an expedition of local climbers. I thought plants from the region seemed apropos."

"Very apropos. Yet the ones you selected are all specific to the Chanku diet." He held his hand out to her. "I realize you don't know me, but please try to trust me. The others are returning. I sense them drawing near. You might be able to sense their arrival as well."

Keisha stared at his hand a moment, gathered what courage she had left and wrapped her fingers around his larger ones. His olive skin looked pale against hers, his large fingers dwarfing hers. He tugged her easily to her feet, pulling her up with a single, graceful motion that drew her close to his chest.

She tried to sense the others. Sensed only Anton. Felt the beat of his heart, the soft exhalation of his breath. Smelled the clean, musky scent that made her own heart rate speed up.

She dropped his hand and stepped away. Only then, when she'd put some distance between herself and Anton, did she become aware of the others coming up the front steps, the sound of their footsteps ringing in her mind, wisps of conversation floating, barely heard.

She glanced quickly at Anton, then practically ran out of the greenhouse. "Your friends are back. I guess I should let them in."

She heard Anton's quiet laughter as he followed her across the yard.

Chapter 14

"I know it's asking a lot of you to come with us, but please consider it." Alexandria set her coffee cup down on the place mat in front of her and smiled at Keisha.

"I have my work. . . . I don't know any of you. . . ." Keisha held onto her cup, clutching it with both hands.

Stefan took a swallow of his coffee. He looked so much like Anton, it was just plain eerie, but the men insisted they weren't related, other than through their shared Chanku heritage. "You said the designs are almost complete. If I remember correctly, you also said they have to go through an approval process that should take about six weeks. Come with us, just for a month. Give yourself a chance to know us, give us a chance to find out more about you, to convince you to join us. Whether you like it or not, you are one of us."

He's telling the truth, Keisha. We all are. Please, look into our minds. We're all completely open to you. Look into our minds and see that we mean you no harm.

Keisha's hands trembled. To have Anton enter her mind so easily . . . she closed her eyes and took a deep breath. The connection was both frightening and, at the same time, comforting. With her eyes still closed, she tried again to sense the thoughts of the others in the room.

As if a veil had lifted, she suddenly caught their conversation flitting through her mind.

She's been badly traumatized, Stefan. It's not fair to push her.

She's a lot stronger than she looks, my love. She needs us as much as we need her.

Alexandria's right. We will not force the issue. I don't want her hurt. If she says she's not ready, we're not going to push her. This must be her decision, and her decision alone.

Anton! Alexandria worried about her, but Anton was the one willing to give her space, the one who saw her troubled soul and understood. For Anton, she would make this decision. Nodding slowly, she looked at each of the three people in the room.

"I will go, but only if you promise me a room of my own, a quiet place where I can be by myself, and a return ticket if this doesn't work."

"It's yours." Anton slowly held out his hand to her, not to grab it, but to shake and seal the agreement.

Keisha took his hand, felt the warmth, sensed the innate honesty of the man. Beyond that, she felt his need, his desire for her. She almost slipped her hand free, but she looked into his eyes and stilled.

Need. Such need and naked vulnerability, she thought her heart would break. Where she feared, Anton needed. Where she worried, Anton wanted.

She fought the urge to pull her hand free, almost turned and ran, but a small whisper of thought entered her mind.

Anton needs you. We all do, but Anton most of all. He is the one who rediscovered the Chanku. He is the one who brought Stefan and me together, who brought all of us together. You need to find yourself, and Anton should be the one to help you. Please, join us.

Keisha jerked her head in Alexandria's direction. The woman's face held no sign of their discussion. It had been totally private, words between two women. Kindred. She felt a warmth under her heart she'd not known before. Alexandria nodded, an almost imperceptible movement, but enough to let Keisha know it had indeed been her speaking.

Keisha glanced once more in Anton's direction. He studied her, his eyes wide open and yet so sad they made her want to cry. He seemed to think she would turn them down, would change her mind, though she'd already accepted. He seemed to be afraid of losing her.

Slowly, Keisha nodded her head. "I will go with you. I need to know you. More than that, I need to know myself."

"It's lovely." Barefoot, dressed like Xandi in a soft, blue silk sarong tied over one shoulder, Keisha stared out over the vast mountain range, tinged with pale gold and silver in the last glow of evening. She and Xandi shared a quiet moment on the large deck off the western side of the house. "I've never been to Montana. I thought it was all cowboys and buffalo."

Xandi laughed. She'd shadowed Keisha since their departure, a comforting presence with so many new experiences. "It is beautiful, and this is my favorite time of night. After dinner, Anton, Stefan and I usually shift to our wolven forms and run. We've explored every inch of the forests around us."

"You really do shift, don't you?" Keisha turned and leaned back against the deck railing, her wine glass clasped between her fingers. "I still can't believe it, though after seeing what you did yesterday, I know I have to accept. Will you run tonight?"

"If you don't mind being left alone. Oliver will be here, but the three of us might be away for hours. Otherwise we can stay here until you feel more settled."

Keisha took a deep breath. "I think I would like to see

you shift. I want to feel what you feel when it happens. It might make it easier for me to accept."

"Are you sure?" Xandi's eyes practically bored into hers. Keisha nodded. Immediately Stefan and Anton joined them on the deck, and she realized they'd been listening to the conversation.

Anton stepped close to Keisha. "I don't want you to fear us. There's so much for you to learn, but I admire your willingness to see something that, for want of another word, is impossible." He smiled, then slowly began to unbutton his shirt.

Keisha glanced quickly away, in Xandi's direction. She was already naked, having only a silk sarong to unwrap. Stefan was slipping out of his pants, his shirt already neatly folded on a deck chair.

"What?" Her hand went to her throat, and she choked back a nervous giggle. She hadn't expected them to undress first, hadn't really thought of anything, but suddenly she was surrounded by three of the most beautiful people she'd ever known, all naked and grinning at her.

"We can shift while wearing clothes, but it makes a big mess. I hate to iron." Xandi laughed, then suddenly it was happening all over again and she was melting, shifting, stretching and reshaping. It happened so fast, Keisha forgot to link to her mind, but she twisted around and caught Stefan's thoughts as he went through the same process.

It all made sense. Strange and unusual, so hard to imagine, but when she linked to his mind as he shifted, Keisha realized she'd done this before.

She was the wolf.

She truly had killed three men.

She spun around to watch Anton shift, but he stood beside her, still in his gorgeous human body.

"Are you all right? I can stay here with you."

Compassion flowed from him in waves. Compassion

and warmth, so strong, so loving, Keisha basked in his healing strength.

"No. I want to go with you. I want to shift." She felt a sob catch in her throat, realized the two wolves standing beside her and the man directly in front of her were caught unaware by her decision.

Are you sure? You don't have to, not so soon, but if that is your wish, we'll help you. All of us.

Xandi's soft question washed away Keisha's fear. "I know how to shift. I've done it before, though I must have blocked the memory, but I remember doing it now. I remember the power of the wolf. I want that power again."

Shift with me. Link with my thoughts, feel what I do and let your body flow. It will be disorienting. You may experience a bit of nausea. Just relax and follow my lead.

Keisha nodded, her mind so completely linked with Anton's, she no longer sensed the other two, no longer felt the wooden deck beneath her bare feet. Slowly she loosened the knot holding the sarong over her shoulder. It slipped to the deck, brushing her bare feet with shimmering coolness, a cobalt blue puddle of silk. She stood shivering in the warm evening, more aware of the molten heat in Anton's eyes than of her own nudity.

His look was pure male appreciation, but he quickly banked the smoldering lust in his eyes and took Keisha's hands in a light grip.

She felt the first tingling awareness that something about her body was changing. Following Anton's lead, she concentrated on the shifting of bone and muscle into new lupine shapes. It happened so quickly, so completely, she was hardly aware of the shift completing before she was sitting on the deck, blinking at the coal-black wolf staring back at her.

Fascinated, she held up her front paw, turning it this way and that, to study the thick pads, the sharp claws. Her fur was very dark brown, as dark as Anton's was black, though she noticed a reddish glint when she moved, as if there were fire hiding in the depths of her coat.

Her heart pounded. She wanted to run. Wanted to leave Keisha Rialto behind. Wanted to outrace the victim and find a new self in the darkness of the nighttime forest.

Stefan leapt first, sailing over the railing and landing in the thick lawn that circled the house. Xandi followed him, her muscles bunching as she cleared the three-foot fence with ease. Anton nudged her shoulder.

What the hell? Keisha followed, amazed her brain knew how to make this strange shape function with such fluid beauty. She landed in the soft grass beside Xandi, with Anton coming down just ahead of her.

He yipped, turned, nipped Keisha on the shoulder and took off running.

The night was clear and warm, the forest scents intriguing, the strength and power of her wolven body a pure, unadulterated joy. Speed—unbelievable speed—as they raced through the woods, leaping over creeks, slipping beneath brush and following trails barely visible along creek beds and canyons.

And always the link, the constant flow of information from one to the other. Sharing the scent of live things rushing out of their path, sharing the pure joy of the hunt. Keisha had never before felt this sense—of being one with the pack. Had not realized the power inherent in the pack link, the sensual beauty of streaking through the dark forest with eyes that pierced the night, with a brain that understood each different scent, each rustling sound, each tiny squeak and chirp.

They ran for hours, their bodies finding a rhythm that gave them strength. Keisha wanted to go on forever, but Anton's quiet presence beside her was a reminder she should take care, at least this first time. Still, the pale rays of dawn streaked the sky when they finally flopped down on the damp grass in front of Anton's huge home, tongues lolling, eyes sparkling, tails too tired to hold high.

Stefan rolled over on his back, his shaggy gray-streaked coat matted and dirty from their rush through a boggy swamp. With a teasing glint in his amber eyes, Anton leaned over and nipped Stefan's shoulder.

The act was rife with sexual overtones, a sense of dominance and submission.

Xandi did the same to Anton, leaning her furry body close to his, then nuzzling Stefan as well. Keisha sensed it then, the strong, linked sexuality among the three of them. Anton turned and looked at her, his eyes wide, his mind open.

He shared the intimate relationship he had with both Alexandria and Stefan. Shared the sensual connection among all within the pack, the physical intimacies that were as natural to them as the shift from human to wolf and back again, the almost hedonistic rushes of desire that followed each of their runs through the forest together.

Keisha understood and accepted, aware at once of her own sense of heightened sensuality, her recently dormant libido raging almost beyond control. Somehow shifting, taking the form of the wolf, had reawakened the sensual side of her nature. A sensual side she was still unable to accept.

She felt no jealousy, only a sense of sadness, an awareness that what the other three shared so freely was not for her.

She wasn't ready. Not yet. The assault was too recent, her body too newly healed.

Exhausted, she pulled herself to her feet and padded up the stairs to the deck. In a fluid motion, as if she'd shifted for years, she regained her human form and picked up the sarong she'd left the night before. She wrapped it lightly around her torso.

Her hair fell forward. She reached up to push it out of

her eyes and realized it now cascaded in loose, corkscrew curls to her shoulders. Her hand paused over the unfamiliar texture. Gone was the short, coarse, tightly kinked hair she'd known all her life.

Her laughter sounded shaky even to her own ears, and she knew her smile was just as wobbly. "Well, I guess this explains why I can't keep a braid do for any length of time. They keep working themselves loose. It must be the wolf in me." She bit her lips and blinked back the tears that filled her eyes. Everything was changing—her body, her mind, even her hair. It was too much, too intense. Too fast.

She took a deep breath and stared solemnly at Alexandria, Stefan and Anton, not even sure where to begin. "Thank you. Thank you all for something more amazing than anything I have ever imagined. It's going to take me a while before I can really accept what has happened here tonight. I need to shower now, and to sleep. I want to replay every second of the night." She started to leave, then turned around, grinning. "And I wanna do it again, okay?"

Anton shifted and raced up the stairs. He grabbed her hands in his and held them firmly. "Are you okay? We didn't mean to upset you. Our feelings for one another are so natural, so much a part of who we are . . . I didn't think. The last thing I want to do is make you feel uncomfortable."

Keisha laughed and slowly looked him up and down. His body was streaked in mud and wet grass, his cock partially erect and jutting out from its nest of dark hair. He was masculinity incarnate, so beautiful she wanted to touch him.

When she was ready.

"Yesterday, seeing you like this would have terrified me. Today, it makes me miss what I'm not quite ready for. You're not making me uncomfortable, Anton. You're helping me feel again." She cupped the side of his face in her palm. "Give me time, please. Just a little bit of time."

He leaned over and placed a very chaste kiss on the side of her face. "For you, anything. Good night, Keisha. Sleep well."

Keisha left Anton standing on the deck and went straight into the bathroom. Smiling, she turned on the shower and stepped beneath the spray. Her cheek still tingled from the tender brush of his lips.

Chapter 15

The sun was just peeking over the mountains when Keisha finally crawled between the cool sheets. Her room was off by itself, a beautiful space of peace and quiet, with a huge window and a view of the forest.

She still couldn't believe she'd run through that forest, keeping pace with three beautiful wolves, their sleek coats rippling, tongues lolling between powerful jaws. She missed the feeling now, the sense of family she'd shared from the moment she became the wolf. Sighing quietly, snuggling into the thick down comforter, she let her mind drift, searching for Anton's already familiar touch.

She found him, his mind seeking hers much as she sought his. The realization that he was looking for her made her smile.

Where are you? Would he answer?

I'm getting into bed. We ran far last night and I'm tired. Are you alone?

There was a long, thoughtful pause.

No, I no longer sleep alone. Xandi and Stefan share their bed with me.

She knew that. She'd sensed the link between the three, though hadn't completely accepted it for what it was.

Oh.

Would you like to join us?

Join them? Sleep with three strangers? Never. No. She couldn't do anything like . . .

Not physically. Mentally. Maintain the link with me. Share the love with me. Stay there, in the privacy of your room, but feel the love the three of us have for each other . . . and know that you can be a part of it whenever you're ready.

You would allow that? I would feel like a voyeur.

Keisha sensed the sound of his laughter, knew Xandi and Stefan shared the emotion.

You would be a voyeur. Is there anything wrong with that if you've been invited to watch?

It didn't feel right. But it did. Dear Lord, it felt so right for her to be a part of whatever the other three shared. Keisha wrapped the blanket tighter around her shoulders.

No matter how it feels, we will share with you. You are our sister, Keisha. Our sister, our lover, our newest mate. Be with us tonight. Not in body. You're not ready for that. Share with us in spirit.

She was still trying to comprehend Anton's words when she suddenly realized she was in the room with Anton, Xandi and Stefan. The window was open, and the drapes floated softly on the morning breeze. Sunlight filtered through partially drawn shades. She saw through Anton's eyes, knew he shielded her connection from the others, though they were well aware she was with them.

It was Stefan who moved first, leaning over Xandi and kissing her, his mouth moving over hers, his tongue parting her lips and slipping inside. Anton lay beside Xandi, close enough to encircle her in his arms as she and Stefan kissed.

Keisha realized, though she watched through Anton's eyes, she identified with Xandi. She felt Anton's growing passion, realized he was moving closer, his hand stroking Stefan's lean flank, his mouth searching out Xandi's taut nipple.

I want to be with Xandi. Do you think . . . ?

Anton's laughter was a gentle sound in her head, then Xandi was laughing with him.

Link with me, little sister. I have more fun than either of these guys.

Before she could compose an answer, Keisha was aware of Stefan's lips on hers, of Anton's mouth suckling her nipple. She felt the hard length of Anton's cock pressing against her thigh and Stefan's equally hard penis poised at the mouth of her pussy.

Her body stiffened, began to tremble. Her heart pounded a staccato rhythm, and she was flooded with images of her assault, images of terror and pain and . . .

Xandi's soothing thoughts overpowered her fear.

Keisha, it's okay. Take a deep breath. It's not your body they're touching. It's mine. Keep the separation clear in your mind. Relax . . . you're alone in your room. It's my body they're taking. Remind yourself, you're just a little bug on the wall, watching.

Keisha sighed, her taut muscles relaxed, and she nodded her head against the pillow, knowing full well Xandi couldn't see her but would know her feelings. *A little bug on the wall. I can do that.*

I know you can. Stay with us. Enjoy. Experience love without fear, the touch of two men who want nothing more than to please a woman. Let yourself be the woman, through me. No one will hurt you.

Rationally, I know that. It's hard to accept.

Rationally, did you ever think you'd take the form of a wolf, racing through the forest? Gentle laughter followed Xandi's dry comment. *Sweetie, if you can accept that, you can accept anything. Darn!*

Keisha heard more laughter. *Look what's happened. While I've been talking to you, the guys have found other things to do.*

Once more Keisha saw through Xandi's eyes. Stefan

and Anton lay facing one another, embracing, their mouths locked together in a passionate kiss. Anton's back was to her, his muscles rippling with each tilt of his hips. Xandi focused on the smooth line of Anton's buttocks, followed the crease to the deep, dark red tip of Stefan's engorged cock, sliding between Anton's muscular thighs, riding smoothly in the slick sweat generated by their heated, straining bodies.

Mesmerized by the vision she saw through Xandi's eyes, Keisha lost herself in the eroticism, the sensual magic, of two strong men loving each other. Their bodies were beautiful, glossy with sweat, all lean, hard muscle and masculine perfection. Stefan's cock slipped between Anton's thighs, the head larger, dark like a ripe plum, the tip glistening with the first drops of fluid. His fingers splayed across Anton's muscled back, holding the other man close to him, as the two rocked together in perfect rhythm, buttocks clenching, bodies straining.

Keisha felt the first stirrings in her own body, the tension in her belly, the needy ache in her womb. Still caught in Xandi's view, she reached down between her legs and found that she was wet, the tissues of her labia thick and unbelievably sensitive. She smiled to herself when she discovered even the once tightly woven nest of curls between her legs felt softer than it had before. Slowly, she stroked back and forth over her swollen clit, matching the rhythm between Anton and Stefan.

Xandi shifted her position near the men, moving behind Stefan so that Anton's face was now visible. His eyes were closed, his lips parted, still damp from Stefan's kisses, so lost in passion that Keisha knew at once how he would look thrusting into her. Now, though, he jerked his hips faster, harder, matching Stefan's tempo. Xandi changed her focus, showing Keisha the taut line of Stefan's buttocks, the dark, moist head of Anton's cock riding between his lover's thighs.

Xandi slipped lower on the big bed, reached down and

raked her fingernails across Stefan's buttocks, flicking a nail over the head of Anton's cock. She scooted closer and slipped her hands between Stefan's legs. Gently, she squeezed his testicles, then found Anton's and massaged his as well.

Joined by a strangled cry, both men stiffened, pumped hard against each other and climaxed. Keisha could practically feel the pulsing, throbbing orbs in her own hands. Panting, Stefan rolled away from Anton, and both men lay on their backs, laughing, gasping for air. Xandi straddled their legs, a hand wrapped around each cock, and slowly brought them down with smooth, pumping strokes, using their own semen to lubricate her erotic massage.

She leaned over and ran her tongue the length of Anton's cock, then did the same to Stefan. "Okay, boys, our turn."

Anton raised his head, one eyebrow cocked. "Our turn? Our who?"

Practically sobbing with frustration, Keisha thrust her fingers deep inside her wet and swollen pussy, then trailed them across her clit. So close! She was so close to coming, just from watching Stefan and Anton make love to each other. Watching them through Xandi's eyes. She'd never dreamed two men together could be so damned sexy.

Sexy and dumb as a pair of stumps.

Who our? Who the hell did he think she was?

"Our, as in mine and Keisha's. She's still with me."

A slow smile spread across Anton's face. Keisha suddenly felt his familiar touch in her mind. *I thought you'd gone. I didn't feel you with me anymore.*

I was with Xandi. I've never shared anything remotely close to what you and Stefan just did. I had no idea it would . . .

Turn you on? Make you hot enough to want to share yourself with us? Stefan thinks you're absolutely gorgeous. You know I want you, Keisha. I've wanted you since the first moment I saw you.

The need in his mental touch sent shivers across her flesh. Shivers as much from desire as from the latent fear she'd not been able to shake. *I'm not ready, not yet. I'm not ready to let you touch me, but I am ready to feel what Xandi feels.*

Anton's soft chuckle trickled across her senses, followed by a slow, mental drawl. *Then we'd better make sure Xandi feels real good, don't you agree?*

Xandi's laughter rippled into their thoughts. *I think Xandi's going to like that very much. Hang on, Keisha. The boys appear to have recovered.*

It was more than a little decadent, lying in bed with morning sunlight filtering through the blinds, her body naked and wanting, two fingers buried deep between her legs in anticipation of another woman sharing sex with two men.

Keisha practically laughed aloud when Xandi's thoughts surfaced once more in her mind.

This isn't decadence. This is . . .

Stefan's thoughts interrupted. *This is for you, Keisha. From all of us. Call it a welcome home gift.*

He leaned over Xandi, his long hair undone and trailing across her breasts.

Keisha quivered as the silken strands touched Xandi's nipples, followed by Stefan's hot mouth. Fighting the terror, the sudden urge to withdraw from Xandi's mind, Keisha held onto the link, mentally worked her way through the fear and allowed herself to feel with Xandi, to experience every touch, every kiss, each subtle stroke and lick and taste.

Xandi had told her Stefan was, like Anton, a magician. Right now his mouth was working pure magic on Xandi's breast. Keisha arched her back as Stefan's tongue flickered back and forth across the sensitive tip, then moaned when he suckled the swollen nipple deep inside his mouth.

Hands stroked her thighs, swept the length of her

calves, teased closer and closer to Xandi's waiting pussy. Keisha held her breath, so caught up in the sensation of Anton's hands separating the folds between the other woman's legs that she actually moved her own fingers out of the way.

She heard his satisfied chuckle in her mind, knew this was exactly what he hoped would happen. Grasping the sheets on either side of her, Keisha arched her hips against the cool morning air. Anton's fingers penetrated Xandi, in and out, spreading her juices, slipping along the crease between her buttocks.

Stefan suckled Xandi's other breast, plucking at it first with his fingers, building up his own rhythm. At the same time, Anton spread her legs wider apart, leaned close and blew his hot breath over her clit.

His fingers slipped deeper between her buttocks, penetrating her behind, just as his firm lips found her clit. Alternating strokes between his tongue deep inside her pussy and his two fingers thrusting slowly in and out of her ass, he caught Stefan's rhythm. He also caught Stefan's growing cock in his free hand, connecting the three of them physically, the four of them mentally.

This time there was no thought of anyone or anything other than Xandi, Stefan and Anton. No fear beyond the unknown, beyond the fact she'd never experienced anything remotely like this in her life. Keisha twisted and undulated against the sheets, her body reacting as Xandi's did, her sex pouting and swelling, the fluids dampening the dark nest of curls between her legs.

Her breasts ached, her nipples tingled, with the shared sensations of Stefan's lips and teeth and tongue, of his fingers rubbing and plucking, his mouth suckling.

Anton's tongue speared into her, over and over again. His fingers stretched her backside, slipping in and out, deeper, further, with each thrust. Xandi's back arched, her keening cry filling the room, her mind completely linked with Keisha's. Keisha cried out as well, her breath caught in her throat, her mouth stretched wide as she gasped for air, sharing each pulsing shudder of Xandi's climax, sharing her own with the rest of the pack.

Sobbing, gasping, laughing, Keisha lay alone in her bed, struggling to catch her breath. Her pussy clenched and released, her breasts ached for more of Stefan's touch, and she wanted Anton's lips back where they'd been, suckling Xandi's pulsing clit, so she could feel more of the same.

Xandi's soft chuckle flitted through her mind. *Again?*

Oh, God, yes! I've never . . .

Neither have I. That was pretty spectacular. Would you like to join us?

Keisha tensed. *I don't . . .*

There's no rush, little one, Anton's soothing voice gently intruded. *Let us love you through Xandi for a while. When you're ready, you can join us.*

Keisha immediately relaxed. There was no feeling of pressure, no anger. Merely pure acceptance.

Unconditional love.

She stayed with Xandi as the other woman rolled Stefan over on his back and took his fully erect cock into her mouth. She savored his spicy flavor, tested the ridges and textures with her tongue, felt the hard testicles within his sac when Xandi rolled them gently between her fingers.

When Xandi straddled Stefan's lean thighs and lowered herself on his straining cock, Keisha gasped at the sense of fullness, the slick entry so deep inside that the smooth crown of his penis brushed the mouth of Xandi's womb.

She sighed with the other woman, felt her settle her hips and adjust to the man inside her, then wondered what was coming next as Xandi leaned forward.

Anton knelt behind her, his cock riding in the crease of her ass. She felt him stroking her backside with his cock, knew he held himself in his hand as he slipped a condom over his erection. Xandi knelt forward, still impaled on

Stefan. Keisha gasped when she realized what Anton had in mind.

He thrust his fingers inside Xandi, finding entrance alongside Stefan's cock, finding her lubricating moisture as well. He rubbed it slowly, sensually, around the sensitive tissues of her behind, once again slowly forcing entrance with first one finger, then two. He stretched her further, all the while rubbing back and forth with the head of his cock, teasing the entrance, then slipping past.

He paused for a moment, and Keisha realized he was stroking lower, finding Stefan's testicles and including them in his sensual massage as well. She held her breath, waiting to see if he was going to take Xandi the way she thought he might, wondering how much pain there would be.

Suddenly, like a dark fog, memories overwhelmed her. Sensations, fear, remembered, the terror of her assault, the pain, the wrongness of everything associated with her body, with the act of sex.

She wanted to scream, wanted to tell them no, that this was wrong, that this same act, without love, without care, had been part of her brutal assault, part of the incentive to bring the wolf to life.

She'd been brutally raped by three men. Three men who'd taken her at the same time, forcing themselves into her mouth, her vagina, her rectum, tearing her flesh, ignoring her agonized screams, hurting her, laughing while they . . .

We love you, Keisha. You are one of us. There will be no pain. Only love. If it hurts you to share this, we will stop, but we won't sever the link. You are with us. Let us help you heal.

Keisha heard Xandi's voice, but she sensed Anton and Stefan as well, knew they were waiting, giving her time and strength.

I'll try. I promise. I'll break the link if I can't handle it.

Whatever you wish. It will always be your choice.

The sensual massage began again. The feather-light touches, the sense of fullness from Stefan's cock held tightly within Xandi's warm sheath, unmoving, waiting.

Once more she felt Anton's fingers rubbing circles between her buttocks. Keisha forced herself to relax, even though it was Xandi waiting for penetration. The soft, damp head of Anton's sheathed cock found the opening, bumped slowly against the taut muscle, pushed and released, pushed again and released, forcing entrance but never to the point of pain.

Xandi leaned forward, adjusting her body and burying her head on Stefan's chest. Keisha heard his heart beating, felt the love surrounding the three of them . . . the four of them. She was there, in everyone's thoughts. A part of their lovemaking.

Anton breached Xandi's tight opening, and his cock slipped slowly inside, trapped by the taut ring of muscle. He moved forward, mere fractions of an inch, then retreated. Forward again, finding space within Xandi's body, pressed close against the thin tissues separating him from Stefan's cock—two men, loving her, wanting her, making love to her.

Without pain. Gently, with love, with compassion and caring—and totally without pain.

Keisha sobbed, her body rising to the gentle thrusts of both Stefan and Anton. She realized she'd rolled to her stomach, buried her face in her pillow and raised her buttocks, mimicking Xandi's position. Mentally she took both men, sensed Xandi's growing climax, realized the tension in her body was no longer fear, was instead the growing, gasping need to come, to give herself over once more to another mind-shattering orgasm.

Stefan climaxed first, followed quickly by Anton. Xandi was next, her body rippling and shaking with the power of her orgasm. Keisha shared each climax, each peak of unbelievable passion, her body tightening, straining for release, struggling to break through the anger and fear that held her apart from the pack.

We love you. Be one with us.

Three separate voices speaking as one. Three very special people, claiming her as their own.

She felt it then, starting deep in her middle and spreading out to her toes, her fingers, the top of her head—all-consuming, a spinning vortex of heat and lust and incredible, unbelievable rapture.

Keisha raised her head and screamed. This time, the cry ripped from her heart, a profound, agonizing wail of innocence lost, of passion and pain, of fear, acceptance and overwhelming love.

Gasping, sobbing, her entire body convulsing with the power of her orgasm, Keisha pressed her face against her pillow and collapsed into the twisted sheets. She drew her knees up close to her chest, her tears flowing uncontrollably, her body shuddering and trembling as she rocked herself back and forth.

Dimly she heard the door burst open, sensed Anton's presence, his worry and concern as he gathered her up in his arms, held her against his chest like a baby and rocked her. Instead of fear she felt comfort and knew, even in the most deeply wounded part of her mind, that part still suffering the trauma of the rape and assault, that this man loved her. Loved her and would always protect her, would never harm her in any way.

Slowly she felt the tension flowing out of her body, realized her arms were rising, winding over Anton's strong, solid shoulders. She pressed her cheek against the soft skin where his shoulder met the column of his throat and felt the rapid beat of his pulse. When she raised her hand to cup his cheek, she found his face wet with tears.

Anton?

Don't ever frighten me like that again.

I'm sorry, I didn't ...

I love you, Keisha. I felt the pain, the horror in your soul. I never meant for ...

No! She turned in his arms and held her palms against the sides of his face, forced him to look directly at her. "All I have felt for the weeks since the attack is fear—fear and loathing, not only of every man I've seen, but of myself. You three have brought me back, given me that sense of who I am, of the woman I thought might be gone forever."

She pulled his face down to hers and kissed him, very softly, very briefly, on the mouth. Before he could respond, she backed away. "I still have a long way to go, but I know now that I can heal. You've given that to me. You, Stefan and Alexandria, but most of all you."

Anton wrapped his fingers around her right hand, brought it to his mouth and kissed her palm. "We have all the time you need."

Very gently he set her back on the bed, straightened the twisted sheets and fluffed her pillow. "Sleep. It's been a long night, and you need at least a couple of hours' rest. I'll call you later for brunch."

Keisha crawled between the cool sheets as Anton turned away. Morning sunlight caught the smooth line of his back, the curve of his buttocks, the strong muscles of his thighs and calves. He was beautiful, not merely in body, but in spirit. She felt his compassion, his love, his heartbreaking need.

Need for her. Anton was every bit as alone, just as lonely, as she'd ever been in her life.

Without giving herself time to think of the consequences, Keisha pulled the sheets back beside her. "Don't go. Please. Stay with me."

Anton halted in mid-step, turned slowly around and stared at her. There was nothing sexual in the naked desire she saw in his eyes, nothing to frighten her or make her feel threatened. There was love, pure and simple.

"Are you sure?"

Smiling, she shook her head and smoothed the down comforter back across her legs. "No. I'm not at all sure. I know I'm not ready for sex, at least not for anything physical. Not yet. Knowing that, are you willing to stay?"

Smiling, Anton slowly crawled into the bed next to her, pulled Keisha into his arms and tucked her head under his chin. "Just try to get rid of me, sweetheart. I'm yours, whether you want me or not. I'm yours, and I'm staying."

She inhaled, drawing his now familiar scent deep into her lungs. She heard the steady beat of his heart, sensed the flow of blood in his veins and knew she'd come home. Sighing, Keisha relaxed within the strength of his embrace.

There was nothing more to say. Nothing that could make this moment more meaningful, more powerful, for her. She sensed Alexandria and Stefan hovering just beyond her consciousness, concerned, loving, aware of the man holding her so protectively.

Surrounded by the pack, Keisha let her worries go and drifted off to sleep.

Anton felt her body relax, heard the soft sigh as she gave up her struggle for consciousness. He let his thoughts touch hers and found only peace, the quiet of a mind at rest.

There would be no dreams, no nightmares, no frightening shifts from human to wolf and back again without her own determination and knowledge. He carefully adjusted his body around hers, protecting her, holding her close against his heart.

Need for her simmered just beneath the surface, a need so strong it frightened him with its intensity. His cock throbbed, hard and erect, but he willed the poor beast into submission. Keisha would tell him when she was ready. Only she would know when she was healed enough to want the physical expression of his love.

He imagined they would be spectacular together. Knew already she would welcome both Alexandria and Stefan into her bed as well when the time was right. She was capable of great love, great passion, and already felt a strong bond with him. Smiling, nuzzling the tousled curls spilling across her pillow, Anton finally allowed himself to relax.

Keisha filled an emptiness he hadn't known existed. He'd never felt such emotion for another person, not even for Alexandria or Stefan, two people he loved more than he had ever imagined himself capable.

Keisha sighed and snuggled close against his chest. A slight smile curved her lips. In sleep, her hand stroked the length of his back, trailing fingers along his thigh, coming to rest on the curve of his hip. She tilted her pelvis closer, bringing herself into contact with his suddenly wide-awake cock.

Definitely, they were going to be spectacular together, when the time was right.

Holding that thought, holding Keisha in his arms and her love in his heart, Anton drifted into sleep.

PART FOUR

Keisha

Chapter 16

Running. Always running. Grass whipping face and chest, paws torn and bleeding. Searching for someone? Evading someone? Not sure. Never certain if running after or away from, only certain of speed. Constant, lung-bursting, heart-throbbing speed. Must run, faster . . . faster.

Someone follows, someone . . . no. Something new, someone shadowing, someone strong and true, dark as night, heart pure as gold, running alongside, a safe, strong shadow, running close in the night.

"Ouch! Meanie! That hurts!"

"Stop complaining. I've never done this to a white girl before. Your hair's so straight, it's hard to braid. Maybe I should just quit."

"Please! Don't stop now."

Anton paused outside the open door and smiled at Stefan when he heard the women's laughter in the kitchen. Stefan merely grinned and shook his head.

It was such an amazing sound, the soft lilt of Keisha's laughter.

He heard her giggle again.

"Xandi, you say that all the time. 'Please, Stefan. Don't

stop now. Please, Anton. Don't stop, Anton. Oh . . . Anton . . .' "

The last was said in a low, breathy wail.

"I heard that." Grinning so wide he felt like an absolute fool, Anton shoved the door open and walked into the kitchen. Alexandria sat on a kitchen stool, her tightly braided hair gleaming like polished copper, caught in a brilliant beam of morning sunlight. Keisha stood behind her, eyes twinkling, as she braided one last row in Alexandria's hair.

"Heard what? This little girl whimpering 'cause I'm braiding her do a bit too tight? She is such a wuss." Still laughing, Keisha tugged the strands tighter, finished up the last row and fixed a small blue bead to the end of the braid.

Alexandria shook her head, and the beads adorning the ends of dozens of braids clattered together. Then she tilted her chin, making the myriad colored beads drape to one side, and smiled seductively at Stefan. From the harsh intake of the other man's breath, Anton had a feeling she'd gotten the desired effect.

"Damn." Stefan walked around her, staring at the totally new look. "You did this, Keisha? It's gorgeous."

"Thank you. Of course, it's all gonna fall out the minute she shifts." Hands on her hips, Keisha stood back to survey her work.

"I just wanted to see how it would look." Alexandria forced a sulky pout.

She couldn't hold it. "Where's the mirror? I wanna see!"

Keisha passed her a small hand mirror. "It really does look good on you. Wish there was a way to make it hold through a shift, but it all pops right out. All that work and *poof!* You end up tripping over a scattered bunch of beads!"

Alexandria turned to Anton. "You haven't said anything. What's your opinion, oh exalted leader?"

Anton cast her a sideways glance. " 'Exalted leader'? Moi? I understood you were the alpha bitch in this pack."

Alexandria snorted. "Yeah, right. C'mon. What do you think?"

"I think Keisha's an artist. You look absolutely beautiful." He trailed his hand over the tight row of perfect braids sweeping back from her forehead. "You look just like a red-headed Bo Derek. Remember her in that old movie *10*?"

"Oh, yeah." Stefan nodded. "Now if she were wearing that same skimpy little bikini . . ."

"You see me naked all the time. What good's the bikini?"

"I enjoy unwrapping the package." Stefan moved closer and tilted his head just enough to catch Alexandria's lips with his. She practically melted against him, all teasing suddenly lost in the lush sharing of lips and tongue.

Anton looked over the two of them at Keisha. The laughter had disappeared from her face, and her body trembled. Sending a subtle block to Stefan and Alexandria, Anton reached around them to lightly grasp Keisha's hand and lead her from the kitchen.

He closed the door softly behind them and grabbed her when she burst into tears.

"I'm sorry," she whispered, sobbing against his chest. "I don't mean to be that way. I don't."

Lightly stroking her back, Anton smiled against her hair and silently reveled in the tight clasp of her arms around his waist. She had no idea how far she'd come. No idea at all.

"Sweetheart, don't cry." He kissed her tousled hair. When she raised her head, he used his thumbs to wipe the tears from beneath her eyes. "Look at me and think of what just happened. You've spent almost three hours braiding Alexandria's hair. Touching her, being close to her. Right now your arms are around my waist. You're holding onto me for comfort."

She nodded, but she didn't pull away. Another positive step.

"Are you afraid of me embracing you like this?"

Almost shyly she shook her head.

"That's because you trust me. I think what just happened in there—when you saw them kiss—I think your body reacted to the inherent sensuality, and it frightened you. Does that make sense?"

"Of course it does." Pushing away from his embrace, Keisha stomped across the room, whirled around and stalked back to him. "Everything you say makes sense, dammit. It still doesn't keep me from freaking out every time I see you guys kiss. Every time you crawl into bed with them, and you guys make love, I want to be there so bad it hurts, but I lose it. I've stood in the doorway and felt my heart pound and my pussy practically weep from wanting to be with all of you, and I still fall apart!"

"It's going to take time."

"I'm tired of waiting." She flipped her hand beside her face, opened her mouth, then shut it. "I want to do more than just hug, more than sleep in your arms as if you were my big brother. I want to fuck. I want to enjoy sex again, not run away when things start to get hot. I can't keep playing the voyeur, getting my rocks off in your heads when the three of you screw. I can't go to a therapist. Counseling won't work when I can't say what's going on."

She glared at him, as if her condition were all his fault. "I can just hear myself now. 'Oh, it's a bit confusing, doctor. I'm not really human. I'm actually a shape-shifting Chanku. And I really, really want to screw my pack mates, but the silly little rape thing keeps getting in my way.' Anton . . ." She practically wailed when she asked, "What can I do to get past this?"

Once again Anton wished he had been the one to kill the bastards who did this to her. Choking back a low, angry growl, he spread his arms wide. Keisha threw her body against his, taking his comfort, taking his love. Avoiding the attraction that was tearing him apart.

He held her while she cried. Murmured words of love, kissed her dark hair and fought his own tears of utter and profound frustration. At times like this it was all he could do to keep from going uninvited into her head and tweaking her memories, changing her past, in order to help her accept her present.

Unacceptable. Even so, there had to be something he could do to help her. She'd been here for three weeks now. Her body had healed. Her sense of humor blossomed. Her ability to touch and be touched was returning.

Yet the only way she'd been able to accept the sexual nature of their relationship was through a mind link with Alexandria. Joining mentally with the other woman, experiencing the sensual touch, the deeply intimate acts, the three of them shared, not as an actual participant, but as a mental voyeur.

Maybe . . . maybe Alexandria was the key.

My love, do you ever feel sexually drawn to Alexandria?

Xandi? Keisha lifted her tear-streaked face away from his chest and frowned. *I guess I never thought about her in that way. She's beautiful. I love being in her head when you guys are all together in bed, love the feel of sharing your bodies. I just wish I didn't lose it when I'm in the same room with you!*

"What if you were in control? What if it was just you and Alexandria, alone together? What if the two of you made love? Would you find that at all appealing? She's not male, not a threat. She loves you as much as Stefan and I do. She is a gentle, caring lover, filled with compassion as well as passion. As Chanku, you should find her as sexually appealing as you would any male."

He allowed the sentence to linger. Holding Keisha in a loose embrace, he watched the thoughts unfolding in her brilliant amber eyes.

Xandi? Blinking owlishly, Keisha opened her mind to the idea of sex with another woman. Obviously she'd never thought of herself as lesbian, though she'd often noticed women who she felt were sexually attractive. It wasn't as farfetched as it sounded, not really. Xandi was beautiful, sensual . . .

With her mind linked to Xandi's, Keisha had been more intimate with this woman than she had with any other human alive. She'd participated in group sex, enjoyed the other woman's responses and made them her own. There'd never been a feeling of wrongness, never a sense of shame.

How could she feel shame with someone as loving, as giving, as Alexandria Olanet? And if what Anton said were true, that the Chanku were polyamorous by genetics, they saw sex as a way of showing their love for the pack, then her feelings for another woman within the pack were right and normal.

How come she hadn't thought of this before?

Ah, but you have. I know you've pleasured yourself during the links with Alexandria.

You do? Struggling out of his light grasp, Keisha glared at Anton. "You snooped!"

He laughed softly and brushed his hand over her hair. Damned if she didn't lean into his touch! Jerking herself upright, away from the magnetic pull of his fingers, Keisha took a deep breath, prepared to tell him exactly what she thought of him coming uninvited into her head.

"Yes, I was snooping," Anton said quickly. "I've been worried about you, afraid you were withdrawing from us. When I realized you were finding sexual satisfaction in the privacy of your room, I was not so worried anymore."

He cupped her chin in his big hands, his fingers warm and firm. "I want you healed, my love. I want you able to come to me, to share your body with me. Someday to share with all of us, with Stefan and Alexandria as well, so that there are four of us together, four of us as intimate as any two people can be. I want you to love me, to love them. Most of all I want you as my mate, as the one who will bear my children. I want you with me, for all my life. Before that can happen, you must be whole, a complete woman, without fear."

The breath whooshed out of her lungs. Anton's hands trembled against her face, and his jaw was tightly clenched. She'd had no idea—none at all—of how much of a future he envisioned, how deep his feelings ran.

What of hers for him? Blinking back tears, she reached up and touched the side of his face with her palm. "Give me time, Anton. Just a little more time. I want to say I love you, but not until I can come to you with a body and mind free of fear."

The disappointment in his eyes made her wish she could draw her cowardly words back. He merely nodded, leaned over and kissed her gently on the forehead, then turned and left the room.

Keisha felt as if he took the sunshine with him, took the air she needed to breathe, the love she needed to exist. Stumbling in her haste to leave this suddenly cold and dreary place, she raced down the long hallway to her bedroom.

Chapter 17

Oliver brought her meals, a silent visitor, warning of his presence with a soft tap on the door. She felt so foolish, hiding away like this, but Keisha realized she'd put the day to good use.

Xandi had been always in her thoughts. A silent, sensual image. Keisha found herself thinking about things in connection with the other woman she'd never imagined, thinking about things sexual, thinking about wanting to touch herself.

More important, she realized she wanted to touch Xandi.

The sun had begun to set. It was time to shift, time to join Xandi and the men for their run through the forest. Time to lose herself in the mentality of the pack, to hunt as one, to merge her consciousness, for a while anyway, with something primitive and wild.

She wasn't ready. Didn't want to bare herself to the others. Not now. Not when she still felt fragile, unsure.

A soft tap at her door brought Keisha out of her musings. She wasn't at all hungry, but it must be Oliver with an evening snack.

"Come in." She scooted up in her bed, resting against the pillows.

Xandi opened the door. "It's me," she said. "The guys have gone. I . . . I didn't want to mess up my braids. I decided not to shift tonight."

Keisha laughed. Suddenly everything seemed to come together. "Braids, hell. Anton told you to seduce me, didn't he?"

At least Xandi had the good grace to blush. "Well . . . okay. Yeah. But I brought wine!" She held the bottle aloft as she closed the door behind her.

"Been there, done that, bought the farm." Keisha sat straighter against the pillows. "The first time I got laid, he got me good and drunk. Knew I'd do anything. Of course I wanted to do anything . . . everything. I was sixteen. What did I know?"

"A hell of a lot less than you know now." Xandi walked into the room, sat on the chair by the bed and set out two crystal goblets. She carefully uncorked the bottle and poured the chilled Chardonnay into each glass.

"I'd like to make a toast to you, but instead I'll toast to us. Will you drink?"

Keisha stared at her a moment before taking the offered glass. "I'll do more than drink. I've thought of you all day. First, though, tell me what Anton said to you. Believe me, that's a conversation I wish I'd heard."

"He said only what I hoped he'd say. I've wanted you ever since we shared a link, Keisha. I won't lie to you—I've never been with a woman. But I've dreamed of making love with you almost since the beginning."

Taken aback, Keisha stared at Xandi, looking for any sense of deception. "I find that—"

"Honest Injun," Xandi interrupted. She held her hand over her heart. "I felt weird about it at first, believe me." She dipped her chin and blushed. "Especially when I actually fantasized it was you one time when Stefan was going down on me."

"Chanku?" Keisha barely breathed the word.

"Yes . . . and no. I'm sure it's the reason why I'm

equally attracted to a woman as I am to men. I liked you immediately, the first time I saw you. As I've gotten to know you, I've grown to love you. Love your strength, your resilience, your ability to accept the unacceptable. I've wanted to be more like you, wanted to touch you. At the same time, I knew you weren't ready. I think you're ready now. I think you want to explore as much as I do."

She did, as much to satisfy her curiosity as anything else. At least that's what she told herself. Holding the filled goblet in both her hands, Keisha tipped the glass and drank deeply. When she'd emptied her glass, she held it out to Xandi for a refill.

"I know there's an inhibition left in there somewhere. One more glass should put that baby to sleep."

Xandi snorted. Then she carefully poured the golden liquid, filling the goblet one more time. She refilled her own, set the bottle down and held her glass out to Keisha.

Keisha lightly tapped her glass to Xandi's in a toast. "Here's to us, sister."

"To us. To exploring new territory." Xandi took a sip of the wine. Her gray eyes sparkled over the rim of the glass. When she set the half-empty goblet down, her tongue swept across her upper lip.

Evening shadows filled the room. The women stared silently at one another. Keisha realized she was fantasizing, imagining what each of them could do to please the other. The images—graphic images of their bodies together—filled her thoughts. Lush and sensual, the sweet eroticism of her fantasies gave Keisha the feeling they truly were about to explore new territory.

As the room darkened, she became more aware of the sound of their hearts beating, of Xandi's familiar scent, the soft sound of her breathing, the gentle clatter of the beads she'd braided into Xandi's long hair. The beads clicked together with every move Xandi made, no matter how slight.

Suddenly Keisha realized the sound had moved closer.

Xandi now sat beside her on the large bed. Close, not touching, yet Keisha felt the warmth of her body, imagined their bodies together, soft and sensitive in the same places.

Keisha set her goblet down on the bedside table, only marginally aware it was once again empty. Xandi drank her last swallow of wine, setting her goblet down again as well. Slowly she turned to Keisha. She slipped her hand under the soft cotton tank top, following each of Keisha's ribs, stroking softly until her fingers rested beneath her breast.

Keisha inhaled sharply as one of Xandi's fingers found her suddenly erect nipple. Moisture pooled between her legs when Xandi simply rubbed her fingertip gently back and forth, bringing her nipple to a tight, taut, sensitive peak.

The room darkened, yet Keisha's enhanced Chanku vision threw everything into sharp relief as she slowly wrapped her fingers around the hem of her shirt and pulled it over her head.

Xandi never altered the soft caress of her nipple, but now that both breasts were free of the cotton shirt, she leaned closer to Keisha and licked the very tip of the other one.

The tiny beads at the ends of her hair tickled the round swell of Keisha's breast. The soft clicking sounds they made as Xandi's head moved across her chest echoed in the room. Her tongue was hot and moist, licking just the very tip of Keisha's tightly puckered nipple.

Once more Keisha forgot to breathe. She sat rigidly, leaning back with her legs crossed Indian fashion, supporting herself with her hands tightly fisted in the blankets, as Xandi licked her nipple once more, then slowly sucked it between her lips and pulled it into her mouth.

"Ahhhh . . ." Keisha tilted her head back and thrust her breasts forward. Xandi sucked harder, using her tongue and teeth, nibbling and suckling, while her hand continued its soft caress of Keisha's other nipple.

The beads tickled, clicked, tickled more.

Neither woman shared her thoughts. Keisha wasn't ready for such intimacy, didn't want to know what Xandi was thinking, only wanted to experience her own pleasure, selfish as that might be.

Trembling, she lay back against the pillows and spread her legs wide, making room for Xandi between her thighs. Xandi went with her, slowly pleasuring Keisha's breasts with lips and tongue and teeth, with soft fingers and the warm palm of her hand. The beads felt like more tiny fingers, touching, teasing, slowly warming to the heat of Keisha's body.

After long moments, Xandi slowly released Keisha's nipple, breaking the strong suction with a soft *pop*. She licked the moist tip, blowing cool air across it, then kissed her way down, along Keisha's ribs, slipping her loose sweatpants off over her hips when she reached the waistband with her mouth.

The tiny beads rolled and clattered, crawling behind Xandi's mouth, following like an army of little mouths, as she kissed and licked slowly across Keisha's flesh.

Keisha arched her hips and felt the cool night air against her wet pussy and puckered nipples. Felt Xandi's lips and tongue trailing the soft skin beneath her navel, a sharp nip on her inner thigh, the sweep of a warm tongue along the crease where thigh met groin.

Heard the beads, felt one brush against her clit, another rest for a moment in the indentation of her navel, others skitter across her thighs, between her legs.

Suddenly the direction Xandi's mouth was taking coalesced in a white-hot flash of understanding and desire.

You don't want to . . . can't possibly want to . . . oh, Lord, woman!

Oh, but I do.

Keisha raised her head and looked down. Xandi knelt between her legs. Her eyes glittered, the shiny beads swinging slightly with each breath she took, mesmerizing, hypnotic. Keisha had never realized before how those beads would feel against a body, how they'd stimulate and entice.

Somehow Xandi had removed her sarong, and her naked body gleamed in the darkness, her full breasts with their dark nipples swaying as she leaned forward and once more licked the sensitive bit of flesh on Keisha's inner thigh.

The beads tickled . . . clattered and clicked. The sound somehow caught the rhythm of Xandi's lips, emphasized each nip and lick.

Xandi slipped her hands beneath Keisha's rear and lifted her, then tucked a fat pillow under her hips to hold them up. She lightly patted Keisha's flat belly, ending the pat with a long, slow stroke down between her legs, completely bypassing her clit.

Groaning, Keisha raised her hips in blatant invitation. Damn, she'd never felt so turned on, wondering what might come next, wondering just how far Xandi planned to take this. With a guy you knew, you'd get the perfunctory lick between the legs, then a good, hard poke with a thick cock. Not that she'd complained. But this was so weird, knowing the person kneeling between your thighs knew exactly what parts to touch, what buttons to push.

If she'd only get on with it! Xandi leaned forward, but instead of going for her pussy, she pressed her breasts against Keisha's, dragging her nipples over her darker set, pressing her pubic bone against Keisha's clit, lightly rubbing her practically smooth pussy across the sensitive flesh and thatch of tightly curled dark hair.

The beads clicked and clattered, louder, faster, with each movement Xandi made.

Practically hyperventilating, Keisha fought the need to wrap her arms around Xandi and hold their bodies together. This was Xandi's show, Xandi's chance to experiment, and it felt good. Felt so damned good, and somehow forbidden and wrong, and so right and beautiful, all at the same time.

The contrast of pale flesh against dark, of tightly curled pubic hair against Xandi's almost bare pussy, of tightly puckered nipples sweeping against nipples and the accompanying music of the beads went beyond anything Keisha had ever imagined. Caught up in their differences as much as their sameness, she was stroking Xandi's breast, bringing it to her lips, suckling the other woman's flesh deep into her mouth, before she even realized what she was doing.

She'd never imagined what this would be like, never thought of what a man felt when he sucked her breast. She thought she could spend all day suckling the sweet nipple, tugging it with her teeth, wrapping her tongue around the pebbled tip, using her lips to compress and hold tight.

Xandi moaned, and her mons came down hard against Keisha's, then she pulled slowly away, slipping once more down, down lower, between Keisha's widespread thighs, dragging those damned beads, those tiny little fingers of sensation, slower, lower.

Hardly daring to breathe, Keisha waited. She felt the soft puff of air, the first tentative lick of Xandi's tongue against her needy flesh. Her hips jerked in response. She bit back a nervous giggle. Closed her eyes.

Xandi licked her once again, slowly this time, using the flat of her tongue to sweep between the engorged folds of Keisha's labia, the very tip of her tongue to tease her protruding clit. She suckled Keisha's nether lips deep into her mouth, tugging at them, then releasing. She kissed her inner thighs, staying away from her clit, until Keisha begged for release.

Finally, her breath rasping from her heaving chest, unable to form a coherent word, Keisha linked.

What are you waiting for, bitch?

Xandi laughed out loud. *C'mon. Admit it. You're more turned on now than you've ever been with a man.*

Oh, shit, yes. She writhed against the blankets, bucking her hips toward Xandi's mouth, begging with her body, her mind, her moaning appeals, for release.

Xandi spread Keisha's legs wider, grabbed her butt in one hand, then slipped the fingers of her other hand deep into Keisha's pussy. Keisha felt her muscles clamp tightly around Xandi's fingers just as the other woman leaned close, teased her a moment with the dangling beads, then drew her clit into her mouth, suckling it as she had Keisha's breast.

Xandi moaned against Keisha's clit, a deep sound of pure desire and need. Her tongue pressed harder, her fingers probed deeper.

Sensation. Pure, unadulterated sensation.

Keisha's legs trembled, her hips bucked against Xandi's mouth. Overwhelming stimulation—so much at once! One hand kneading her buttock, tongue and teeth taking her clit, slick fingers thrusting in and out of her pussy, all in perfect rhythm with the swaying beads, the hypnotic clicking and clattering, moving faster . . . faster. All framed in a mental sense of love and acceptance, flowing over her like an aphrodisiac.

Higher, farther, than she'd ever flown, Keisha felt her body arc, stiffen, heard the cry from deep in her chest, felt herself come apart like shattered glass in a mind-blowing, breath-stealing climax.

Lights behind her eyes flashed, and her body went numb. Her arms and legs were solid cement, but her toes and fingers tingled, as if from an electric shock. The only part of her that moved was her pussy, tightening rhythmically around Xandi's fingers.

Ohmygawd. Keisha dragged in one deep breath after another.

That was fun.

Xandi's deadpan comment made Keisha chuckle.

Oh, I'd say so. For me anyway. Give me a minute, then it's your turn.

You don't have to. The guys will be home soon.

I want to.

Are you sure?

Yeah, I'm sure. Maybe not the same way, but I want to make you come. I want to watch your face.

Yours was beautiful. I've never before seen a woman's face when she's climaxing.

Your fingers are still inside of me.

I know. I'm wondering if I can make you do it again.

Keisha laughed and tightened her pussy around Xandi's fingers. "Bitch."

"Alpha bitch to you, sweetie."

Keisha twisted free and rolled Xandi to her belly before the other woman had a clue what was coming. Laughing, she sat on her butt and pinned her down with knees clamped tightly to her hips, holding her arms over her head.

"We'll talk about the alpha bitch role later."

Xandi did a half-hearted bounce to throw Keisha off.

"It'll take more than that." Before Xandi could react, Keisha had her hands tied to the headboard with a nylon stocking. They were both giggling hysterically by the time she got Xandi's feet spread apart and tied to each bedpost.

Then she flipped on the bedside lamp, throwing a soft glow across the room, and shoved a big pillow beneath Xandi's belly, raising her buttocks high and showing her sex to its best advantage.

"I never noticed before what a nice ass you've got." Keisha slapped one round cheek with the flat of her hand.

Xandi jumped.

"Slap a black girl's ass, it doesn't turn that nice shade of pink. Yours is really rather attractive." She slapped the other cheek, harder this time, and bit back a giggle. She'd left a perfect handprint on each cheek. They practically glowed.

She couldn't believe she was actually spanking another woman!

"You've been bad, little girl. Very bad." Keisha leaned over and dragged her nipples along Xandi's back, then licked the indentation along her spine, just above her waist. Xandi's skin tasted slightly salty.

Keisha licked her again.

Xandi moaned and pressed her belly against the bed.

Keisha scooted back and ran her fingers between Xandi's legs. Her pussy was soft and engorged, slick with fluids. Keisha ran her fingers back and forth a couple of times, dipping them into her vagina once before withdrawing her hand and showing it to Xandi. "Oh, my. You're wet. Isn't that a punishable offense?"

Xandi giggled. "Oh, my. I sure hope so. I've been very bad." She wiggled her hips as much as the restraints allowed.

It looked to Keisha as if Xandi definitely wanted a spanking.

Chapter 18

Xandi still tasted Keisha's fluids on her tongue, a salty, earthy taste that made her want to taste her again, made her wish she'd spent longer with her mouth between the other woman's legs, buried in her slick pussy. But this wasn't so bad either.

She'd fantasized before about being tied up, though certainly not by another woman! There was something so decadent about this, stretched out buck-naked on her belly— well, naked except for the beads in her hair—with her legs spread wide, her butt in the air and her arms stretched out straight, hands tied to the bedposts.

Keisha knelt out of sight between her thighs.

Slap!

Oh, shit! It hurt, but there was an immediate reaction she'd not expected, a rush of hot moisture between her legs.

The second slap on the opposing cheek felt even better. Xandi's skin tingled, and her entire butt warmed.

"Bad girls who think they're alpha bitches need to be punished, don't you think?"

"Uhm . . ."

Slap! Slap!

"Don't you agree?"

"Yes, ma'am, but you'd sound more alpha if you'd quit giggling . . . ma'am."

Keisha snorted. Xandi bit her lips to keep from laughing out loud. She felt really stupid tied up like this, hoping like hell the guys wouldn't find them. Really stupid, like two kids playing sex games . . . stupid, and horny as hell.

She was warm all over, waiting for the next spank.

Keisha didn't make her wait long.

She slapped her hard, first one cheek, then the other. Quick, stinging slaps with the flat of her palm, low on Xandi's buttocks one time, higher the next, alternating cheeks and intensity, finding a rhythm that kept Xandi just enough off base she wasn't sure where the next one would land.

Every once in a while, Keisha would stop altogether, just long enough to drag her fingers through Xandi's engorged labia, dipping into the liquid pooling there, finding more *proof* she'd been a "bad girl."

Harder, faster, until her bottom stung and tingled, and her pussy begged to be filled. Writhing to meet each slap as much as she wanted to avoid them, Xandi bucked and twisted, fighting the nylon bonds, begging for the climax that hovered just out of reach.

Close, so close, to the edge, she . . . Keisha suddenly stopped.

Damn!

"I think that's enough, don't you? Your bottom's such a pretty shade of red. Clashes with your hair, though. Such a shame."

Her body trembling with the need to climax, Xandi turned her head and saw Keisha reaching into the drawer of the bedside table. She pulled out the biggest, most realistic-looking dildo Xandi had ever seen.

"Let's see how this feels. I've been saving it for one of the guys. That is, if I ever get my nerve back." Keisha laughed, stroking the lifelike rubber cock. It was the color of dark coffee, with prominent veins and a bulging crown. "I'm suddenly feeling really nervy."

She twisted the base, and a low hum filled the air. Xandi watched until Keisha disappeared from her line of vision. Her pussy clenched, waiting to take the lifelike vibrator.

Instead of inserting it, Keisha dragged it slowly across Xandi's sensitized buttocks, caressing her hot skin with the cool, ribbed toy. Xandi felt each vibration, each soft sweep, as if her entire body were being touched.

Moaning, lifting her hips, she begged for release. "C'mon, Keisha. I didn't make you wait this long!"

"Yes, you did! I was begging! My pussy was weeping, and I was desperate. Your turn to see what it feels like."

She slowly ran the vibrating cock between Xandi's widespread legs, barely touching her clit.

Giggling nervously, Xandi jumped and bit back a scream. "You bitch!"

"Alpha bitch to you, sweetie. C'mon, say it, or I leave you here."

"I never knew you were this mean!"

"Say it. C'mon. 'Keisha's the alpha bitch.' You can do it." Once more she slowly dragged the vibrator across Xandi's sensitive cheeks.

Xandi's pussy clenched, and she felt moisture trickle over her clit.

Keisha lightly touched the vibrator to Xandi's ass, rubbing back and forth across the puckered opening, then sliding it down lower, between her legs, brushing her clit.

Xandi almost came when it touched her ass, and if Keisha had lingered just a moment longer on that sensitive little spot, she . . .

Keisha turned the vibrator off and stepped away. "Have it your way."

Oh shit oh shit oh shit . . . Sobbing, laughing so hard

she could hardly talk, Xandi twisted and bucked her hips. "Alpha bitch, alpha bitch, Keisha's the alpha bitch. C'mon, don't leave me like this!"

Keisha slapped her once more on the butt, hard. "Don't leave me like this, alpha bitch, ma'am," Keisha said, then burst into laughter. "Wow, I didn't know I had it in me. I am *so* good!"

The hum returned when Keisha twisted the vibrator back on, and Xandi felt the long, slow slide of the massive, shuddering cock head easing between her legs, deeper, deeper, stretching, probing, then coming to rest against the mouth of her womb, where it vibrated and hummed.

"Ahhh . . . bless you, Ms. Alpha Bitch." Xandi closed her eyes, savoring the fullness, the heat and the vibration. Keisha knew exactly what to do with the big toy, slipping the vibrating dildo slowly in and out as she rubbed Xandi's clit with her fingertip, harder, faster, building up speed and pressure.

Xandi felt the first coil of her climax, a hollow, needy feeling deep in her womb, felt the hard thrust of the vibrating cock and the warm sweep of Keisha's fingers over her clit.

Her body stiffened, the sensations all coalesced into one, hot pulsing sense of fulfillment, and the climax boiled up and out of her body. Screaming, she jerked at her restraints and bucked against the thick dildo vibrating her sensitive tissues. Her pussy tightened around it in quick, convulsive spasms. Keisha held the cock hard and deep inside her.

Sobbing with her release, Xandi trembled as she slowly came down from her orgasm. She gasped for air when Keisha replaced the rubber vibrator with her own soft tongue, lapping gently at Xandi's sensitive tissues, bringing her once more to a smaller, lighter orgasm.

She came once more when Keisha's practiced fingers found the perfect spot between her legs to stroke. Closing her eyes, Xandi let her entire body go liquid as the rhythmic tremors finally slowed and stilled. Sagging against her restraints, she closed her eyes and reveled in Keisha's loving touch.

She must have slept, at least for a little while. Xandi suddenly realized she was awake, her hands and feet no longer tied, and Keisha sat on the bed beside her, legs crossed, her chin resting in her palms.

"Wondered if you were ever going to wake up."

"Wow... I feel totally... totally fucked." Xandi laughed. "Damn, woman. You're good. Who needs the guys?"

Keisha smiled shyly. "Feels weird, doesn't it? Waking up next to a woman. I've been sitting here staring at you, thinking of how you made me feel, how good the sex was ... how different. As good as it was, I still need the guys, though, don't you? I mean, some of the time when you were touching me, I thought of Anton. I wondered what his tongue would feel like, licking me, how his fingers would be inside of me." She looked away and sighed. "I guess I wanted not to be afraid of his cock. I want it to feel as good as what you and I just did."

Xandi sat up, brushed the beaded strands back behind her ears and took Keisha's hand. "I understand. As good as you are with that rubber cock, it's not the same as Stefan's." She stared at Keisha for a long moment. "How are you? Are you okay with what we did?"

Keisha's broad grin told her everything.

"Oh, yeah. More than okay. I had sex, I had a mind-blowing orgasm, I gave my partner at least two—"

"Three ... and counting."

"Three orgasms, I licked a woman's pussy—and liked it—and not once did I feel threatened or scared, or think of what happened before. I don't know if I'm ready to make it with all you guys at once, but I finally feel as if I'm getting *me* back."

"How about we break into it gently? When the guys get back, they're really going to be ready to fuck. You know the feeling, after a good run, especially if you've hunted. Come with me. Link with me. Stay in the room, touch if you want, but don't feel as if you have to participate. Think you can do that?"

"I can try." Keisha took both of Xandi's hands in hers. "Thank you. It's hard to believe it's been only three weeks since we met. All of you are so important to me. So patient. Thank you for helping me through this."

She leaned close to Xandi for a quick kiss. Xandi captured her mouth, moving her soft lips over Keisha's fuller ones, teasing the seam between them with the tip of her tongue, then finding entrance into the warm, wet cavern of her mouth.

Suddenly Keisha moved closer and wrapped her legs around Xandi's waist until she was practically sitting in her lap. Their breasts rubbed together, nipple to nipple. Their mouths discovered new tastes and textures, and Xandi realized she wasn't nearly as sated as she'd thought.

She wrapped an arm around Keisha's waist to steady her, then reached between them to find Keisha's clit. Keisha did the same, rubbing her fingers through Xandi's moist tissues, moaning against her mouth.

Tongues twisting, bodies writhing against searching fingers, they found a rhythm and held it, held it until Xandi broke for air, gasping out her scream of release, with Keisha following close behind her. Gasping for breath, they leaned against each other, giggling and panting, their fingers still buried deep in one another's bodies.

"Holy shit!"

"Stefan?" Xandi slowly turned and stared at the door. Stefan stood in the doorway, with Anton just behind him. Both men wore gym shorts and nothing else, as if they'd just come from the shower. Their bodies gleamed in the soft glow from the bedside lamp.

The front of each man's shorts tented straight out.

The looks on their faces were priceless.

"Hello, boys." Keisha slowly removed her glistening fingers from between Xandi's legs and waved. "You're late. The party's over. I was just heading for the shower."

Still panting from her climax, Xandi grabbed Keisha's hand. "No, you don't. Remember what we talked about?"

"Oh. Yeah . . ." Keisha looked around, as if searching for a way out. She dipped her head and nodded, then took a deep breath. "Okay. I can do this."

"Do what?" Carefully adjusting himself, Anton sat down on the bed next to them. He played with the colorful beads dangling from Xandi's braids, but made no attempt to touch Keisha.

"When we—you, me and Stefan—go to bed tonight, Keisha's going to join us. Not to participate, just to be in the room, in my head, linked like we usually are, but physically in the same space with us."

Anton smiled at Keisha. "Are you ready for this?"

"I think so . . . I hope so. If not, I'll get the hell out of Dodge."

Still leaning against the doorway, Stefan laughed. "I've never quite compared our lovemaking to *High Noon* before. I'll have to think on that."

"You do that, Sheriff." Anton stood up. "C'mon. Let's get something to eat."

Xandi slipped off the bed and bent over to reach for her sarong. She was barely aware of Stefan's bark of laughter before she felt a stinging slap to her behind.

"Ouch! What was that for?"

Stefan leaned close and kissed her soundly. "As rosy red as your butt looks, I thought maybe you enjoyed it. What have you girls been up to?"

Grinning, Keisha slid off the bed and grabbed her clothes. "Wouldn't you like to know?"

Xandi leaned close and whispered in her ear. "I think he'd rather we showed him, don't you? Bring the nylons . . ."

Keisha slipped them into her pocket as they headed for the kitchen.

Chapter 19

"So you're telling me we've got two alpha bitches now?" Stefan grinned at Anton. "One was enough to drive me nuts."

"Two is two too many." Anton gently pulled Keisha onto his lap, pleased when she didn't attempt to get away. "Don't you agree?"

She swiveled around, rubbing her bottom against his cock as she twisted to look him in the eye. Anton bit back a moan of pure frustration.

"Xandi and I will work it out between us. You two beta males just stay out of our power play."

Stefan stood up from the dinner table. "Personally, I intend to work it out between Xandi's legs. Do you two intend to join us?" He held his hand out. Grinning broadly, Alexandria took it, then reached over and palmed his erection through his soft, cotton pants.

"Down, boy. Behave." She tugged Stefan's hand and led him from the room.

Keisha stiffened in Anton's lap, silently nodded and stood up. He stared at her a moment, until she turned away and refused to meet his eyes. He tried to read her thoughts, but she'd completely blocked her mind.

He almost wished he had the guts to mesmerize her. Just use the powers of his mind to entrance her out of her fear, but that was a coward's way of coping. Keisha was not a coward. If she ever found out—and she would find out the first time they linked—she would forever resent him. Even worse, he would always wonder if she really loved him, or loved him because he made it so.

Controlling her thoughts with a set of false memories was not an option. Instead he held out his hand, until she slowly placed hers within his grasp.

Stefan and Xandi took the lead. By the time Anton and Keisha entered the bedroom, the other two were already undressed and wrestling playfully on the bed.

Keisha hung back at the doorway, her fingers still tightly grasped in Anton's hand. He heard the quick rush of her breathing, felt her rising panic.

Suddenly, before he could react, Keisha shifted, became the wolf, and, claws scrabbling for purchase on the hardwood floor, bolted from the room.

"You two stay here. I'll go after her." Anton shifted and took off at a full run. He saw Keisha race through the open door, leap over the deck railing and make a mad dash for the thick forest. Anton followed at an easy lope, knowing he would never lose her scent.

She needed this time alone. Once more he would give it to her, but not at so great a distance he couldn't protect her if the need arose.

It was well past dawn when he tracked her to a small woodland pond. She lay in the thick grass, her fur matted and covered with mud, her paws raw and bleeding.

Anton flopped down beside her with a canine grunt, stretched out his long legs and laid his head across her shoulders. He felt her sigh, waited for her to open her mind to his.

I'm going back to San Francisco as soon as I can get a flight. My month is almost up. I need to go back to work on my project.

Let me come with you.

No. I need time alone, time away from all of you, the intensity of your feelings for one another . . . your feelings for me.

I love you, Keisha. I will wait.

It's so unfair! She scrambled out from beneath him, standing squarely in front of the water. *You're so patient, and I'm such a fucked-up head case! It's not fair to you.*

I didn't ask it to be. I only want what's best for you. I want you to heal.

One week. Give me a week alone. I'll call you then and let you know if you can come. If it's worth it for you to even make the trip.

Her head hung low, her body trembled. Anton sat up on his haunches, then stood. He licked her muzzle and nudged her shoulder in the direction of the house. *Okay. One week. I don't think you can forget me in a week.*

She took off at a tired, wobbling run, but he caught her thoughts as she passed by him.

I couldn't forget you in a lifetime. Not if I lived forever.

Keisha tipped the cabby an extra ten dollars when he carried her bags to the front door and waited until she got inside and turned on the lights. She'd been terrified of coming home to her townhouse alone at night, terrified of leaving the safety of her friends' love.

Terrified of staying.

She leaned against the door, staring down the well-lighted hallway at the beautifully decorated entry, the attractive front room. She'd loved this place from the moment she bought it. Now it just felt empty . . . lonely and empty.

Would it ever feel like home again?

Home now was high in the mountains of Montana, where the air was cool and the forest dark and deep and welcoming. Where she could run freely with her pack, feel the night air against her furred body, stretch her legs out and race the wind.

Race the wind with Anton beside her.

Already she missed him. He'd taken her to the airport, held her tightly before she boarded the plane, kissed her forehead when she turned her lips away from his.

She loved him. Of course she loved him. But how could he know that?

She hadn't told him, certainly couldn't show him.

That, of course, was the problem. Until she could come to him freely, make love to him as a whole woman, she was useless to him. Anton deserved better.

She carried her bags up to her bedroom, checked on her studio, made sure the greenhouse watering system had kept her plants alive, then went back inside.

The night called to her. She opened the door to the fenced backyard and took a deep breath. Anton, Stefan and Xandi would be running right now. Running as a pack beneath the nighttime sky, following the trails of deer and rabbits, leaping creeks and fallen logs, baying and yipping with the pure joy of the hunt.

She smiled, imagining Xandi's beads scattered all over the planks on the deck, and hoped Oliver wouldn't slip on them when he came to work in the morning.

Slow tears coursed down her cheeks as she sat in the dark on the back porch step. The sounds of the city were all around her, the stars lost in the bright reflection of a million lights. Before Keisha was even aware of what she'd done, she became the wolf.

A single leap took her over the tall fence, into the narrow alley that was a direct link to the only wilderness within miles. She ran low to the ground and fast, weaving in and out of shadows, until she leapt the last barrier between herself and the freedom of the forest that was Golden Gate Park.

She circled Stow Lake, found the spot where her memorial garden would eventually grow if the commission accepted her entry, then raced the length of the park, staying clear of roads and lights. Watching, always watching, hiding in shadows, avoiding sleeping transients and their skinny, underfed dogs, curling her lip in disgust at the smells of unwashed humanity, overfilled trash cans, the detritus of too many people in too small a space.

She dreamed longingly of the thick forest and fresh air of the Montana mountains, missed the sense of brotherhood she'd known with her pack, searched fruitlessly for the sense of freedom she'd discovered under the wide Montana sky. She ran until her muscles ached, until each breath screamed in her lungs, until her footpads were raw from the asphalt and gravel paths.

Well before dawn, she retraced her path, slipped quietly through the sleeping neighborhood, leapt her backyard fence and paused in the silence near the greenhouse. Something seemed out of place. Something was not quite as it should be.

Her Chanku senses went on high alert as she checked the yard, sniffed the back door, which was still slightly ajar, just as she'd foolishly left it. Hackles rising, she squatted and peed by the back step, marking her territory.

Nothing. She sniffed the air once more, growled quietly and made one last pass around her yard. Still feeling oddly unsettled, she slipped inside to become Keisha once again, in the privacy of her home.

Sleep was a long time coming. Her burglar alarms were set, the house secure.

Her dreams, when they finally came, were lonely and unsettled.

It was three days before she was willing to face the huge pile of mail that filled the box she'd left beneath the mail slot. She thought of calling Anton first, but it was an hour later in Montana, and she knew he'd be running with the pack. Other than a call to let him know she'd arrived safely, they'd not spoken.

Damn, but she missed the nightly runs, the thrill of the chase when they hunted, the tight mental link of the pack when they saw their prey come into sight.

She'd run just one other time since her return—run without intention or direction. It wasn't at all satisfying without the pack. Instead it was lonely, unsettling. She missed the connection, the sense of family.

She missed Anton most of all. So serious and patient, a direct counterpoint to Stefan's more playful yet sweetly caring nature and Xandi's nurturing soul.

Anton needed her, if only to lighten him up. Smiling, the sense of Anton strong in her heart, Keisha poured herself a glass of wine and went back to her front room with the box of mail under her arm.

It took almost an hour to sort through everything. She filled a bag for recycling with junk mail, separated out the stuff she needed to run through the shredder, checked the statements for the bills paid automatically out of her account, dismissed the political ads and added them to the recycling bag.

One slim envelope dropped out of the small pile remaining in her lap. She leaned over and picked it up off the carpet. There was no postmark, no stamp, no return address. Her name and address were neatly typed on the front, but someone must have slipped it through the mail slot on his or her own.

Curious, she slit the top of the envelope with a kitchen

knife and dumped out the single folded sheet of paper, then forgot to breathe when she read the message.

I know about the wolf.
Call me.

Keisha stared at the telephone. The letter she'd received the night before lay on the table next to another piece of paper, which had Anton's phone number written across it in his big, scrawling hand. She touched the numbers and bit back the tears.

Then she dialed the local number. There was no need to involve Anton. She'd put a stop to this now.

"Hello? Carl Burns here."

"Mr. Burns, my name is Keisha Rialto."

She heard soft laughter on the other end. It made the hair on the back of her neck stand up.

"It's true, isn't it?"

"What, Mr. Burns? I have no idea what you're talking about."

"The wolf, Ms. Rialto. You are the wolf. You killed three men. Somehow you can shift, become a ferocious beast. A killer. You're a werewolf, right?"

"That's absolutely preposterous. Who are you? Wait . . . I know. You're that tabloid reporter, aren't you? The one with the vivid imagination?"

The image of that faked newspaper photo was forever seared into her brain. How could he do this to her? All she wanted was to heal, to get past all this. "Please, leave me alone. If you persist in bothering me, I will take out a restraining order against you, and I'll make sure it's enforced."

"You'll shift again, Ms. Rialto. The moon will be full. Maybe something will happen, and you'll shift. When you do, I'll be there."

"Are you threatening me, Mr. Burns?" She realized her

hands were shaking and prayed it wasn't showing in her voice. She couldn't let him know how much he frightened her.

"Not at all, Ms. Rialto. Have a nice evening. Enjoy your run in the park."

Chapter 20

Keisha sat on the floor of her studio in the dark, knees drawn up under her chin, the drawings of her memorial project scattered about her on the hardwood floor.

The commission had accepted her entry, which meant she had to stay here in San Francisco, at least until it was completed. She should be thrilled, celebrating, jumping for joy. She should be on the phone to Anton, who would celebrate with her.

She should be happy.

All she really wanted to do was go home. Home to Montana, to Stefan and Alexandria and, most of all, Anton.

Home to the people who loved her.

She wanted to run free in the forest, feel the wind on her muzzle, the damp earth beneath her paws. She wanted the sense of power she experienced when she ran as a wolf, the physical strength, the aggressive nature, which became, in essence, a focus for her energy.

Instead, she was a virtual prisoner here in her townhouse, afraid to venture out as a human, much less as a wolf.

Now that she knew how to shift, she craved the feeling. Now that she knew she was being watched, she couldn't risk giving in to her true animal self.

Images of the torn and mutilated bodies of the three men she'd killed flashed through her mind. She shuddered, well aware she recalled more of that fateful night each time she drew the memories forth. More detail, more blood.

The Chanku were an ancient race, their rules of survival primitive and violent. Like the wolves of the forest, the Chanku hunted. When they were threatened, they killed.

Keisha did not want to kill again.

She couldn't call Anton. He'd have no sense of remorse over killing Carl Burns. She didn't want murder on his soul, and she knew he would want to protect her. Neither did she want to expose him to her misery, to a woman who wouldn't take the risk to become whole.

She glanced at the scattered drawings, at the project that had consumed her, given her so much satisfaction, before the attack. Work on the memorial garden was scheduled to begin in two weeks. All she could think of now was the fact that she had time to go back to Montana, time to spend with others of her kind.

She knew if she went, she'd never return to San Francisco.

She wanted Anton here. Wanted to feel his warm, undemanding body next to hers. Wanted finally to find the strength to tell him how much she loved him, how very much he meant to her. Wanted to make love to him without fear, without the horrible memories slipping in and stealing her soul. Wanted to ask him to stay, at least until she completed this project, sold her townhouse and moved home with him to stay.

She wanted . . .

Something moved just outside, on the front porch. Keisha sensed life, someone or something male. Rolling onto her knees, Keisha slowly crept across the floor of her studio and looked down from the open window.

The shadow on her porch was obviously not a potted plant. It slipped out of the darkness, still partially hidden from view. Could it be Burns? She'd never seen the man, couldn't identify him at all, but dammit, if he had the temerity to come to her home . . .

Furious, barely controlling the Chanku's violent nature, the almost overwhelming desire to shift and become the predator, Keisha stomped down the stairs, prepared to do battle. She flung open the front door.

"Hello, sweetheart."

Anton!

Sobbing, she threw herself into his arms. He half carried her across the threshold and closed the door behind them.

"Keisha? What's wrong? Has something happened? Are you okay?"

I missed you. I didn't think I would, not like this, but Anton, I've missed you so much!

I couldn't stay away, my love. I was certain I sensed your need, then realized the distance was too great, and I was merely projecting my own need, my own desire.

He knows about the wolf. He's threatened me.

"Who?" Anton's anger was suddenly a palpable third party in the entryway. "Who's threatened you?"

Gasping for air, Keisha struggled to get her breathing under control, to cut the flow of tears. "His name is Carl Burns. He's the tabloid reporter who wrote the story about me being a werewolf. He contacted me, told me to enjoy my runs in the park."

"You've shifted?" Anton stepped back but kept his big hands solidly clasped about her shoulders.

Keisha nodded. "Twice. I had to. I missed all of you so much more than I thought I would. I figured if I shifted, I might feel closer to you, feel like part of the pack, but it was so lonely. I went to Golden Gate Park and pretended it was your mountains, but it's not the same without you."

"Oh, sweetheart." He wrapped his arms around her and held her close.

She sighed against his broad chest, inhaled his familiar scent and realized there was no fear in her. Not now, not with Anton here to protect her.

"I got the project. The memorial for the park. I start in two weeks."

"That's wonderful!" Anton stepped back but kept his hands on her. "I knew you'd win. You're talented as well as beautiful."

She dipped her head. "You're biased, but thank you. I wish I could enjoy the feeling more, but I've been so worried. What about the reporter? He could ruin everything."

"Leave him to me." The low snarl behind Anton's voice left no doubt how he would handle things.

She couldn't let him kill.

I know. However, it's very tempting. He tilted her chin up and forced her to look at him. The naked desire in his amber eyes practically stole her breath.

"Come away with me. You've got a couple of weeks before you have to start work. I have a cabin up in Humboldt County, just a few hours north of here. The redwoods and ferns grow thick, there's no one around, and we can run as much as we want without fear of observation. We'll figure something out. Please, say you'll come."

She couldn't speak. How could he know exactly what she needed? "Tell me what to pack. I can be ready in five minutes."

He wasn't going to give her a chance to know fear, not this time. Anger, hot and heavy, boiled just beneath the surface, anger he struggled to hold under control. Anton had Keisha's single bag loaded in the back of the rental car just minutes after his arrival. If the reporter were watching, he'd have a hard time following the nondescript sedan up busy Highway 101.

If he followed them, actually found them, Anton figured Burns would regret it . . . but only for the time it took

Anton to kill the bastard. Anton would rather deal with an angry Chanku bitch any day than let the reporter expose her.

Within half an hour, Anton was skillfully negotiating the rush-hour traffic across the Golden Gate. Once they got through the heavy commuter traffic in Santa Rosa, they sped through the wine country, took a jog to the west at Cloverdale and caught the twisting, narrow coast highway heading north. Just past Rockport, they cut east through miles of stately redwoods to Benbow. At Garberville, Anton took another road back to the west. It was growing dark, and Keisha had long since fallen asleep.

He studied her throughout the long trip, wishing he could find the secret to help her overcome her fears. It was such a temptation to use his mind, his powers to mesmerize, to compel her to want him, to help her forget the attack.

If he did that, he would be every bit as guilty as the men who had assaulted her, would always wonder if she were drawn to him of her own accord or because he had planted the compulsion within her heart.

That was unacceptable. Keisha would love him on her own . . .

Or not at all.

And that's just as unacceptable.

Many narrow, unnamed roads, locked gates, private thoughts and private roads later, he pulled up in front of a small, well-kept cabin. He'd called ahead to have it stocked and prepared for his arrival. It helped that he'd owned the property for years, and the caretakers were trusted friends.

Keisha stirred in the seat beside him, stretched, opened her eyes and looked about her curiously. "Where are we? How long have I been asleep?"

"We're at the cabin. It's not all that far from the King Range National Conservation Area and about as private as can be. There's no way your reporter or anyone else can find you here. You're safe, and I want you to relax. Think you can do that?"

She stared at him for a long moment, her amber eyes like golden disks, glinting in the pale starlight. "I always feel safe with you. Always."

He nodded, deeply moved by her trust. "C'mon, we'll get something to eat. Then the Chanku are going to run for as long as they want. No one will disturb us."

Everything was as he had expected. The generator was fueled, the refrigerator was stocked, and the stove was working fine. The cupboards had plenty of provisions. Anton fixed a quick meal, while Keisha unpacked their few belongings, wrapped herself in a comfortable sarong and explored the cabin. There was a single room for the kitchen and living area, one bedroom with an enormous bed and a serviceable bathroom with a tub-and-shower combination.

Her eyes were constantly drawn back to the bed. Was she ready? Could she make love to Anton without flashing back to her attack? She wanted him. She knew she could experience sexual pleasure. Xandi had certainly proved that.

Somehow, some way, she had to get over her fear of men and of sex.

Anton called her to come and eat. He'd prepared fresh salmon, a salad and pasta, skillfully using the gas range that dominated the small kitchen.

"Ah, and he can cook, too! I didn't know you were so talented."

"I'm a man of many talents, my love." He tapped her nose with his fingertip, and she rewarded him with a smile.

"Actually, I love to cook. It's easier to let Oliver take over when I'm at home, but cooking is a pleasure I enjoy." He leaned close and kissed her, a light touch of lips to cheek. "I enjoy it almost as much as running through the forest with an alpha bitch at my side."

Keisha giggled. "I guess Xandi talked, eh?"

"Alexandria did more than talk. She showed Stefan exactly what you did with those nylons of yours. And the flat of your hand. He couldn't sit down the next day, though I didn't hear him complaining. In fact, he smiled an awful lot. It was truly disgusting. I chose not to join them that night."

Keisha's laughter shifted to a contemplative smile. "I had no idea I could find sexual pleasure with a woman. It was absolutely amazing. Xandi said the Chanku . . ." Her voice trailed off.

"The Chanku are a polyamorous people. We find sexual satisfaction with both sexes. It's part of who we are—an important part."

"It's a part of me, but I'm still not whole. Anton, can you love me the way I am?"

She looked desolate, as if her soul were shredded. Somehow, some way, he would bring her through this. The Chanku were a strong and powerful race.

A vengeful race . . . yet adaptable. He would find a way.

They finished their meal in silence. His thoughts were anything but quiet.

Chanku? He set down his fork and neatly folded his napkin, then touched the side of her face, gently forced her to look at him. *My love, when you shift, when you are the wolf, do you fear your sensual nature then? Do you fear me?*

Slowly, eyes unblinking, she shook her head. *I have no fear when I am the wolf. No fear at all.*

Run with me tonight. The forest calls us. I also think it heals that which is broken. Are you willing?

Keisha stood and shifted in the same motion, then waited uncertainly in front of the closed door. Anton laughed, stood up and walked to the door. "It's always a good idea to open the door first. Paws are no good for that sort of thing."

He opened the door and stepped out onto the narrow

front porch, carefully removed his clothing and shifted. His muscles bunched, and he leapt over the railing, landing lightly in the thick ferns beyond the cabin.

Keisha followed, her leap almost as far, her body primed and ready to run.

The night called them. The forest and its myriad scents beckoned. With a sharp yelp and a nip at her shoulder, Anton took the lead.

Chapter 21

She lost track of the miles they ran, the trails through the towering redwoods they followed, on soft, spongy earth that was damp and pungent beneath her paws. It was new and fresh, a rebirth to feel so free. How she'd missed this!

At one point, Keisha scared a buck, a huge creature with spreading antlers. It raced away, and they followed, no threat this night, as they'd both fed so well at dinner. Still the run was exhilarating and left both of them panting, tongues lolling, eyes bright with wolven laughter.

After the chase, Anton kept the pace at a comfortable speed, so the miles disappeared beneath their feet but Keisha never felt pushed or stressed.

Finally he paused in a small, secluded glade. He circled the meadow, sniffing for any sign of danger, lifted his leg and pissed to mark territory along the perimeter. Nothing would intrude where wolves rested.

They might have been on another planet, so far from human habitation, so deep within the primeval forest.

Trees older than recorded time towered above them, their roots cushioned in beds of thick, springy moss. Ferns grew six feet high and more, and thick vines made bridges over creeks and fallen logs. It was a place of magic, truly a place of healing.

The forest heals that which is broken.

Anton's words had become her own private mantra. *I am broken,* she cried. *Heal me!*

They flopped down in the thick bracken, tongues lolling, eyes glowing in the pale starlight. Keisha had never felt so aware of her wolven body before, nor as aware of the big male beside her. The strength of their muscles, the thick pads on their paws, the dark nails they used to dig and climb and run.

She rolled over on her back and nipped at Anton's muzzle. He licked her face. She nipped again.

He rolled over as well, so that his furry body pressed against hers, nose to tail, tail to nose.

She felt his tongue between her legs and jerked at the contact. He'd never approached her sexually in wolven form before. He licked her again, slower this time. She might have been frightened, had she been human.

She was wolf. An alpha bitch.

She lay back and spread her legs.

Anton rolled over and stood up, his shaggy head hanging low, his eyes intense, watching. His mind was closed to her, but his intentions were obvious.

He meant to have her.

She was Chanku, the wolf. Not a victim of rape, not human. Her fears couldn't touch her now. Powerful, in control, the alpha bitch.

Growling, the snarl a low rumble in her chest, Keisha rolled over and rose to all four feet. She presented her bushy tail to Anton, swinging it slowly, enticingly, back and forth.

A deep growl emanated from Anton's wolven throat. He raised his foreleg and pawed her hip.

His claws were sharp. They left ruffled furrows in her pelt.

Keisha refused to give ground. Instead she turned and looked at him over her shoulder, linked with him.

Take me now, as a wolf, not a woman. The woman is broken. The wolf is whole.

He shook his head, denying her words.

You are not broken. Never, in my eyes. I love you. You must know, my love, that among the Chanku, if I take you as a wolf, you are mine forever. Have you noticed that Stefan and Alexandria mate as wolves? I do not join them. Only in human form are we so promiscuous.

I love you, Anton. Do you truly want me?

For all time, my love. Forever.

Then take me now. Make love to me. Show me your goodness and your strength. Wipe out the memories and give me new ones, fresh, loving memories, of you and me together.

He needed no further urging. Nipping at her shoulder, he established his dominance with a single slash of his teeth, the rake of his paw across her back, as he mounted her.

The frustration he'd felt as a human male was intensified in wolven form. He found her soft opening on his first thrust, driving deep, hard, entering Keisha as she braced her legs to take his much heavier weight.

He heard her soft grunt as he filled her, a sharp yip when he finally buried himself deep inside. He tried to link and found a barrier thick as a stone wall. Then the sensations took over, the clenching heat of her channel, the coarse fur along her spine rubbing against his chest. He pumped quickly, taking her as a wolf takes a mate, filling her with his rapidly swelling cock, readying her for his seed.

Once embedded in her warmth, Anton thrust hard and deep, over and over, until his swollen cock tied the two of them together. He felt her body stiffen, knew the sexual knot in his wolf's penis could frighten her with her loss of control, the sense of entrapment.

He took his chance then—prayed it was the right

move—and shifted. Still tied to Keisha, he resumed his human form.

And realized she'd done the same thing. He held a woman in his arms, her buttocks pressed against his belly, his cock buried deep inside her hot sheath. They lay together in the soft bed of moss and bracken fern, tied together in love and passion.

He shuddered with the last tremors of his climax and felt the lingering spasms in Keisha's body. Gently he brushed the tangled hair away from her face and held her close, her back fitting perfectly against his chest, her hips seated in the cradle of his. She turned her head and gazed back at him with so much longing in her eyes, so much love, he buried his face in the hollow of her throat, broke down and wept.

She twisted her upper body so that she could see him, looked into his face, into the amber eyes of the man she loved, and marveled at his tears. With her hands still shaking from the tremors of her climax, Keisha brushed the moisture away from his eyes, leaned closer and kissed Anton on the mouth.

Whatever fears, whatever worries, she'd had melted away in the beauty of his tears, in the depth of love she felt for this most amazing man. His cock was still embedded within her heat, and the connection felt right. It was perfect. When she kissed him, she felt him swell once more within her, knew he wanted her again.

"I love you. Forever. Make love to me again. Love me as a man loves a woman."

His body trembled, and he closed his eyes as if in prayer. Very gently, he withdrew from her clasping sheath and rolled her to her back in the crushed bed of ferns. Kneeling between her legs, he brushed the hair back from her face.

He started to speak, cleared his throat and tried again.

His eyes glittered in the starlight, filled with unshed tears. His voice broke, cracked, strengthened. "When I first saw you, your hair was so tightly braided, I had no idea how thick it was, how beautiful."

She frowned. All she could think of was putting that beautiful cock of his back between her legs. The fear that had held her for the past month felt like a bad dream. She wanted him inside her, now. And he wanted to talk about hair?

"It's changed. I've changed." She knew she sounded impatient. She couldn't help it. "My hair was so kinky, I had to wear it braided or keep it short. Becoming Chanku changed it. It's softer now, more like Xandi's."

"You've always been Chanku. Shifting to the wolf must have altered your hair, much as it's altered the rest of you." He ran his hand over her tousled mass of black curls and waves, leaned over and held a handful of her hair to his face and inhaled, then smoothed it back from her face once more.

"You are stronger, more powerful. You will never be a victim again." He laughed as he leaned down and kissed her, his lips moving skillfully over her mouth, his tongue barely teasing hers. She felt his hard cock brush against her belly, and her pussy wept.

He ended the kiss and sat back on his heels. "You truly are the alpha bitch in the pack. Even Xandi defers to you in many ways."

She tightened her knees against his hips. "What are you driving at, Anton? Why aren't we making love? You've been wanting this for weeks." She bit back a nervous giggle. "I'm ready, okay? So are you. Just look. Your poor cock's standing there, looking very impatient with both of us."

She tilted her hips once more in blatant invitation. His erect cock grew even larger, pressed upward against his lean belly. What was he up to? His introspective comments made her uneasy, unsure of herself. Her pussy was wet and waiting, her nipples puckered into tight, sensitive little buds, and all of a sudden he wanted to talk?

Why did he still look so sad?

"I've dreamed of this since the moment I saw you. I've slept with you in my arms, knowing you were afraid of anything more than my support and companionship. Let me savor this a minute, okay? Let me look at your body, taste your flavors, inhale your scent. I want it all, my love. All of you. I want your love, your passion, the very thoughts in your mind. I don't intend to rush until you're ready to drop all your barriers."

"Oh." She gazed up at him, understanding for the first time the true depth of his need. She'd blocked his thoughts so thoroughly, seeking the one protection left to her, the sanctity of her fears still locked in her mind.

The fear was gone because of Anton. The trauma, the assault, the brutality, no longer controlled her heart, her mind and her soul. Finally there was truly room for love in her heart. She dropped her barriers, linked with Anton and gasped with the intensity of emotion roiling within his thoughts.

Gasped, then smiled, finally accepting his need, his desire, his unconditional love.

Accepted, and returned every bit as much.

Love washed over her, spilled out of Anton and bathed her. He leaned close and took her nipple into his mouth, suckling it deep, and she felt reborn. His tongue licked the very tip, his teeth nibbled and nipped, and she cried out at each fresh sensation.

He quickly kissed his way down her belly, nuzzling in the thatch of tightly curled hair between her legs, licking her swollen lips like a starving man at a feast.

She was almost frantic when he lifted her with broad palms beneath her buttocks, raised her hips to his mouth and curled his tongue inside her, lapping like the big wolf he was.

Moaning, body trembling, Keisha reached for his arms and held on tight, practically curling herself into a ball as he licked and sucked her tender folds.

He took her to the edge, took her one step closer, then stopped, raised his head and leaned over to kiss her. She tasted herself on his lips, suckled his tongue into her mouth, groaning with each new taste, each new sensation.

Her pussy clenched, wanting. His cock bumped against her, just as desperate.

What are you waiting for? She glared at him.

An invitation?

Oh, shit. Fuck me! Now, Anton. I can't wait any longer. Gasping for breath, she lay back in the soft ferns and grabbed onto the stems, anchoring herself. He drove deep and hard, his cock finding its way home in one sleek thrust. He bumped hard against the mouth of her womb and sighed.

I feel as if I've come home.

You are home. We both are. She reached up and touched his beloved face, felt the emotion in his heart and mind, and accepted, finally, what Anton had told her all along. He was the one, her mate, the single most important person in the world for her. Lifting her hips to hold him even closer, she wrapped her arms around his lean, muscular back and hung on tightly.

In the deep woods in the dark of night, in the strong, steady arms of the man she loved, Keisha healed.

Chapter 22

Four days later, just at sunset, they crossed back over the Golden Gate Bridge. The lights of San Francisco glittered against a pink and mauve sky, and the buildings faded from peach to gray in the dying light of the sun.

Keisha stared at the familiar skyline and missed the mountains of Montana, the tall trees of Humboldt. She definitely missed the little cabin.

She and Anton had truly discovered one another over the past few days. There wasn't an erogenous zone on either body that had gone untouched, an orifice that hadn't been stimulated, a taste that hadn't been sampled. She felt well and thoroughly fucked, as wonderfully satiated as she'd ever been in her life.

So in love with the man beside her, she almost hurt.

She looked down at her left hand, grasped tightly in Anton's right, and felt the first sense of tension since they'd left the cabin.

"He'll be waiting, you know. We won't be able to shift. He'll see us."

Anton turned and smiled at her, looking more feral than when in wolven form.

"I know. I look forward to meeting Mr. Burns." He looked ahead, skillfully maneuvered around a stalled truck, then turned back to Keisha. "I doubt he'll enjoy it as much as I intend to, though."

He squeezed her hand in reassurance, then returned his attention to the heavy commuter traffic. Keisha sat back against the seat and watched the road ahead.

A car was parked in front of her townhouse. Anton's senses went on alert. He had to consciously tamp down the need to shift, to become the predator he was at heart. *I believe Mr. Burns is waiting for us now. Do you recognize the car?*

Keisha shook her head. Perspiration beaded on her brow. *It's been in the neighborhood off and on since I returned. I don't recall if it was here before my trip to Montana.*

If it is him, follow my lead. Stay in my mind if you must, but don't question anything I say.

You're not going to kill him, are you?

No, though I've thought about it. It would be most satisfying to gut the bastard, but it would make a horrible mess. He turned his attention from the car at the curb to the woman beside him. *It's important, Keisha. Will you do as I say?*

She turned, showing no fear. She laughed out loud. Saluted. "Yes, sir!"

This was the woman he loved.

Finally relaxed, now that the battle had come to him, Anton pulled into the driveway.

A portly, middle-aged man immediately got out of the car at the curb. From the rumpled appearance of his clothing, he looked as if he'd practically lived in his vehicle over the past few days.

"Ah, Ms. Rialto. I was sure you'd return eventually." He held his hand out, totally ignoring Anton.

Big mistake. Anton barely controlled the low growl starting deep in his chest. His skin shivered and twitched with his desire to become the wolf, the predator in his nature almost overwhelming his civilized self.

"I'm Carl Burns, reporter for the—"

"We know who you are, Mr. Burns. Thank you for coming." Anton bit back the snarl and stuck out his hand, intercepting the other man's hand in a tight shake. Burns' bluster turned to confusion.

"Thank . . ."

"It's wonderful of your newspaper to acknowledge Ms. Rialto's memorial garden. It was truly an honor when her design was selected."

"But that's not why . . ." Burns shook his head. "I'm not here to . . ."

"Come this way." Still speaking, Anton put his hand on the other man's back and guided him up the stairs. Claws appeared, then receded. His spine rippled with his need to transform, to kill. "I'm sure you'd like to get some shots of Ms. Rialto's drawings, maybe information about the exotic plants she's selected? It's really quite exciting." He turned to Keisha. "Sweetheart, hand me the key, would you?"

Shaking her head, biting back a grin, Keisha turned the keys over to Anton, grabbed their luggage and followed the two men up the steps. She felt Anton's struggle, knew the wolf was close. The fact his anger was so near the surface yet so tightly controlled made her feel more loved and protected than she could imagine.

She closed the door behind them. The moment it clicked shut, Anton grabbed Burns by the throat and shoved him up against the wall. There was a feral gleam in his eyes, and he bared his teeth, but somehow, to Keisha's surprise, he controlled his rage.

Instead of the wolf she feared, it was a very angry human watching the reporter gasp and squirm, his feet dangling six inches off the floor, his face turning purple from the choke hold Anton continued to tighten.

"You will not write about the wolf. The wolf does not exist. If you persist, you will die. It's a simple choice to make, Mr. Burns."

Burns' eyes bugged out, his hands scrabbled at Anton's muscular wrist, and his feet scraped at the wall. Keisha held her breath, wondering how far Anton would take this, knowing full well she couldn't let him kill the reporter no matter what she had promised Anton, no matter how great a threat he posed to all Chanku.

Suddenly Anton took a deep breath and released his hold on Burns. Gasping for breath, the man slid to the floor. When Anton leaned over and grabbed his hand to pull him to his feet, Burns appeared transfixed for a brief moment.

Then he was shaking his head, absentmindedly rubbing his throat before straightening his coat, apologizing for his clumsiness in tripping over the carpet.

Keisha wasn't certain how Anton had managed it, but he had Carl nodding and smiling as if nothing at all had happened in the entryway of her home. The reporter pulled out his notepad and jotted down information, even grabbed his camera for a quick photo of her drawings in the up-stairs studio. He also took a picture of Keisha, standing beside her greenhouse.

She almost laughed when he had her hold some of the very grasses that helped her become the wolf. Anton stood behind the idiot, his canines practically clicking in frustra-tion. Keisha sensed the fury simmering just beneath the surface of Anton's civilized behavior.

Burns left a few minutes later, obviously unaware of how close to death he'd come. The minute he was gone, Keisha grabbed Anton by the back of the shirt and spun him around. "Would you mind explaining to me what just happened? You practically strangle the man, then he acts like it's all his fault and we're his new best friends. What the hell is going on?"

"Why, Mr. Burns merely stumbled in the entryway before he interviewed you about your memorial garden."

With his smile he was innocence personified, but the effect was ruined by the snarl in his voice.

"That's not exactly why he was here. How come he totally ignored the fact you tried to kill him?"

"If I'd tried to kill him, he would be dead."

"That's not the point, and you know it. Why didn't he ask about the wolf?"

"Merely an implanted suggestion, m'dear. A form of hypnotism, if you will."

"What?" she practically shrieked, took a deep breath and tried again. "You're saying you used mind control? How?"

His look was pure *Anton*, all testosterone-driven male, proud of himself and of his ability to protect his mate.

Keisha growled.

Anton took a deep breath and answered. "You forget. Before I was a wolf, or before I knew I was a wolf, I was a very powerful wizard. Those skills are part of me, learned through many years of study. I merely convinced Mr. Burns that a story about your lovely memorial garden in Golden Gate Park was the entire reason he'd been trying to reach you. And you, my lovely lady, have been terribly elusive because you're very shy by nature."

"Yeah. Right. Shy." She snorted.

"Not very ladylike, however."

"Will he ever remember? Will he come back?"

Anton nodded, kissed the end of her nose. "He's going to find his notes, references to you as a wolf. He doesn't have photos, or he would have used them to blackmail you. I imagine, however, that he has a lot of information in his files. It may confuse him at first, but eventually he'll remember. Hopefully by then we'll be long gone."

"What about the bruises on his throat?"

"I'll let him wonder about them." Anton looked away for a moment, the fury radiating from his elegant frame almost palpable. He took a deep breath, and Keisha heard him grinding his teeth together. "I wanted very much to kill him, but it would create too many problems for you." He swept his hand over her hair. "I think you're safe now."

"What if he finds us?"

"If he comes after us, I just may eat him."

From the feral gleam in his eyes, Keisha wasn't sure if he was serious or teasing. "You don't . . ."

"Nah. Too much fat. Bad for my cholesterol."

Laughing, she threw her arms around him and kissed him hard on the mouth. "Anton, I love you. As soon as the project is over, take me home, please."

"You've got it." He kissed her back.

Lord, but she loved the taste of his mouth, couldn't wait to taste the rest of him. *Mind control.* He could make someone think whatever he wanted . . .

"Anton?" She pulled away, moved out of his embrace. "Why didn't you ever try that on me? The mind thing. Why didn't you just convince me I wasn't raped, I didn't kill those men. It would have been so much easier for you."

His pensive smile told her how much he'd thought of just such a thing. How difficult it had been for him not to help her.

"Not easier for you, though. It would have taken away a very powerful part of who and what you are. You needed to come through this by your own choice. You're a survivor. I would not cheat you of that victory. It's an amazing testimony to your strength that you've done this on your own. I love you the way you are, who you are. I don't want someone I've helped create. I love you, Keisha Rialto, fears, flaws and all."

"Flaws? You're saying I have *flaws*?"

"Well, you do have an odd habit of thinking you're in charge of things."

She threw herself into his embrace. Once again, as always, he caught her. Just as he would always catch her. She whispered against his lips, kissing him between the words. "As soon as the project is over, you're taking me home to Montana. There's so much more for me there than here."

Anton nuzzled her hair, then raised his head and grinned at her. "You're right. You can't forget Xandi . . . and there's still Stefan."

Stefan? Stefan, with a body and face so much like Anton's, with a quirky sense of humor and limitless compassion—and an obvious interest in sex.

"You wouldn't mind, wouldn't feel jealous, seeing me with another man?"

"Do you feel jealous when I make love with Xandi—or, for that matter, with Stefan? When I have Xandi's breast in my mouth and Stefan's cock deep inside me, do you want to stop what we're doing?"

She shook her head, picturing exactly the scene he described, realizing it no longer held fear for her, only desire. "No. I want to be there with you. When I linked with Xandi, I wanted so badly to be a part of your lovemaking, but I couldn't be. I was too afraid. The fear's gone now, though I imagine I'd like to sleep alone with Stefan first, before we do it as a group. I need to start slowly. Would that make *you* jealous?"

"It would make me very proud to see how far you've come. To know you truly embrace the part of you that is Chanku. I love you." He kissed her again, much more thoroughly this time.

"C'mon. I know a few things Stefan enjoys. How about I show you what you need to do?"

She laughed. "So I'm getting instructions now? You would presume to . . ."

Anton swept her up in his arms, kissed her mouth and headed for the bedroom. "I *presume* you love me. I presume you're mine forever and beyond. I presume you can't wait to make love. And I presume the bedroom is down this hall?"

"You presume correctly." She wrapped her arms around his neck. "On all counts. I sure hope Stefan appreciates how much we're willing to sacrifice for his pleasure."

"Oh, he does. I'm sure he does." Anton tossed her on the bed and kicked the door shut behind them.

PART FIVE

The Gift

Chapter 23

Stefan set the phone back on the table and sighed. Anton and Xandi had arrived safely in Portland in spite of an unexpected snowstorm. The house seemed so empty with them gone. He hadn't expected to miss them this much, but hearing Xandi's sweet voice made his heart hurt.

A week, no longer. It should take only a week for Xandi to sign off on the lease for the apartment she'd once shared with her ex-fiancé, formally resign from her job, pack her belongings and make the long drive in the rental truck back to Montana.

If Anton hadn't had business in Portland, Stefan would be the one with her now, but Anton had business there and Stefan didn't, and it only made sense that Stefan be the one to stay here with Keisha.

Keisha. Stefan watched her through the large front window.

She leaned over the deck railing, her slim body silhouetted by the setting sun, her once kinky black hair now falling in soft, tousled waves past her shoulders, its new texture a direct result of her Chanku heritage.

She looked so lonely out there, so alone. He'd grown used to seeing Anton by her side. Always touching, protecting, loving her. Keisha was such an enigma. Fun-loving, brilliant, beautiful—yet still so conflicted, Stefan's heart ached for her.

He pushed himself to his feet and poured a couple of glasses of wine. Keisha looked up at him and smiled when he shoved the door open with his shoulder and joined her at the railing. The freezing air practically took his breath away, but the clear sky and brilliant stars were worth the chill.

"Beautiful out, isn't it?" He handed Keisha the glass of Chardonnay, watched her throat constrict when she took a small sip, nodded when she smiled at him.

He opened his mind, but found her thoughts blocked. Unlike the others, Keisha kept her barriers in place more often than not. He wasn't certain, but he suspected that her rape and assault were never far from her mind, that she still suffered the trauma of her attack.

Looking at her, at the pensive, faraway look in her eyes, he imagined it was still very much a part of her. Stefan sipped at his wine, then set the glass on the railing. "Xandi just called. She and Anton are settled into their hotel room. Anton's got appointments all morning long, and Xandi's hoping to close out the lease and take care of her formal resignation. Packing her belongings will take longer, and they'll have to rent a truck to move everything here. It looks like they won't get home until at least Friday."

"That long?" Keisha frowned as she sipped at her wine. "That's Christmas Eve."

"I know. Weather's been pretty sketchy, too, but they'll leave as soon as they can."

"I'll worry about them all week." Keisha blinked and looked out across the snow-covered meadow.

Stefan saw the glint of tears in her eyes. He touched her chin with his fingertips, turned her face to him. "They'll be fine. We'll be fine. Wanna go run?"

Her eyes widened. "Oh. I guess I never thought of you and me running. I figured we'd wait until they got back."

Stefan began working the buttons down the front of his flannel shirt. The freezing air made his fingers clumsy. "You're kidding, right? Go a week without shifting? C'mon." He slipped out of his clothing, aware of Keisha's hesitation, her sudden shyness. It wasn't easy to keep from grinning at her. "Keisha, we've shared the same bed. We've been naked together. We've shifted countless times together."

"I know." She dipped her chin so he couldn't see her eyes. "Anton and Xandi have always been here."

"Are you afraid?"

Challenged, she glared at him. "No. No, I'm not afraid." She whipped the sweater over her head, slipped out of her jeans and shifted, her amber eyes glowing in the early twilight. *I'm fine. What're you waiting for?*

The barriers were still there, still blocking her innermost thoughts. He shifted.

Nothing. Let's go.

The week-old snow had formed a hard crust, enough to support their weight as they raced across the frozen meadow. Stefan quickly took the lead, but Keisha followed closely behind, to the right of his flank.

He ran hard, leaping fallen logs, skimming along the icy surface of creeks and bogs, his mouth wide, tongue lolling, ears sleeked back against his skull. Without warning, Keisha nipped his flank and sped past, her eyes bright and tail streaming out behind.

She hit the surface of an old mill pond where the ice was thick and the surface broad. Stefan ran directly into her, bowled her over, so that she slid on her back across the ice, before scrambling to her feet.

She rushed him, eyes gleaming, jaws wide, ducked her head as she reached his belly, dipped her snout under his chest and flipped him expertly over on his back.

Stefan landed hard, slid into a snowbank and came up with his face covered in ice crystals. Snorting, he shook his head.

Keisha stood about ten feet away, feet spread wide and planted firmly. *Gotcha! Don't ever mess with the alpha bitch!*

Alpha bitch! You still pulling that crap? He heard her laughter in his mind as he jumped, covering the distance between them in a single leap, and bowled her over before she could react.

The impact took both of them halfway across the pond. A tangle of gaunt willows against the bank stopped their slide. A huge drift of snow cascaded over their heads.

You okay? He heard Keisha wheezing for breath. He scrambled out from under the snow, shifting to his human form as he moved. The cold hit him like a fist, but he reached into the drift and pulled the wolf free.

She shifted, laughing so hard he realized at once the wheezing hadn't been a problem at all.

Also naked, she wrapped her arms around her slim body and shivered.

"Shit. I'm freezing." Keisha shook her tangled hair, and snowflakes cascaded all around. "Let's get back. It's really cold tonight."

They shifted together. The run back to the house was more leisurely, the sense of family stronger than ever. Keisha seemed to relax and really enjoy herself.

Still, Stefan felt the barrier, the sense of secrets Keisha couldn't—or wouldn't—share. He was still wondering how he could help her when they finally reached the house, gathered their clothing and went inside to shower.

Chapter 24

"Why are you so quiet?" Stefan paused as he cleared the dishes from the table. "Didn't you enjoy dinner? Oliver outdid himself."

Keisha blinked, caught dreaming. "Oh . . . I'm sorry. Dinner was excellent."

Stefan held the plates out of sight. "What did we have?"

"What?" Oh, lordy, what had she just eaten? She blinked. "For dinner? Uh . . . we had . . . I ate . . ." Keisha felt her skin heat up, knew she was probably blushing. Caught, she slumped in her chair. "I don't know. Sheesh, I feel really stupid."

"You're worried about where you're going to sleep tonight, aren't you?"

Did he have to look so damned smug? How could he know what she was thinking? Her blocks were tight, not a thought escaping. "I . . ."

"With me, I hope, but you know you don't have to, and I won't mind if you don't."

She took a deep breath. "I want to. Sleep with you, I mean. It's not like we haven't before."

"Yeah, but the others have always been nearby, or with us."

He set the dishes near the sink, walked back to the table and knelt beside her chair. It was so eerie looking into Stefan's eyes—eyes exactly like Anton's. He seemed to be weighing something when he took her hand in his, turned it and traced her lifeline with his fingertip, following the dark crease in the lighter flesh of her palm.

She felt each stroke all the way to her womb.

It was such a sensual act, the callused tip of his finger slowly, gently tracing that deeply etched line, back and forth, over and over. Mesmerized, she watched him while her pussy clenched, and she felt the hot moisture gathering, readying her.

"Stefan?" She placed her other hand over his, stopping the motion before she embarrassed herself and jumped him right here in the kitchen.

He covered her hand, so kneeling there, their hands sandwiched together, he looked like he was proposing. His eyes were luminous, his expression troubled.

He licked his lips. When he swallowed, she watched the muscles of his throat contract, mesmerized by the fluid motion. He was beautiful, every bit as gorgeous as Anton, just as sensual, just as caring. And Lord help her, but she loved the man. Not in the same way she loved Anton, but the feelings were there, so strong and true, they made her ache.

"Keisha?"

He looked troubled. Almost sad. She tilted her head, studying him, not daring to read his thoughts. His hands were warm, strong, holding hers tightly.

"Sweetheart, have you ever talked to anyone about what happened to you? Have you told Anton, your therapist, anyone, about the wolf? About your attack?"

What? She hadn't expected that question. Not in a million years! "Of course I have." She tried to tug her hands free, but he held on. After a couple of tugs, she gave up. "Anton knows I was raped. So do the police, the therapist and, after that newspaper article, half the known Western world." She choked back a sound that could have been a sob. She hoped he thought it was laughter.

Stefan stared at her a moment longer, then he smiled and stood up. Held out his hand to her. "C'mon. We don't need to have sex, but I want you beside me."

"You sound like Anton." This time the laughter was easy when she took his hand. "That poor man. He was so frustrated, and all I wanted to do was snuggle."

"Snuggling's good. Fucking's better, but snuggling works."

He grinned at her, perfect white teeth, brilliant amber eyes, the most gorgeous black hair shot through with silver, a body to die for. Without a doubt, the sweetest, most lovable guy she'd ever not fallen in love with . . .

But I do love him.

Not the way she loved Anton. No, though just not as deeply, every bit as fiercely. "How'd I ever get so lucky?" She flashed him a smile as she let him pull her to her feet. "Let's finish the dishes first. I hate to leave a mess for Oliver."

She watched him, sneaking glances to her right as he carefully dried each dish she handed him. Maybe her brain wasn't too sure, but her body definitely wanted more than snuggling. By the time the counters had been wiped down and the last dish put away, Keisha's taut nipples were rubbing themselves raw against her sweater, and she was afraid her jeans would show the dampness between her legs.

Stefan flipped off the light switch, turned and took her hand. His nostrils flared. She knew he'd caught her scent, knew just how aroused she was, knew how much she wanted him deep inside her. Keisha felt the awareness leap between them, felt it curling hot and live in her belly, flowing through her veins like liquid fire.

A low growl slipped from between his lips. Slowly he

tilted her chin up, positioned her perfectly for his mouth, then took her in a long, slow kiss. He brushed his lips across hers, dampened the seam between her lips with the tip of his tongue.

She opened for him, suckling his tongue into her mouth, tasting the flavors so much like Anton's, yet so unique to Stefan. He slipped his arm beneath her hips and lifted her easily, still kissing her, his tongue a warm and welcome violation.

She moaned. Could she come from just kissing? Stefan shoved the bedroom door open with his foot and deposited Keisha on the bed. Still fully dressed, he lay over her, kissing her mouth, the part of her throat exposed by her sweater.

There was something wonderfully decadent about making love fully dressed—decadent but woefully unsatisfying. Keisha tugged at the soft flannel shirt tucked into his jeans, felt the pressure of his hips against hers as he kicked his shoes and socks off, slipped out of his pants, ripped the shirt off his shoulders.

Completely naked, gloriously aroused, Stefan knelt between her jeans-clad thighs, his huge cock trapped in his hand. Slowly, he pumped back and forth, all the way from the base to the thick, dark crown.

"Are you going to undress?"

She giggled, suddenly nervous, her mouth dry. Instead of answering, she leaned forward and licked the very end of his cock. He shuddered, his hand stopped all motion.

She licked him again, then arched back and raised her hips, putting pressure on his testicles. He groaned and settled himself closer against her. There was something empowering about Stefan's nudity, the contrast to her clothed body. Something wild and carnal, to be fully dressed while he was naked.

Keisha leaned forward and licked his right nipple, then

dragged her teeth across the hard little point. He groaned, pressed more tightly against her, arched his back to bring his chest closer to her mouth.

She repeated with the left nipple, almost preternaturally aware of his racing heartbeat, the blood rushing in his veins, his harsh intake of air. Moving slowly, Keisha slipped out from beneath his parted thighs and pushed Stefan to his back. She straddled his hips, trapped his erection beneath her pussy and slowly rubbed her jeans-clad body over his.

Even through the denim she felt his heat, the hard ridge of his cock, the solid strength of his muscular thighs. On each backward sweep, the broad, plum-colored head peeked out between her legs, then disappeared as she swayed forward.

She palmed his nipples with both hands, supporting herself as she continued rocking, back and forth, moving slowly, smoothly, against his rigid flesh.

The seam of her denims hugged her clit, his erection forcing the fabric tight against her pussy. Keisha gasped. Her body tightened, her breath caught. Awash in the familiar coil of heat and need and lush sensitivity, she strained against him, riding this gorgeous naked man to completion.

Faster, uncaring how rough her jeans might feel to him, taking control, she turned her body loose. Back and forth, with Stefan's hands now clasping her hips, helping her ride him hard and fast, his cock suddenly jerking, spurting, shooting his seed all over his belly. The sight of his climax tipped Keisha into her own. Her body convulsed, spasmed. She arched her back and pressed down hard.

Her pussy clenched against the emptiness, as if searching frantically for more. Her heart pounded.

Stefan laughed. "Shit. Haven't done that since I was a teenager. Feels good, but not nearly so good as . . ."

He flipped her to her back. Still boneless from her own

climax, she could barely move her hands. Giggling, gasping for air, she helped him tug her jeans off, helped when he pulled her sweater over her head.

Could only lie back and moan when he fastened his mouth between her legs, stabbed into her with his tongue, licked her sensitive clit. Gently, so very gently, he brought her back to the edge, brought her to crying, quivering need before kneeling between her legs and slowly, surely, driving his newly erect cock deep inside.

This was what she needed, this hot, stretched feeling of total fulfillment. Raising her hips to meet his, she took him deep inside. The thick head of his cock touched the hard mouth of her womb on each downward thrust.

His fingers clutched her buttocks, holding her close. He thrust hard and fast, harder, until she shattered once more, until her arms and legs trembled and her pussy clutched his cock.

She felt him dragging his fingers through the moisture between her legs, then the soft slide as one finger found her ass, pressed lightly against the puckered flesh, then gained entrance. Still caught in the throes of climax, her mind missed the significance of his slow, tantalizing thrusts as first one finger, then two, then finally three, stretched the taut muscle.

When the head of his cock pressed against her, she freaked.

"No!"

What the fuck did he think he was doing? Screaming, crying, she shoved him with her legs, pushed him away and scrambled to the far side of the bed. Huddled there, crying, lost in shame, so embarrassed she wanted to fall through the floorboards and just disappear.

Stefan sat back on his heels and watched her. He offered no comfort, didn't try to hug her, as if he realized any movement on his part might send her over the edge.

She fought for control, hugged her arms around herself

and took deep, steady breaths. Looked anywhere but at Stefan.

"Mind telling me what just happened?"

Keisha shook her head. Stared at her toes and felt more naked than she'd ever felt in her life.

He grabbed his jeans off the floor and pulled them on. Then he threw a soft afghan to Keisha. She wrapped it tightly around herself. Hid within its multihued folds.

"I asked you earlier if you'd ever talked about the rape and the wolf with anyone. What just happened is linked to your assault, isn't it?"

She nodded. Still couldn't look at him.

"Wait here. I'll be right back."

She watched him go and thought her heart would break. Couldn't tell him she'd had the same reaction when Anton had tried anal sex, though she hadn't remembered why then.

This time, the memories were clear and true. Brutal and bloody, so horrible she couldn't tell anyone how afraid she was—not for herself, but for them.

One other man had taken her that way, and because of him, three men had died horrible deaths. Screaming in agony, bleeding, terrified to the final moments when their torn throats were no longer capable of sound.

Chapter 25

Alexandria awakened, sated, sleepy—alone. The hotel room was dark, the bed beside her empty. She sensed movement, sat up and focused through the gloom with her enhanced Chanku sight.

A wolf prowled. Large, predatory, it paced back and forth beneath the covered window. Twelve floors up, there was no risk of it jumping, but still it paced.

Anton? What's wrong? Can't you sleep?

No. I sense Keisha. She's troubled. I feel her.

She's a thousand miles away. You can't possibly . . .

Yes. I can.

She felt his very human sigh. *If you say so.*

He snorted, a very human sound from the large wolf now standing in the middle of their room. *I realize Stefan will tell me if she's in trouble, but I can't ignore the fact I sense her. It's frustrating, knowing there's nothing I can do from so far away.*

You can come back to bed. I'll let you pretend I'm Keisha. "C'mon." She patted the sheets beside her.

He sighed again, took a single leap and landed on the bed. Still in his wolven form, Anton curled up beside Alexandria and draped his muzzle across her breasts.

His head was heavy, comforting. She drifted off to

sleep, her fingers slowly rubbing the soft fur behind his ears.

Stefan carried two brandy snifters filled with Anton's special stash of aged Scotch whiskey. What he had to do with Keisha was going to take more than a couple of glasses of wine.

He'd been so close to linking with her at the moment she had lost it, so close he'd actually picked up shadowy visions of her thoughts, terrifying images that left his heart pounding and his stomach in turmoil.

If what he'd seen had actually happened, it was no wonder Keisha hadn't fully recovered.

He pushed the door to the bedroom open. She hadn't moved. Still huddled in the corner of the bed, her back pressed against the headboard, the crocheted blanket wrapped tightly around her body, she looked like a little girl awaiting punishment.

He sat down next to her, reached inside the twisted blanket and grabbed her hand. Carefully unfolding her clenched fingers, he placed the glass in her hand.

"Drink this. It's just to calm you down. We may have a long night ahead of us."

"I don't want to . . ."

"Drink."

He watched while she took a deep swallow, gasped and coughed, stared at him with hurting eyes, then sipped again, slower.

He took a chance. Crossed his fingers and hoped Anton wouldn't kill him for what he intended to do. He glared at Keisha. "Okay. You can put the glass down now. I don't give a shit what you don't want to talk about. Keisha, I love you. Anton and Xandi love you. We are damned tired of seeing you hurting, knowing you have so much bottled up inside that it's keeping you from being the woman

you're meant to be. Let me help you. I'm not totally without skills."

"No . . . no, I don't want . . ."

"Keisha!" He grabbed her shoulders, stared into her
tear-filled eyes. "Look at me. You remembered something
tonight, something that has scared the shit out of you.
Don't say it, don't even go there, but please, let me into
your mind. Drop the barriers. Let me see what's got you
under its control."

She dipped her chin so that it almost rested on her
chest. Her voice was nothing more than a broken whisper,
and it ripped his heart out.

"I don't want to hurt you," she said. "I knew I did
something awful, but tonight I remembered. It was worse
than I thought. I'm afraid of what I'll do . . . "

"Show me." He felt like a liar using his mind like this,
the skills to mesmerize that Anton had been teaching him,
but he used them anyway, nudging Keisha gently in the direction he wanted her to take.

Exhausted, frightened, already feeling the Scotch in her
system, she was an easier subject than he expected. She
raised her head and stared blankly at him, totally under
the spell of his suggestion. At his subtle command, she
dropped her barriers, removed all the blocks she'd so carefully maintained and let him in.

It was all he could do not to vomit. She shared her rape
and its bloody aftermath, linking completely with Stefan.
He was Keisha, straddling one man, her insides raw and
bleeding from repeated penetrations as her attacker brutally shoved into her from below. Another man held her
head while he drove his cock down her throat. The pain
was excruciating, the gag reflex overwhelming, but there
was nothing she could do. No way to fight back, not with
her hands tied behind her with wide strips of tape, her hips
roughly held by the man beneath her.

Fear, blinding, overwhelming fear and pain, so much pain her body began to shut down, to find another state, another existence. Then the sensation of someone else, the third man, behind her. Groping her, grabbing her hips, spreading her buttocks, then agony—blinding, unavoidable agony—as he forced entrance, shoving himself deep inside, tearing, ripping her flesh.

She wanted to scream, but the cock in her mouth kept her mute. She wanted to die, but her life force was too strong.

She wanted to kill. Wanted the taste of their blood, the sounds of their death screams. Wanted to live. Stefan felt it then, the shift that had saved her, the crackling of bones and straining of sinews unprepared for such an act. The shift that happened so quickly, her attackers were suddenly screwing a full-sized she-wolf, a wolf that did exactly what any wild animal will do when it's frightened or in pain.

She attacked. The cock in her mouth was simple. She simply snapped her jaws and jerked her head, tearing the man's genitals from his body. Turning with lightning speed, she ripped out the throat of the man who sodomized her, at the same time disemboweling the one beneath her with her hind feet. The claws tore into his gut, shredding skin and tendon as if it were paper.

Her attack was fast and efficient, though only the man who'd had his throat torn died instantly. The others screamed for what seemed a long, long time. Exhausted, still in wolf form, Keisha stood alone in the middle of the blood-soaked room, her head hanging almost to the floor. Blood poured from her body, but she finally staggered to the door, only to discover paws were not made for dead bolts and doorknobs.

Exhausted, weak from loss of blood, she finally collapsed against a wall as far from the three men as she could get. Her mind shut down completely, blotting out the moans and screams. She laid her bloodied muzzle against her crossed paws and slept.

Her mind was completely blank during the shift back to human form, but Stefan became aware of a loud pounding on the door, of the smell of blood and death in the room, of the death rattle of the last of the attackers as he finally died from loss of blood. Then all was confusion and disorientation as the police broke through the door and reality once more intruded.

Stefan realized he had somehow reached for Keisha, held her in his arms as both of them cried. He'd never imagined the horror she'd lived through, knew Anton had no idea how brave and strong his mate actually was. He tried to tell her those things, tried to impress upon her the power of the wolf, the strength and bravery it had taken for her to fight back when fighting was all but futile.

He released the link and held her close. She shuddered and tried to pull away, but he rubbed her back and whispered silly phrases in her ear until she finally calmed down. Her heart rate slowed, her tears ended. Finally, exhausted, both of them slept.

Keisha awoke, blinking against the bright morning sun. She'd slept all night! The horrible nightmares that had troubled her sleep since her assault hadn't appeared. She'd slept soundly, her mind free of fear. The terror was gone.

She'd dreamed of Anton.

She blinked, focused on Stefan sitting beside her on the bed, a steaming cup of coffee held in his hands. He smiled and held the cup out for her to take a sip. It was wonderful, hot and strong, with enough caffeine to wake the dead. She smiled and handed the cup back to Stefan. "Thank you."

"You are an amazing woman, Keisha Rialto. Absolutely amazing."

She shook her head. "How can you say that? I killed three men. I lost control. They didn't die cleanly, Stefan."

He took a swallow of the coffee and grinned at her. "You were true to your nature. You were brave and fearless, and I'm so proud of you, I can hardly stand it."

"What?" Startled, she stared at him. "What do you mean? I'm a murderer."

"Beats being a victim. You were being systematically, brutally tortured by three vicious thugs. They let you see them, so we know they intended to kill you. You were able to save yourself because you had the courage to take action. You did what comes naturally to the wolf. You had something shoved down your throat, so you bit it off. You had two other men restraining you, so you retaliated in the only way a wolf can—with your teeth and your claws. You're amazing." He kissed her.

She didn't kiss him back. She felt too stunned to react. "All this time I've known I did something awful, but I had no idea what. Last night, when you tried to . . ."

She sighed. "Well, it all came back to me. Everything, all at once." She took another sip of his coffee. "Dr. Aragat's magic potion?"

"Hey, if it works . . ." He brushed her hair back from her eyes. "Are you okay?"

She looked at him, sighed deeply and smiled. "Yeah. Actually, I feel really good. It's either the coffee or your therapy session."

"The true test will be whether or not you can take a man from behind without freaking out. I hope you realize you scared the crap out of me."

"I scared Anton too. But when it happened with him, I had no idea why I lost it. I knew it had something to do with the assault, but not exactly what."

"Now that you know, how do you feel about it? What if I were to take you like that? Would you be able to handle it?"

"Probably, but you're not going to find out. At least not yet." She grinned at him, fully awake now.

"Why not?"

"I'm saving myself for Anton. We may have a very open relationship, but I know it hurt him that I couldn't enjoy everything with him, that I still had this huge block in my mind. Do you understand?"

"Yeah." He leaned over and kissed her nose, then moved lower to feast on her full lips. Finally he came up for air. "It's okay. I'll get it out of your hide in a lot of other ways."

She lay back and spread her legs, then crooked her finger, inviting him in.

Never one to turn down an invitation, Stefan accepted.

"They're late."

"I know." Stefan turned away from the window. Snow fell steadily, glistening multicolored in the glow from the twinkling Christmas lights. Anton had called hours ago. They should have been here by now.

The meal was cold and forgotten. Oliver had long ago returned to his cottage. The main highway was closed due to the storm, but Anton and Xandi should have been on the private road hours ago.

"Do you sense them?" Keisha wrapped her arms around her middle and looked close to tears.

Stefan stepped up behind her and wrapped his arms around her. "No. I've tried, but they're still too far away."

"Or dead." Her voice shook.

"No. They're okay." They had to be okay. He tried to imagine life without Xandi, without Anton, and knew he never wanted to be so alone again. Knew Keisha felt the same way. Together, they were family. Together, they could conquer anything.

Just look at what Keisha had conquered this week. They'd talked again, later, about the details of her attack.

She'd screamed, she'd cried, she'd even struck out, angry at Stefan for making her face things she would rather have kept hidden in the back of her heart.

He'd finally convinced her those memories were merely festering, stored away as they'd been. Made her see the good that had come from her horrible attack, the fact that it had forced her to find the wolf inside herself, something she might never have discovered.

It had not been an easy week. They'd spoken to Anton and Xandi nightly by phone, but neither Keisha nor Stefan had mentioned the impromptu therapy sessions.

Now they worried.

The blizzard worsened. Snow blew sideways, obscuring even the railing around the deck. Keisha stared at the phone. Stefan paced. Finally he headed for the door.

"Wait here. I'm going down the road, see if I can pick up anything. My Chanku senses are stronger there."

Keisha reached for her top buttons as if preparing to shift.

"No. Stay by the phone in case they call. I won't go farther than I can link with you. If I find anything, I'll let you know. Keep in touch with me. Shift if you think it will increase your senses, but don't leave the house."

She nodded, accepting his decision, though he knew she hated the thought of being here alone.

Before she could change her mind, Stefan undressed, opened the door and shifted.

Be careful.

He felt the biting cold even through the thick winter coat of the wolf. His broad paws sank into the drifted snow, and he found it was almost impossible to locate the road, much less make any headway, but he forced his way forward, eventually taking to the trees beside the road, where the snow wasn't as thick.

Something was wrong, horribly wrong. He'd sensed it the moment he shifted—the fear, the pain. He tried to judge time and distance, but it was impossible. Drawing him on was the sense of Anton and Xandi. He shared his feelings with Keisha, drew on her for strength as he covered the long miles leading to the highway. The temperature continued to fall as he raced forward, as the sense of wrongness grew stronger.

He might have missed the truck altogether, so deeply buried was it in the drifts, but the motor still ran, and the thick cloud coming from the exhaust caught his attention.

They'd gone off the road. How long ago he could only guess, but he shifted, ending up naked in the biting cold, but it was the only way he could wrench open the door on the passenger side of the truck.

The fumes from the exhaust were overpowering, seeping into the cab, poisoning the unconscious figures within. *Keisha! I need you. Bring the four-wheeler with blankets. Lots of blankets.*

He dragged Xandi out onto the snow, then grabbed Anton. Both were unconscious, barely breathing. Fighting panic, Stefan checked Xandi's pulse, then blew air into her lungs. She coughed, gasped, struggled against him. He moved quickly to Anton, giving him the breath of life, begging him to awaken.

The four-wheeler sounded muffled in the storm, but he called out to Keisha, using the mental link they'd strengthened over this long week to reach her, to bring her directly to them.

She pulled up close in the small vehicle. She'd attached the garden trailer Oliver used around the grounds.

Are they alive?

Barely.

She threw a bundle of warm clothing to Stefan. While he dressed, she spread blankets in the bed of the trailer, fashioned a warm cocoon for Xandi and Anton, then helped Stefan load the two into the back.

Stefan reached for Xandi's mind. Found nothing. He

tried Anton's and was met with the same unusual lack of consciousness. He looked at Keisha and knew she'd tried to reach them as well. Were they too late? How long had they been exposed to the deadly fumes?

Breathing around a huge lump of fear in his throat, Stefan helped Keisha cover Xandi and Anton with the blankets. Then, with their precious cargo well-protected, they headed back to the house.

Chapter 26

Day broke slowly, a watery gray dawning, nothing like the picture-perfect Christmas mornings featured on cards, but Keisha couldn't remember a better Christmas in her entire life. Stefan, as wolf, lay curled up next to Xandi, who slept peacefully beside Anton.

Keisha sat in the rocker next to the bed. She'd wrapped herself in the multicolored afghan against the morning chill. Now she sipped her cup of coffee and grinned like a complete idiot while tears streamed down her face.

They're okay, Stefan. I sense their thoughts. Their dreams are normal, their thoughts clear and coherent. I'd almost given up.

Stefan raised his shaggy head and blinked. Keisha saw his eyes narrow, knew he reached for Xandi. Slowly, as if waking from a long dream, Alexandria opened her eyes and sat up.

"Stefan?" She touched the wolf beside her. "Keisha? What happened? There was a horrible storm. We lost the brakes on that last hill and . . . Anton?"

"I'm here." Shoving himself upright, Anton shook his head and groaned. "My god, what a headache! We're home? How?"

Throwing her blanket aside, Keisha launched herself

into his arms. Anton grunted, but hung onto her as she sobbed and hugged him with her arms around his neck, her legs wrapped just as tightly around his waist.

Stefan jumped down off the bed, shifted, leaned over and kissed Xandi, then picked her up. "Ya know, sweetheart, I'm getting a bit tired of rescuing your lovely butt from car wrecks in snowstorms." He kissed her again. "You and I need time alone together, mate. Just as they do. Don't ever scare me like that again."

He looked back at Keisha and winked. "Merry Christmas, kiddo. Looks like you got what you wanted . . . which means you get to give him what he wants. Glad to see you back among the living, Anton. You two scared the crap out of us." He kissed Xandi hard on the mouth, then carried her out of the room.

Anton swept Keisha's tousled hair back from her face. "What was that all about?"

"Link with me, Anton. Completely."

He frowned, but did as she asked. The look of wonder that crossed his face brought on an entirely new rush of tears.

"No barriers. No blocks of any kind. What happened?" He brushed her hair back from her eyes once more, the unabashed love in his almost her undoing.

"Stefan helped me through some of the trauma, some of the stuff I haven't been able to deal with. It was pretty awful. Stuff I didn't even know myself, probably could never have shown you because I love you too much."

Anton kissed her. She could drown in those kisses. Could never get enough of his taste, his scent. His love. Then he pulled away, held her face in his hands, looked at her with so much love, so much feeling, it took her breath away.

"Stefan's given you a very special gift, my love. He's returned your spirit, that part you've been hiding from me since I've known you. But what did he mean by your gift for me? You're all the gift I'll ever need."

She tried to bite back her grin, but failed. "Not until you're feeling better. I want you strong and healthy."

The reality of the past hours suddenly caught her. "Do you know how close you came to dying in that truck? The fumes were horrible!" She tried to look indignant, but the thought of their comatose bodies brought a fresh round of tears. "I was so afraid, Anton."

He tightened his arms around her. "We must have been knocked unconscious when the truck slid off the road. Then the exhaust fumes leaking into the cab kept us out. If Stefan hadn't come along when he did . . . "

"Maybe we should call him Santa, not Stefan." Keisha giggled when she felt Anton's hand creeping inside the waistband of her sweats. She wriggled, settled herself closer against him and felt the hard ridge of his cock, swelling in the valley between her legs.

"I'm feeling much better, by the way."

"I noticed." She pressed harder, her muscles clenching against his growing erection.

His fingers crept lower.

"I thought you had a headache." She wiggled her bottom once more when his fingers found the crease between her cheeks, slipped lower, discovered the heat between her legs.

"What headache? I'm getting ideas."

"So am I." Then she opened her thoughts, let him see what Stefan had done, how he'd helped her accept the violence, the true nature of Chanku.

Then she showed him very explicitly what she wanted . . . what she now fantasized and no longer feared.

Eyes alight with desire, he kissed her. Feasted on her mouth as if her breath alone would keep him alive. Still he managed to strip her clothing off her body. His right hand found her breast, his left trailing along the line of her hip, cupping her buttocks and pulling her close against him.

She rolled her hips, rubbing the wet folds of her pussy against his cock, waiting for him to fill her. Instead Anton slipped out of her grasp. Stacking pillows in the middle of the bed, he bent Keisha over them.

Her mouth went dry. Too soon, too sudden! A thick coil of fear clutched her heart. But instead of entering her the way she feared, the thick head of his cock slipped easily into her waiting pussy. He moved slowly in and out, teasing her with the controlled rhythm, with the soft touch that wasn't nearly enough.

His fingers found her clit, and he rubbed and tugged much too gently. She bit back a moan and shuddered as the tension built, as her body cried out for more. His soft laughter filled her mind just as he withdrew his cock and rested it between her buttocks. Slowly, still so very slowly, he rubbed his solid cock up and down against her ass, stroking lightly at first, pressing so close she felt the hot weight of his balls against her pussy.

He didn't change his cadence at all . . . didn't touch her except with his cock. His hands grasped her hips, held her close. Her pussy cried out for contact. He dipped his fingers deep inside her, then quickly withdrew, but when his wet finger lightly brushed the tightly puckered ring of muscle at her ass, Keisha knew another erogenous zone had suddenly been added to her body.

Instead of fear, she trembled with anticipation. Instead of pain, she felt only pleasure as Anton pressed and rubbed with his moistened fingertip, pressed and rubbed again, and finally breached the tightly puckered opening. He slipped his finger in and out. Keisha wriggled against him, wanting more, wanting relief from the building pressure of pending climax.

He added another finger to her behind, slowly stretching her, making her ready. She shivered, tilted her hips just so, giving him greater access. His fingers moved inside her, and she raised her hips to meet each gentle thrust.

His cock rested against her back, his balls rubbed over her buttocks, his fingers slowly fucked her from behind. She shivered in pleasure, not in fear, in anticipation, not in pain.

She arched her back and moaned. *Are you trying to drive me insane?*

He laughed out loud. *I want you ready for me. I want you so desperate, you'll take me deep inside without pain, without fear.*

I'm ready, dammit! Any more ready, and I'll explode! She pressed her face into the mattress, raised her hips in the most blatant invitation she could manage. She felt Anton slowly withdraw his fingers, felt the solid head of his cock as he rubbed it around her ass. Frantic, she pressed back against him as he entered her, only to have him pull back.

She relaxed, her body shivering with need, with anticipation. A sigh escaped her lips when she felt him once more pressing against her, easing his way inside. At the same time, his fingers found her aching clit, rubbed light, wet circles around and around, finding a rhythm that pulled her higher, farther, deeper, into pure sensation.

He was big, much larger than the man who'd raped her, but the thought was merely a shadow that flitted through her mind, not nearly enough to dim the pleasure of taking Anton deep inside her body.

She felt herself stretch, accept. Felt the smooth slide of his hot penis filling her.

Are you okay? He pressed tiny kisses along her spine, a kiss for each word.

Oh, yeah. And I'll be better when you're finally all the way inside of me.

Are you sure?

Slowly Keisha pressed back against him, taking control,

forcing his solid length deeper. The muscles in her pussy clenched. Anton groaned, and she knew he'd felt the contraction.

His mind opened to hers. Keisha almost collapsed under the powerful rush of pure, blind sensuality, the heat he felt inside her passage, the ripple of muscles as he continued his slow, steady entrance. Finally his thighs pressed solidly against the backs of hers. His testicles, tethered tightly beneath his cock, rode in the damp crease of her pussy, and his fingers continued their steady assault on her clit.

He withdrew just as slowly as he'd entered, then filled her once more. Keisha arched her back, forced her hips against his and cried out. The first orgasm left her writhing beneath him. When he filled her pussy with his long fingers, she came again, and when he found a faster rhythm, thrusting into her hard and deep, she cried out a third time and collapsed beneath him.

Only then did Anton find his own release. She felt him strain against her, felt the hot rush of seed filling her, his teeth sharp against her shoulder as he bit down, marking her as his own.

Then she turned her head, found his mouth and kissed him. His face was wet with tears, his lips hard, possessive. She felt his love, his strength, his pure nature, in the beauty of his kiss, in the touch of his body to hers.

Taking her gently, he'd turned her nightmare into something wonderful. She'd thought herself shattered, broken beyond repair, but she was once again whole. She'd feared for Anton through the long night, but he was here, safe, alive, wanting her in every way.

Thank you, my love.

His soft, mental touch brought a smile to her lips. *You need to thank Stefan. It was not an easy week for him.*

Truly a gift beyond measure, Stefan. Thank you.

She sensed Stefan's laughter, his love for Xandi, for all of them.

Merry Christmas, guys. Always glad to be of service.

Then searching lips once more found hers. Stefan faded away, and all she thought of was Anton.

Like to watch? Here's a sneak peek
at Karin Tabke's sizzling
"Stakeout," from
THE HARD STUFF.
Available now from Kensington . . .

"Who said size doesn't matter?" Stevie asked.

Must have been a little man with a little . . .

She whistled admiringly at the package, grateful for the unexpected perk.

Grinning, she dragged her eyes for a breathless second from the high-powered telescope and looked over her shoulder. The last thing she wanted was for one of the task force guys her lieutenant insisted on saddling her with to think she was some hard-up sexpot.

She laughed out loud. Okay, maybe she was. It had been too long since she last felt the sinful pressure of a man between her legs. And it wasn't because she was a prude. Unfortunately, the most intriguing prospects were the same ones she'd sworn off for years: cops.

She'd learned the hard way not to be the company inkwell. Too many hassles. Too many knowing grins from her fellow officers, followed by suggestive wolf whistles.

Nope, she made damn sure she wasn't the hot topic of any lineup. Besides, since her promotion to detective two years ago, she didn't have time for a relationship anyway.

She shrugged and focused back on her subject.

Mario Vincente Spoltori, aka Rocky. Not an original

alias, but hell, the man was a walking hard-on. And she bet he gave granite a run for its money.

She'd been surveilling the *escort* for nearly a week, and finally after tedious hours of watching the paint dry, she got her first look at what the privileged ladies of Sacramento couldn't get enough of.

And mamma mia, there was plenty to go around.

She couldn't blame the ladies who waited months to get an hour of this notorious stud's time. No more than she could help that familiar tingle between her legs. Not for Mario. As delightful as she was sure he was in the sack, she was more straight-laced. One-nighters weren't something she actively pursued. She'd only had one in her life, and although it was the best sex she'd ever had, and she would have followed the guy to the ends of the earth, the whole experience left her feeling . . . well, tawdry.

He never called.

No use thinking about a guy she'd never see again.

Prick.

Shaking her head, Stevie gave rock-hard Rocky her full attention, and for a minute put aside the fact he was the reason she'd worked round the clock for the last three months.

She laughed and thought how ironic her current predicament was. Here she was, a perfectly healthy female, and she was considering paying for stud service. Her life was too hectic for anything less than the occasional quickie. And as picky as she was, her options were severely limited.

Strictly as a woman to his man, Stevie considered Rocky's slick muscles and generous endowment. She sighed. Too bad she wasn't into this kind of stuff.

He bent over, flexing his taut ass at her, and continued the slow slide of his underwear down his thighs before he kicked them off.

Well . . . *maybe* . . . nah. Besides, on her cop salary she'd have to give up a lot of somethings for a roll in the hay with the likes of the Italian Stallion across the way.

"Oh, you selfish bastard."

What a waste. Looked like Adonis was sneaking some of the goodies. As big as his cock was, his hand was larger. He stood stark naked facing her in front of his exposed window and started across the wide boulevard that separated their respective buildings.

He smirked, closed his eyes, tilted his head back, and put on a show. If she didn't know better, she'd swear he knew he had an audience.

Impossible. While his windows were transparent, the small, stuffy office she'd begun to detest had a dark film covering the window, with just a small square cut out for her ever-watchful eyes. No way could he know he was under surveillance.

Stevie dismissed that thought and instead zeroed her attention back on what God had so benevolently given the man. His long dark fingers grasped his rod and in a slow pump he manipulated it to staggering proportions. Stevie licked her dry lips.

Jesus.

His hips ground against an imaginary pussy and he bit at his bottom lip.

Faster and faster he pumped. Stevie's breath held when he splayed himself up against the window, still pumping. Her skin warmed. She didn't want to get sucked in by his erotic display, but she did nonetheless.

She screamed and about jumped out of her skin when the pressure of a large hand squeezed her shoulder.

"Am I interrupting?"

Her shock caused her to lose her balance and fall backward off her chair. As she was trying to catch herself, two large, very capable hands grabbed her. The touch sent shock waves through her body. She had the undeniable inclination to rub herself up against the hard thigh that supported her back.

"Christ, what the hell?" she yelled, collecting herself and sitting up. Quickly she twisted around and pulled her piece.

She felt the blood drain from her face.

Son of a bitch.

"Jack Thornton."

"It's been a long time, Detective Cavanaugh." His grin rivaled a wide-open barn door. He seemed taller, more muscled. The faint smile lines at the corners of his deep-set hazel eyes accentuated his natural mischievous nature.

She braced herself.

Humiliation and excitement riveted through her, running neck and neck for the finish line. Her skin flushed hot and she resisted the urge to lick her dry lips.

Instead, she did what any woman scorned would do. She slapped him. Hard. White imprints of her fingers stood boldly out against the tan of his cheek. Before her hand returned home, he grabbed it. He yanked her hard against him, the connection forcing her breath from her chest. Her sensitive nipples stiffened against the hardness of his chest.

"Was that because I didn't call you or because I wouldn't let you get on top?"

Visions of their sweaty, naked bodies writhing in passion amongst the twisted sheets in her academy dorm room sprang to mind. Jack Thornton could give Rocky across the way a few lessons in pleasing a woman. Her chest tightened while other emotions she chose to ignore vied for playtime.

Stevie's breath hitched high in her throat. "That was because you're an egotistical bastard." She pushed hard against him. He released her. She holstered her Sig.

Thorn continued to grin, but the harsh glare of his eyes belied his mirth. "What's so egotistical about making love to a beautiful woman?"

Despite the warmth of the room, her nipples stood at full mast. Stevie pulled on her jacket. The last thing she wanted was to give his inquiring eyes a show.

"More like seducing a virgin."

Thorn moved in closer. "That was your choice, Stevie, not mine." He grinned like an idiot. "By the way, thanks for picking me."

After so many years, the shock of seeing the only man she'd ever had feelings for forced her off balance. The sensation left her angry, and scared.

He backed up at her fist.

"Go ahead, dickhead," she said, "keep the BS coming, I don't need more of an excuse to nail you."

"I need less of one to nail you." He stepped forward, his face a happy place. "Since we're both in agreement, what do you say, my place after we're done?

"Pig."

"Pride in Grace, don't I know it."

Stevie couldn't believe it. The only guy she'd dreamed about stood in front of her more than willing to go back down that seductive road with her. If her pride weren't at stake, and her heart unwilling to get squashed again, she'd have her running shoes on.

"What are you doing here?"

Casually he walked past her and looked out the tinted window. He gave the long expanse of buildings quiet contemplation. As if he'd just come back from a coffee break, he righted the tipped-over chair, then sat down, and focused in across the way.

"Hmmm, looks like the Italian Stallion over there needs a clean up on aisle nine."

Regaining her composure, Stevie swung the lens from him, and squatting level with it, she zeroed in herself. Geez, Rocky had his chum all over the window. "I swear, you guys just love to spread that stuff around, don't you?"

Thorn pulled the lens his way and refocused. "Yeah, it's

what we do. Men hunt and propagate the species, women nurture and gather. Basic."

Stevie's eyes narrowed. Neanderthal. She'd been too starry-eyed to see it in the academy seven years ago; at least *she'd* evolved since then.

She pulled the lens back her way and focused on Rocky. "That's it, clean up your mess," she said to the gigolo. Then, as if to herself, she said, "I wonder if there was some kind of statute back then about instructors fraternizing with students?"

Thorn leaned in behind her. "No." His hot breath against her ear stirred up old familiar heat. His clean, woodsy scent engulfed her. Her blood thickened in her veins and whatever hormones she had that induced sex surged through her body. She clenched her muscles before they turned to warm mush.

Stevie remembered how she couldn't wait for her defensive tactics classes. Sergeant Jack Thornton was her instructor, and she repeatedly paid with bruises to be his test dummy.

She almost laughed. She'd had such a crush on him from the get-go. Little did she know she'd end up his parting gift.

"How's the wife and kid?"

He pulled away. "You know my divorce was final before graduation." His eyes clouded. "My stepson is with his father."

Stevie inhaled a deep breath and slowly exhaled. She didn't give a rat's ass about his home life.

"What are you doing here, Thorn?"

He grinned and stood back from the telescope. Casually he pulled back his Italian-cut suit and said, "Special Agent Thornton at your service, ma'am."

Renée Alexis presents "Reacquainted."
And it feels so good.
From GOTTA HAVE IT.
Available now from Kensington . . .

The tour along Lake Shore Drive was amazing. Caroline had seen it many times, but never from the window of a Porsche. It was a beautiful, sunny day, a more perfect day hadn't been created, and what made it absolutely perfect was that she would be spending it in Marc's arms. The minute they entered his mansion, she knew she'd wrap herself around him so tightly that they'd make the first human rubberband. She could actually feel Marc sliding that hulking thick meat into her and shattering what was left of her sanity. That was what she needed. No man in her past left an impression upon her the way he did with one evening in a shower. From that point on in her life, wherever she moved to, she made sure the shower was on jam!

Marc took her mind from her bathroom orgasm. "Hey, pretty girl. Whatcha' thinkin' about?"

The side of her dainty little mouth perked up. "I don't think you want to know that."

"Now I really want to know."

Her hand stroked his inner thigh. "Well, I was thinking about showers." She faced him bluntly. "And I don't mean rain showers."

"Girl, I like the sound of that. So tell me, what were we doing in the shower?"

"I didn't get into it that deeply, but there's something about showers that turns me out!" Her hand moved from his leg, to his groin, on to his stomach and caressed his chest. He was still so soft, baby flesh, like she remembered from years ago. "You still feel so good."

"I think it's that aftershave I advertise."

"I have seen that commercial. Sexy, sexy as can be."

"So, finish that shower thing you went off on."

"I was just wondering how it would be making love to you in your shower. I'm sure you have many."

"I have four, and I plan to christen you in all of them."

Her hand moved back to his erection, stroking it, making the linen pants material cause friction against it. She loved the way his muscles tensed, how hot the heat was emitting from those pants. Heat wasn't exactly the only thing she wanted from those pants; she wanted fire, steam, white-hot lava and she wanted it dripping slowly and thickly down his shaft. She tugged at his zipper, then eyed him. "May I?"

"God! Yes."

There was no one on the tree-laden street but them, so he pulled the Porsche to the side of the road. "Why wait for the shower when we can get wet right here?"

"Ummm, I like how you talk, Mr. Marc Brown, king of the Sox bullpen."

"I want to be your king, your every-damn-thing, pretty girl!"

With his hand covering hers, they slid his zipper down. Before the zipper was at half-mast, his tight, seething erection was trying to bust apart all that was in its way. To tease Marc into exquisite hardness, her wet tongue darted at the clothed tip, against the roughness of the Hanes briefs. Marc was ready to go into spasms just from the friction of underwear and her mouth. The feast d' resistance came when she totally took the covered shaft into her mouth, sucking the damp material, making it cling against his rod.

Watching Caroline dine on him made his breathing quicken, his stomach heaved in and out. Her other hand raised his shirt, stroked soft thick flesh and muscles—taming his breathing. His words worked on her as she worked on him. "Damn, this is so fucking good, Caroline. Don't stop . . . don't stop." He reached down and delivered his shaft from the wet material while reclining the bucket seat.

Exposed to her hungry eyes was a shaft so beautiful and cinnamon brown that she almost came. Her fingers glided up and down the thick, rigid erection as it continued to pulsate. The sight of it took her breath away. It'd been so long since her beloved Marc was in her arms; just knowing she'd never mix with him again, never feel any real love from him. But as she stroked his molten flesh, she knew it was real, Marc was real, and her dreams were about to come true once more.

He beckoned her. "Take it, darling."

More than just words, it was action. Caroline's tiny mouth started at his tip, feasting on it, tenderizing it before she dove in for the rest. Marc stroked it up and down for her satisfaction, and his, as her mouth sank deeper and deeper onto it. His thick veins tickled her inner cheeks and throat and she smiled over that fact that he was still way different from what she remembered in dad's medical book. He was an awakening, then and now.

Marc's hips pumped to her rhythm, forcing the shaft deep within her mouth. She was taking it, taking it all but found her comfort zone at the plump, rounded tip. She sipped him, as though he were a fine wine and watched as he erupted from her hand action. He slumped in the seat, staring at his glorious princess. "You are so incredible, Caroline. How'd you learn to do that?"

"I had a good teacher—you. You made me want to be good at it."

"But we only did it once."

"Good teachers need only teach a lesson once."

He kissed her in a long, sucking motion, getting his fill of her before pulling away. "Sit on me. Let me feel what it's like again to be with you. You were so good."

"I was a virgin."

"That meant you were a natural. Come on, sit on me."

Elegant. Decadent
And very, very sexy.
That's THREE by
Noelle Mack.
Available now from Kensington . . .

The maid lugged the bucket through the bedchamber into a connecting alcove, where a gleaming tub stood on lion's paws of bronze. There she lifted the bucket high and poured in the hot water all in one go, a crystalline stream that splashed into the cold water already in the bathtub, sparkling in the candlelight. Steam rose from the tub in delicate wisps.

"Shall I undress you, my lady?" Sukey inquired, looking at Lady Fiona as if she knew perfectly well that someone already had, at least half way. The rumpled state of her mistress's black velvet gown—the disheveled bed, which looked very much as if someone had been clawing at the covers while in the throes of bliss—gave the evening's delights away.

"No. Just go."

Sukey nodded and took her leave, swinging the empty bucket by her side and closing the door quietly enough behind her. Fiona heard the maid's footsteps echo down the hall and return, then patter down the stairs. Evidently the easily aroused Summers had decamped. Fiona had no doubt that Sukey hoped to finish what she'd started.

If she didn't waylay Summers, the maid would have to

find another man to tease. It was a miracle that Sukey got any work done at all.

Fiona undid the ties of her bodice and let the black velvet gown fall into a heap on the floor, stepping out of it. Since Thomas had already done away with her drawers, she was quite naked, not having bothered with stays.

She pushed the dress aside with one foot and walked to the alcove, enjoying the feel of the cool night air on her skin, wearing nothing but the triple strand of pearls. The rim of the bathtub was wide, warmed by the water within, and there she perched, swishing a hand to and fro through the water, anticipating the delicious sensation of a good long soak.

She touched a hand to her tender nether lips, still slick from Thomas's double shots of spunk, wondering if it might be a better idea to wash there first, separately, and deciding that it would.

There was an ewer and a matching basin of Meissen porcelain upon an ebony table in the alcove. Fiona rose, picking up the ewer and dipping it into the tub. She poured the water into the basin and added a soft cloth, wringing it out to just the right juiciness before rubbing it luxuriously between her legs, cleaning herself as thoroughly as a cat.

Stimulating her already stimulated flesh in this fashion aroused her once more. She dropped the washcloth back into the basin and stood before the mirror, legs apart, admiring her proud breasts and curving hips for a few seconds. Then Fiona took her pleasure bud between forefinger and thumb and stroked it, gently pinching it with womanly delicacy, watching herself do it with increasing intensity and speed until she felt soft thrills pulse through her body. She closed her eyes, throwing her head back and letting the deeply sensual feeling overtake her.

It was her third climax of the night and not as strong as the two that Thomas had given her but enjoyable nonetheless. Well, of course, he had certain advantages, she thought dreamily. She couldn't very well spank herself or kiss her own flesh or writhe alone as she did in the powerful grip of his hands upon her waist when he pleasured her long into the night. For now, her fingers took care of the last lingering trace of desire from their time together.

Satisfied, she turned once more to her bath and stepped in, settling into the warm water with a blissful sigh. Fiona watched the candles flicker through half-closed eyes, not thinking of anything at all. Relaxed and happy and de-lighted to be alone, she lolled in the water until it grew cold.

A draft was coming from the bedroom. Perhaps Sukey had left a window open. Lady Fiona shivered and sat up, reaching for a towel and patting the wet pearls that encircled her neck, then rubbing her breasts and arms somewhat dry.

She gripped the rim of the tub and rose from the still water, dripping and looking for her new robe. Ah. There it was, on a nearby hook. The silken folds shimmered in the candlelight, and its elaborate embroidery of full-blown peonies and butterflies shone dully. Hardly a practical gar-ment, but then Lady Fiona owned very few garments that fit that description.

Her wardrobe was designed to be alluring. Workaday woolens and puritanical linens were not fabrics that inter-ested her in the slightest. She preferred sheer things, soft things against her sensitive skin. And if her dress and under-things could be easily removed by her lover du jour, so much the better. Being attended by a lady's maid before and after an amorous interlude had definite drawbacks. Though Sukey, a little hussy if ever there was one, never seemed shocked by anything.

Fiona clambered out of the bathtub rather awkwardly and tossed the towel with which she had dried her neck onto the floor. She picked up another, wrapping it around her hips and rubbing her bottom hard enough to make it jiggle. If Thomas were watching, he would have had her on her knees immediately, her head down and her hands reaching over her hips to spread open for him. He loved to see her cunny when he spanked her this way and watch her bare buttocks quiver under his welcome chastisement— a quivering she could not control and did not want to control, because she knew that the sight aroused him beyond measure.

She loved the feeling of shameful pleasure that pulsed through her, loved hiding her face in her tumbled hair, a woman with no name and no identity for a little while, begging with her whole body and a few gasped-out words, to be fucked by him.

Then, when he could stand her cries no longer, he would ram his hot shaft in all the way, until she screamed his name and came hard, thrusting her hips back, back, back. He very much enjoyed the satisfaction she found in being dominated now and then . . .

**Don't miss the further adventures of
Xandi, Stefan, Anton, and Keisha in
Kate Douglas's new novella, "Chanku Rising."**

SEXY BEAST

Every Woman Wants One . . .

Some men are more than meets the eye . . . much, much
more. And when they unleash a woman's wildest desires—
her deepest, animal hunger—the results are primal, magical,
and undeniably hot! Shape-shifting has never been sexier
than in *Sexy Beast*, an anthology of three novellas from
three of the best new writers of erotica:

Chanku Rising by Kate Douglas

Tiger, Tiger by Noelle Mack

Night of the Jaguar by Vivi Anna

SEXY BEAST

now available from Kensington Publishing.